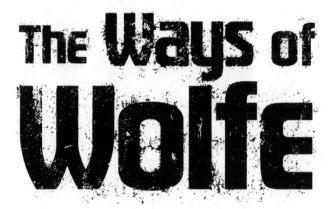

Other Works
By James Carlos Blake

Novels
The House of Wolfe
The Rules of Wolfe
Country of the Bad Wolfes
The Killings of Stanley Ketchel
Handsome Harry
Under the Skin
A World of Thieves
Wildwood Boys
Red Grass River
In the Rogue Blood
The Friends of Pancho Villa
The Pistoleer

Collection
Borderlands

The Ways of Wolfe

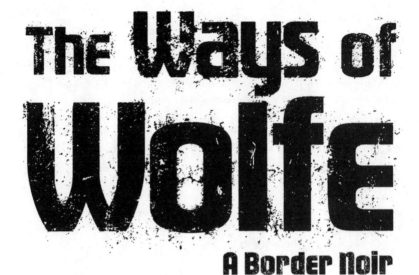

A Border Noir

James Carlos Blake

The Mysterious Press
New York

Published simultaneously in Canada
Printed in the United States of America

First Grove Atlantic hardcover edition: September 2017

FIRST EDITION

ISBN 978-0-8021-2577-4
eISBN 978-0-8021-8941-7

Library of Congress Cataloging-in-Publication data is available for this title.

The Mysterious Press
an imprint of Grove Atlantic
154 West 14th Street
New York, NY 10011

Distributed by Publishers Group West

groveatlantic.com

17 18 19 20   10 9 8 7 6 5 4 3 2 1

In memory of
JAMES DICKERT,
DONALD R. WYLY, JR.,
and
THOMAS E. SANDERS.

Great teachers all.

The past is the present . . . It's the future, too. We all
try to lie our way out of that but life won't let us.
—Eugene O'Neill

These violent delights have violent ends.
—William Shakespeare

All men should strive to learn before they die what
they are running from, and to, and why.
—James Thurber

Who is not of our ways is our enemy.
—Anonymous

PROLOGUE

Dallas, Texas. 1984

Axel Wolfe stole a white Ford Fairmont out of the zoo parking lot, then followed Duro's black Mustang up to I-30 and then eastward a few miles to an exit near a shopping mall. They left the Mustang in the next-to-last row at the rear of the mall's outdoor lot, then took a busy street north for several miles before turning off into a small commercial plaza consisting of a single L-shaped one-story building housing a dozen small businesses, including a jewelry shop. It was twenty past nine and the bright morning was heating up fast on a day predicted to hit the high nineties and maybe break a hundred.

They parked next to a row of shrubbery near the jeweler's—which stood in the middle of the long side of the L layout, its venetian blind down and the slats closed—then went to the Mexican café at the end of the short side of the L and sat in a window booth. All three of them wore light sport jackets. Axel and Billy also wore plain-lens eyeglasses, Axel a false mustache,

Billy a plastic-strip bandage across the bridge of his nose. Duro wore sunglasses he did not remove.

They had a clear view of the jeweler's, about sixty feet from the café on a diagonal line through the parking lot. They ordered coffee from the young waitress and when she brought it they insisted on paying the tab and tipping her then and there. To save time, Duro told her, because they were waiting for a pager notice from a client and would have to hurry off as soon as they received it. He withdrew a laminated bar graph from an expandable attaché case and they affected a relaxed review of it as they chatted in low voice.

The case also held eight sets of plastic flex cuffs, a wide roll of duct tape, and a pair of loaded 9mm Browning pistols fitted with suppressors. Brandished indoors, such accessorized pistols look the size of small cannons, the better to induce unhesitant cooperation. A third Browning, sans silencer, lay under a folded newspaper on the front seat of the Fairmont. Each man carried two extra fully loaded magazines.

They sipped their coffee. No one entered or exited the jeweler's, and its blinds stayed down. A few minutes before ten a yellow Camaro pulled into the lot and parked a few cars over from theirs. The two men in it got out—both in sunglasses, jeans, boots, loose baggy shirts, one of them carrying a slim black document pouch—and went into the jewelry shop.

They slid out of the booth and exited the café with casual dispatch, Billy and Duro bearing toward the jeweler's, Axel toward the Fairmont. At the shop's door, Duro unzipped the briefcase and he and Billy furtively withdrew the Brownings, then went inside. Axel got in the Fairmont and cranked it up and turned on the air conditioner. He took off his jacket and tossed it on the backseat, then lowered the car window and removed his mustache and flung it into the shrubs. He broke the fake glasses in two and wiped the lens on each half with his shirt and flung the glasses into the shrubs too and raised the window. A station wagon pulled into the lot and parked and a man got out and went into a locksmith's shop. A trio of gesticulating girls came out of a nail salon and got in a small sedan and departed. Now there was no activity at all in the plaza. No one in view. Time seemed arrested. He fingered the pistol under the newspaper.

Then out they came, Duro in the lead, the briefcase under an arm and hiding his gun hand, Billy right behind him and shutting the door as he exited, holding his gun under his jacket, both of them moving with the same cool briskness as before. Billy got in the back and Duro slid into the shotgun seat. Axel backed out, drove up to the exit, and melded into traffic.

"We're *rich*!" Billy Capp cried, flinging his mustache and glasses out the window and then closing it. "God *damn* if we ain't!"

⁕

"They're standing and talking at the counter, and you shoulda seen their faces, *all* of them—the old jeweler and his guard *and* the two carriers! Their eyes got *this* big when we come in pointing the pieces at them." Billy was telling Axel about it as they headed back to the mall. "Duro says hands up, and every hand just *flew* up. I keep them covered and Duro takes their pieces and sticks them in the briefcase. Pouch was right there on the counter and he checks to see the bonds are there, sticks it in the briefcase too. Tells everybody get on the floor and for me to shoot anybody even *looks* like he's thinking to try something. Cuffs them hands and feet, and then zip-zip-zip, gags them with the tape. Tells one of the carriers he's left his wrist cuffs loose enough he oughta be

able to work free in ten, fifteen minutes if he puts his mind to it,
And we were *out* of there! Man, oh man, went like clockwork!
Feel like goddamn *Dillinger!*"

⧘∞⧙

The shopping center parking lot was shimmering with heat and
packed with cars on this day before the July Fourth holiday. It was
fenced all the way around except at the center's main entrance and
had various entry-exit gates. The sun was glaring off everything of
glass, of chrome. They turned in to the parking lane where they'd
left Duro's car and were almost to it when a small red sports car
shot rearward out of a space directly in front of them. Axel braked
hard but couldn't avoid bashing into it.

"Son of a bitch!" Duro said.

Axel backed up a few feet and stopped as the driver stormed
out—a kid, tall and skinny—shouting, "Jesus fucking Christ!"
He came to the rear of his car and furiously regarded the broken
taillight and dented fender. It was a Porsche 911 Coupe with a
Southern Methodist University decal in the back window. There
wasn't enough room to drive around it. The kid glared at him and
yelled, "*Asshole!* Look what you did!" A pretty girl with a ponytail emerged from the passenger side and stood there, squinting
against the brightness.

"Hell with this," Duro said, opening his door. "Let's hoof
it to my car."

"He'll follow and get your tag," Axel said. "Get a good look
at us."

Duro yanked the door shut. "Then back out into the cross
lane and—"

"*Hey!*" the kid yelled. "*Hey! Over here!*" He was looking
past them and waving his arms over his head.

They turned and saw the police cruiser idling on the cross lane behind them. The sunglassed driver the only occupant. He raised a radio handset to his mouth.

"Of all the shit luck," Billy said. "What's—"

"He's checking the plate," Axel said. "Might've been reported right after we took it."

"*Come on!*" the kid yelled, beckoning the cop.

The cruiser backed up and then slowly turned into their lane and stopped about fifteen feet from them. The cop was talking on the radio.

"What the *hell*, man?" the kid said, shrugging at the cop, palms up.

There was a crackle from the cruiser's activated megaphone. "Everyone in the white car! Exit the vehicle now! Keep your hands where I can see them!"

"He made us," Duro said. "*Go!*"

Axel goosed the Fairmont and rammed the right rear of the Porsche, knocking it out of their way and into an adjacent car with a crash of metal and glass, the girl jumping away with a shriek.

The cop's roof lights came ablaze and the cruiser leaped after them as Axel sped to the end of the parking lane and wheeled onto the lot's perimeter road, tires screeching, then raced along the flanking chain-link fence. There were few cars parked in this farthest reach of the expansive lot. No people in view.

"Get us lost in all them cars in the middle of the lot," Duro yelled. "We'll scoot out and mix with the crowd, sneak back to my car."

"Not with this fucker on our ass!" Billy yelled, looking out the rear window as the cruiser swung into Axel's rearview mirror. The cop was driving with one hand and holding the handset to his mouth with the other.

Duro yelled, "Go for the engine block!" and leaned out the
window and Axel heard the *whamp-whamp-whamp* of the suppressed gunshots, and then Billy was shooting from his window
too.

The cruiser dropped back as if a tow rope had been severed,
steam billowing from under its hood.

"*Yow!* We hit *something!*" Billy said.

The cop braked to a halt and jumped out, drawing his revolver and aiming it two-handed as Axel slowed to make a tight
left into a lane of parked cars and void of people. Almost all in
the same instant, he heard the cop's two shots and the two *thunks*
against the door and felt a jolt in his hip and yipped. Then they
were out of the cop's view and he slowed the Fairmont and turned
right at the next cross lane.

"You hit?" Billy said.

"Okay! I'm okay!" Axel said.

He eased into a parking lane where a scattering of people
were heading toward the mall building or returning to their cars,
a few looking around, maybe having heard the cop's gunshots but
not comprehending what they were.

They slowly wove from parking lane to parking lane toward
the center of the lot, into densely packed rows of vehicles and
heavier pedestrian traffic, Axel's hip throbbing. There was a siren
in the distance.

"Gonna be cops all over real quick," Billy said. "Let's bail
right here."

"No," Duro said. "We leave this barge blocking the lane, the
guy behind us'll get pissed and start a racket, attract attention.
Gotta park it."

The next lane Axel turned into was also jammed with parked
cars but was bare of pedestrians. "There!" Duro said. A car was

backing out of a space just ahead. More sirens now, growing louder. More people looking around, holding shopping bags, standing at pushcarts, jabbering at each other.

Axel wheeled into the vacated spot and cut off the engine and Duro and Billy got out, Duro with the briefcase again hiding the Browning in his hand. Billy's pistol was in his waistband under his jacket. Axel stepped out and almost fell at the stab of pain in his hip. The bloodstain was dark and he pulled out his shirttail to cover it. They were about a dozen rows from where the Mustang was. Duro and Billy sidled over near a handful of people cutting through the parked cars, pushing their carts and walking fast, one of them saying there must've been a terrible accident nearby. Jaw clenched, Axel limped ahead, sopping with sweat.

A patrol car with roof lights flashing rolled slowly into view in the cross lane to their right, the two cops in it checking both ways. Looking for the Fairmont, Axel thought, and paused to peer all about as if in search of his own vehicle. His hand instinctively eased to his waist for the reassurance of the Browning and he realized he'd left it in the car. The cop car moved on and Axel hobbled after Duro and Billy, wincing at every step. They wended through rows of vehicles, staying close to one group of shoppers or another in order to seem part of them. When Axel came abreast of a Latino family unloading goods from shopping carts into a van, a pair of boys in Texas Rangers baseball caps gaped at him—at his dripping face, at the blood now staining his pants below the shirt hem. Axel hurried past them, walking faster, gritting his teeth. Sirens closing in from every direction.

They were but two rows from the one with the Mustang when he stumbled on a jut of asphalt and fell beside a parked pickup. He managed to sit up but couldn't stand. *"Billy!"* he cried.

Billy glanced back and halted and seemed bewildered to see him on the ground. Duro stopped and looked back too. Axel raised his hand toward Billy and said, "Pull me up, damn it! I can walk—just haul me up!"

Billy took a step toward him and then turned and saw Duro hurrying away into the next row of cars. He looked back at Axel and his outstretched hand. Then spun around and hurried after Duro.

Axel was trying to pull himself up by the pickup's door handle when the boys in the Rangers caps came running around the back of the truck, saw him, and stopped short.

"Here!" one yelled, pointing at him. "Right here!"

He let go of the handle and slumped against the truck door.

The boys jumped aside as a massive cop in full SWAT gear came stomping past them, eyes wide, teeth bared, and put the muzzle of his shotgun in Axel's face, shouting, "Gimme a reason! Gimme a reason!"

⁓⧼⧽⁓

There were two police guards posted at the door of his hospital room when he was wheeled in from recovery, still a little groggy. Somebody in plain clothes took pictures of him with a small camera and hastened away. A while later, a pair of detectives showed up. One of them read Axel his rights and then did all the talking. He said they had identified him by way of his prints on a license-to-carry form. Son of a hotshot criminal lawyer in Brownsville and he was gonna need daddy's help for sure.

A jewelry store in West Dallas had been held up that morning and the robbers made off with a load of gems valued at forty thousand dollars. Three perpetrators: a black-and-white stickup team and a white driver. The stickup guys wore dark glasses, but the white guy took his off when he got outside and the jeweler and a customer got a look at him through the window. They'd been shown Axel's photo and were leaning toward a positive ID. They only glimpsed the getaway vehicle but were in agreement it was a four-door of light color, as was the stolen Fairmont Axel crashed into the college kid's car at an eastside mall where he and his partners had stashed another getaway car.

Axel stared at the cop in mute astonishment. West Dallas was across town from the jewelry shop where they'd ripped the bonds.

The SMU student and his girlfriend had positively identified him as the driver of the stolen Ford but they had not had a good look at either of the other two men in the car and could say only that one of them was dark-skinned. But the officer who pursued them in the parking lot had got a fairly good look at the men shooting at him from the windows. He was in his disabled cruiser and talking to headquarters when the same two men sped past him in a black Mustang.

He sent out the vehicle description and a partial-plate, and a cruiser spotted the perps two blocks from the mall and gave chase. The pursuit was marked by an exchange of gunfire and several traffic accidents, and that no one was shot or seriously injured was, in the cop's words, "a fucking miracle." The perpetrators escaped, and some hours later the Mustang was found abandoned on a side street, blood on the driver's seat. Its registration proved fictitious. The two men remained at large. The cop told Axel that things would go a hell of a lot better for him if he told them everything, beginning with who the partners were.

Axel said nothing.

c∞つ

Harry Mack Wolfe arrived that evening, and it was an act of will for Axel to meet his father's eyes. The first thing Harry Mack said, in a whisper at his ear, was, "I would call you a stupid son of a bitch but that would be an insult to your mother, who would be in despair were she alive." He then asked if he had said anything to the police, and Axel assured him he had not.

Wolfe Associates, the family's law firm, was being assisted by a Dallas law partnership of his long acquaintance, Harry Mack informed him. As things stood, Axel was facing felony charges of aggravated robbery and aggravated assault.

Axel swore to him they had not robbed the West Dallas jewelry store, nor had he fired a shot or even brandished a weapon at anyone, nor in any way assaulted anybody.

Even if any of that were true, Harry Mack said, it was his word against that of two eyewitnesses who placed him at the robbery. Eyewitnesses could be unreliable, of course, at times notoriously so, but in the absence of an alibi and contradicting witnesses, they were a potent element in the state's case. And even if in truth they hadn't done that holdup, they *had* stolen a car and his companions *had* fired shots, including at a cop, and *had* caused havoc and severe public endangerment and extensive property damage, and according to the law of parties, as it was known in Texas, Axel bore equal responsibility for all their actions.

"The fact is, there is no question you will go to prison. The only matter at issue is for how long."

Axel's chest tightened but he kept his face blank. His father had not asked exactly what he had been involved in or why. He never would.

As for bail, Harry Mack said that the prosecution had persuaded the judge that, notwithstanding his prominent family, Axel was a flight risk. Someone who was a party to shooting at a police officer and attempting to evade arrest was apt to try to flee the country, and Axel Wolfe had the connections and financial means to do it. The judge could not deny bail but had set it at five hundred thousand dollars.

"We could ask for a reduction and probably get it," Harry Mack said, "but we aren't going to ask because I have no intention of providing the bond in any case. Given the fact of what you've done to be in your present position, I can't help but think that you might be foolish enough to attempt flight and make things even worse for yourself. I think it best you await trial in jail."

"I see," Axel said. "For my own good." In truth it had crossed his mind that as soon as he was bailed out he might take refuge with their Wolfe kin in Mexico City.

His father regarded him sadly. "You're a damned fool, boy. You're very fortunate no one was hurt, but even so you're in severe straits." He instructed him to remain silent with the police, said he would see him again sometime soon, and left.

⚭

On his next visit he brought a sheaf of documents for Axel to sign, including one that granted Harry Mack full control of Axel's assets.

"Unless you don't trust me to attend faithfully to your wife and child's security," he said.

Axel signed.

⚭

The doctor told him he was extremely lucky in that the bullet had but slightly glanced the hip's iliac crest before lodging in muscle tissue. Minute fracture, no major blood vessel damage. He would limp for a while but that would be the worst of it.

⟨∞⟩

A wheelchair conveyed him from the hospital to the patrol wagon that transported him to the county jail. Two days later he was placed in a morning lineup and neither the jeweler nor the customer had any doubt at all that he was one of the robbers. That afternoon he stood in a lineup again and the SMU guy and his girl identified him as the driver of the Fairmont.

⟨∞⟩

Ruby came to visit. The auburn-haired Cajun beauty he'd fallen in love with shortly after they met in college two and a half years ago. She had soon thereafter become pregnant and they had married and he loved her still. Their daughter, Jessica Juliet, was eighteen months old.

Ruby said she couldn't understand how he could've done something so crazy, so reckless, so heedless of his wife and child, his entire family, his whole future.

"How come, Axel? Can you please just tell me *how come*?"

He said he couldn't explain it.

"I'd guess not! How can anybody explain such a thing? But you did it, Axel, and there's got to be a reason somebody does something. Harry Mack says you're sure to go to prison, maybe for years and years. For God's sake, what am I supposed to tell our little girl when she's old enough to ask about her daddy? When she asks why he'd do something that took him away from us like it's done?"

He didn't know. Nor did he know that Ruby's deepest distress derived from having learned that Harry Mack was now Axel's fiduciary and she stood zero chance of availing herself of any Wolfe assets beyond what Harry Mack allotted to her.

She left in tears.

⟨∞⟩

"One more year and you'da had your degree and been in the shade trade," Charlie Fortune said. "But that's not how it went, and how it went's all that counts. Whyever you did it, you had your reason. I want you to know this, though, and I mean *know* it. I'm your brother, Ax. Always will be. Know what I *mean*? I'll say it right out if you want."

"No need," Axel said. "I can hear it."

He put his hand to the Plexiglas partition and Charlie put his to it on the other side.

⟨∞⟩

He awoke nights to the sporadic bangings of iron doors, the loud voices of inmates and jailers, and sometimes could not get back to sleep. He would lie there with eyes closed and see Billy just as clearly as he'd seen him that last time. Would see his face fraught with indecision as he gawked at him on the ground, at his extended hand. Would see him turn and run.

Afraid of being captured?

Or thinking . . . *More for me*?

No. He wouldn't do that. Not Billy. Not to him.

⟨∞⟩

After weeks of bargaining, Harry Mack and his Dallas colleagues at last forged a deal with the prosecution. If Axel pled guilty to aggravated assault, he would be sentenced to fifteen years.

"You'll be up for parole in five," Harry Mack said. "It's a golden deal."

"What's the catch?" Axel said.

"You give them the other two."

"If I don't?"

"They'll add aggravated robbery. You can then plead guilty
to the two charges and get thirty years, or you can choose to
make a trial of it and they lock you up until you're old and gray
and incontinent."

"For a first offense? Even though I didn't shoot, didn't even
have a gun in my hand? Even though I didn't lay a finger on
anybody?"

"That is correct. It's only because it's your first offense that
they're holding it to thirty if you plead to the charges. It, too, is
a more attractive offer than I had anticipated, considering that
some of the gunfire was directed at law enforcement officers and
considering the degree of public peril created by your companions. And by the way, if you choose the thirty, you'll technically
be eligible for a parole hearing after ten years, but they have made
it abundantly clear you will not qualify for that hearing, nor any
other. You will do the full thirty."

"They can do it, too, can't they? See I don't get parole?"

"They want the shooters, kid. If they don't get them, you're
the one to pay. You really have no choice."

He wanted to say he couldn't do it because one of them was
a friend, but that would be telling too much. His father would
muster the investigative forces to check into everybody known
to be his friend and they'd soon narrow it down to Billy. "I can't
rat them out."

"Oh? Is either of them one of ours?"

"One of *ours*? Is that all that counts?"

"A superfluous question. I repeat, is either of them one of
ours?"

Axel said nothing.

"You're an even bigger fool than I thought."

⋘⋙

For several more weeks Harry Mack and his associates strove to achieve a more favorable compromise, calling on every political connection who might be able to assist them. But the prosecution had its own cadre of potent connections and was adamant in its insistence that Axel name the accomplices.

"I strongly counsel you to reconsider," Harry Mack said.

Axel did not.

⋘⋙

The trial date came.

The proceeding was brief.

Axel pled guilty to the two charges.

He was sentenced to thirty years and credited with time served.

He entered prison with twenty-nine years and six months to go.

PART I

CHARLES ZANCO
PRISON UNIT, TEXAS
2008

1

You can't chance it.

The thought comes to Axel the moment he wakes once again from this hot night's fitful sleep. The dim tier light casts a cross-barred shadow on the wall. He has each time wakened with a start, not knowing what time it is or how long he has been asleep. Each time wakened to the hoarse snoring of his cellmate, to the mumblings and sleep whimpers from neighboring cells, once to the footfalls of a guard passing by on the iron walkway, doing the night head count. Each time wakened to the same fearful thought like a low voice in some dark corner of his mind.

You can't chance it.

❦

"Hey, old man, what say we bust out of this zoo?"

That was how Cacho had broached the idea. He was Mexican but spoke English well and with only a slight accent. They had known each other six weeks at the time, and Axel did not yet know that Ramirez was not his true surname.

He had laughed and told the kid to forget it. There was no way. He'd been in prison since before Cacho was born, and he had been privy to a lot of escape plans but never joined any of them. Always for the same reason. Because he knew they wouldn't work. Only a handful of them were ever attempted, he told Cacho, and not one of them succeeded.

The kid gave him a pitying look. "All these years inside and you never *once* tried to bust out?" Axel's advisory did not dissuade him nor diminish his confidence. He was sure there was a way out. "There's always a way," he said. "All we gotta do is figure it."

The "we" made it clear from the start that he considered Axel to be in on it and was in any case counting on his assistance by way of information. Over the following weeks he questioned Axel daily, mining his extensive knowledge of the prison's protocols and procedures, its routines, its personnel.

Axel answered his questions as well as he could. He didn't see any reason not to. He knew the information would lead to nothing, that the kid would never devise a feasible breakout. The Q&A sessions were anyway a pleasant diversion from the daily tedium, and in the course of them Axel surprised himself with how much he had come to learn about this place where he had been for the last ten years—the last four of them as a trusty—far longer than in any of the other prison units where he'd served portions of his sentence.

Besides, he liked the kid, who was the sole exception he'd ever made to his longtime prison practice of befriending no one. All prisons abound with bravado, but hardcore optimism is generally in short supply, and he felt a benign amusement about Cacho's confidence in concocting a successful break. Of course, the kid was only twenty.

His amusement gave way to incredulity when Cacho told him—on a late Saturday afternoon and not quite three months after his first mention of it—that the break was all set and would take place in nine days. It was a visiting day and the kid had seemed antsy ever since his weekly meeting with his lawyer a few hours earlier. For his part, Axel had been feeling low all day, as he always did on visiting days when his brother Charlie didn't come to see him, never mind that Charlie had been there just two weeks ago and that each of his monthly visits was a daylong undertaking for him, having to fly from Brownsville to Fort Stockton, then rent a car for the drive to Zanco.

They had just finished their daily presupper jog around the perimeter of the exercise yard and were still winding down, circling the yard at a walk, when Cacho told him the plan was in place. Axel had stared at the kid's wide smile and said, "Bullshit." But when the kid explained the particulars—and told him his real name was Capote and his older brother was the head of a subgang of a major Mexican criminal cartel—his disbelief gave grudging way to absorption.

"And just *how* were you able . . . well hell, the lawyer, right?" Axel said. "Somoza? Through him, in the visits. You all the time telling me he's working on an appeal."

"How else, man? First time he came to see me he said to find somebody who really knows this joint and get him to tell me everything about how it runs, about the towers and the gates, especially everything about the bosses and the guards. Didn't take long to know that guy was you—been here the longest, been a trusty for a while. You told me the sorta stuff he wanted to know, I told him, he told our guys, they went to work and put the thing together. Somoza brought it to me today. Jesus, Ax, just think, *nine* days, man. Each one's gonna be a month long, know what I'm saying?"

The thing relied on bribery, the oldest and generally most effective of means, and usually the simplest. Axel favored simplicity. He had grown up among people who held it for a rule that the simplest approach was usually best, a view borne out by his own experience. But these bribes involved prison insiders, and that, Axel pointed out, was the plan's flaw.

"You ought to know by now you can't trust anybody on the inside. Not a convict, not a CO, not anybody."

"*I'm* on the inside," Cacho said. "*I'm* a convict. You too. You don't trust *me*? We don't trust each other?"

"Present company excepted."

Cacho laughed. "*Present company excepted.* I love the way you college dudes are always covering your ass with fancy talk. You and my brother sound just alike." In the kid's estimation, Axel was a "college dude" by dint of having completed three years at a university. His brother, he had told Axel, had graduated from the University of Texas.

Cacho said there was no cause to worry about the inside guys. There were only four of them, and none of them convicts. "One civilian and three *corrections officers,*" he said, sardonically emphasizing the bureaucratic term for prison guards, "who are doing what is most *correct* for their greedy-ass pockets."

He told Axel who the COs were and that all of them were already so deeply compromised they couldn't back out without burning themselves too.

"You mean they already took the money?"

"I mean they already took the money," Cacho said. "These hacks don't get paid jack shit. Drop a few packs of Bennies in front of them, they slobber all over theirselves. They'd sell their fucking *mothers* for a hundred G's."

"They really got a hundred per man?"

"Somoza's guy personally gave the money to each one. Said it was the same with all of them. Eyes about bugged outta their heads when they saw it. And they know if they break the deal they get their throat cut. If they break the deal and somehow find a place to hide, they get ratted to the cops, the feds, the press, everybody. They got no out, man. And check this . . . all three of the COs know who the civilian is, but each of them thinks he's the only prison insider. The civilian, he knows there's somebody else in it but don't know who or how many."

"Nice engineering."

"I told you, my people don't fuck around. It's all set. Only a matter of waiting for the insiders' schedules to line up. That'll happen in nine days. *Nine* days! All we got to do till then is think about the fun we're gonna be having in *ten* days. Now come on, gramps, before they shut down the chow line."

He could have opted out any time. Could've said thanks but no thanks and stepped away from the whole business. But he didn't. To the contrary, only a few days later, as they were discussing the details of the thing yet again, he heard in his own voice the same confidence as in the kid's. The same note of conviction that the plan would not fail. And the conviction had held strong.

Until tonight. Until the thought came to him like a whisper on the first of his wakings on this final night before the thing takes place. The thought he's had on every waking since.

You can't chance it.

They'll kill you or catch you. And if they *catch* you—

The cell block lights come ablaze and the PA blares the wake-up call.

It's four o'clock. The daily commotion commences. The vocal din. The shrill chirrings of electric locks and the clashings of iron doors. The harsh squawkings of the PA. The customary cacophony.

The showers are open and breakfast will be served until 5:30. Then comes a cell head count. Then crews to their jobs at 6.

The day is here.

2

Axel Prince Wolfe was three years old when his mother died giving birth to his brother, Charlie Fortune. His sister, Andrea Marie, was two. Their father, Harry McElroy Wolfe, was only a few years out of law school but already the main criminal defense attorney at Wolfe Associates, the family law firm in Brownsville, Texas.

In addition to their practice of law since the early twentieth century, the Wolfes have conducted a variety of illicit enterprises under the collective name of the "shade trade," the main enterprise of which has always been gunrunning, the bulk of it to their Mexican relatives, also named Wolfe and concentrated in Mexico City. For their part, the Mexican Wolfes operate a small and highly secretive cartel of their own, Los Jaguaros, which chiefly sells guns and information of all sorts to other cartels.

By family rule, any Wolfe who aspires to be part of the shade trade must first earn a college degree, which can be in any major except physical education or anything that ends in "Studies." The exception of the "Studies" major is of much more recent vintage than the college requirement itself, which has been in force since the 1930s and is without dispensation. The rationale behind the rule is not only that higher education is a valuable asset in itself—no less so to the criminally inclined than to the legally minded—but also that, in the process of earning the degree, one might stumble onto one's true calling.

Once you reach the age of sixteen, you can, if you wish, spend your high school summers learning the ins and outs of the shade trade's main components, but you cannot take an active role in any actual undertaking. You can learn about gunrunning and other forms of smuggling, about document forgery, about finding people who are lost or in hiding or in captivity. There are any number of specializations you can concentrate on, and you also receive training in the arts of self-defense, such arts of course being equally useful for persuasive or retributive purpose.

From the time he first learned of the shade trade, Axel knew it was the career for him. His father, however, had a greater expectation of him, namely that he go to law school and then join Wolfe Associates. Still, because Harry Mack believed that the more one knew about criminal ways the better equipped one was for the practice of criminal law, he was not opposed to Axel's learning as much as he could during his high school summers about shade trade operations. To avoid argument, Axel agreed to go to law school after getting his bachelor's degree, but in truth he intended to renege as soon as he got the BA and was eligible for the shade trade, regardless of his father's opposition.

His closest bond was with his brother. Axel taught Charlie how to fight, sail, play baseball, fish, shoot, drive a car. The spring Axel graduated from high school, Charlie turned fourteen, and as a birthday present to him, Axel persuaded a companionable girlfriend named Mickey to introduce him to the delights of sex. The exuberant event took place in Mickey's bedroom, and when they at last rejoined Axel in the kitchen, Charlie was beaming and Mickey affecting a glazed-eyed stagger that got a laugh from both brothers. They drank celebratory beers deep into the evening and got happily drunk, another first for Charlie, who couldn't stop staring at Mickey in adoration. At a later hour that night he asked her to marry him as soon as he graduated from high school, in another three years. She giggled in response and Charlie looked so stricken that Axel roared with laughter and fell over backward in his chair. Which made Mickey laugh so hard she snorted beer out of her nose. Which made Charlie laugh so hard he got a case of hiccups that took forever to get under control, and every time it seemed like it was, he'd suddenly hic and they'd all bust out howling again.

It was obvious to Mickey that Charlie venerated his brother. She noted his emulation of Axel's walk, his two-finger grip on a longneck, his mode of sitting with the chair tipped on its rear legs. "That kid," she once remarked to Axel, "would wear a dead rat for a hat if you did. Please don't ever tell him to kill me, because he'd do it without even asking why."

3

Constructed in 1918, the Charles Zanco Unit is one of the oldest prisons in the Texas Department of Criminal Justice. Located in the Trans-Pecos region, in the upper eastern reach of the Chihuahuan Desert, it occupies eight hundred acres in the southwest corner of Terrell County, one of the largest counties in the state and, with fewer than a thousand residents, one of the most sparsely populated. The vast majority of its inhabitants live in Sanderson, the county seat and only actual town, set on Highway 90 and a dozen miles northwest of the prison. The closest town of moderate size is Fort Stockton, sixty-five miles farther north, in Pecos County. Less than seven miles south of the Zanco Unit is the nearest portion of the Rio Grande, or as it's known in Mexico, the Río Bravo. The border.

This is arid, windswept country of limestone hills and rocky plains rampant with scrub brush and cactus and bony mesquites, an outland of spectral mountain ranges carved with canyons and snaking with cottonwood creeks too far-flung to serve for irrigation. The winters are short and chill, the summers long and roasting. The sandstorms can scour the paint off a car. Rainfall is

scant but once in a great while there are thunderstorms of uncommon ferocity, generating flash floods that tear through the
gullies with freight train force. Other than petroleum and natural
gas, the earth here produces little of economic worth. Goat farms.
Small cattle ranches. A scattering of pecan groves.

Although Zanco is classified as a medium-security prison,
popular opinion holds that its surrounding desert presents as
formidable an obstacle to escape as any at the max-security units
in the TDCJ. Even so, the prison was built here only because the
land it stands on was bequeathed to the state by a former lieuten-
ant governor who specified the property could be used for no
other purpose. The institution has neither a cooling nor a heating system. In winter the place is colder within than outside. In
summer it swelters. Among Texas prison guards, an assignment to
Zanco has long been regarded a prime test of one's commitment
to a career as a corrections officer.

∽∾

The prison's population is nearly the equal of the county's, vary-
ing between eight and nine hundred inmates. They are serving
sentences of from two years to life, for crimes ranging from
murder to driving drunk for the third time or more. The grounds
are enclosed by a chain-link fence fifteen feet high, topped
with double rolls of razor wire, and watched over by armed
tower guards. In addition to the cell blocks and administration
buildings, the prison contains a small plant for the manufacture
of state-issue footwear, a large garage for the maintenance and
repair of state motor vehicles, and a kennel for the training of
commercial security dogs. The kennel also houses the prison's
tracking hounds, though in the institution's ninety-year history
there has never been need of them.

❦

There have been only two escape attempts from Zanco, and none in the past forty years. In 1937 a trio of convicts made it out of their cell block and to a darkened section of the fence—it was then only eleven feet high and crowned with barbed wire—and they had scaled it to the top when the spotlights found them and the tower guards opened fire and killed them all. The fence was thereafter made four feet higher and additional barbed wire was added. In the early 1960s the wire was replaced with razor coils.

The more recent effort was in 1968. Four convicts overpowered a pair of guards, held shivs to their throats, and demanded that the warden provide a car and guns for them at the front gate. The car was brought and the inmates shuffled out of the building in a tight group, holding the guards close to them as shields. They were halfway to the gate when a quartet of sharpshooters on the roof fired simultaneously, the volley of head shots dropping all four convicts, three of them dead and the fourth critically wounded. The warden took his time about summoning the prison doctor from his home in Sanderson, and when he arrived he was directed to treat the rescued guards for their scrapes and bruises before attending to the wounded prisoner. When the doctor finally turned his attention to the convict, the man was dead.

Today the front entrance of the Zanco Unit bears a large bold-lettered sign found at other Texas prisons as well:

NO HOSTAGE SHALL PASS THROUGH THIS GATE.

4

He quickly learned to accommodate the desolation of imprisonment. The institutional rules were easy enough to adhere to, and those of the so-called convict code were no burden, either. You minded your own business. You never trusted the guards, never helped them in any way. You did not interfere in another con's interests. You never ratted. He would incur no debt, request no favor, ask no personal questions. He learned how to converse without seeming to seek friendship and how to rebuff those who seemed to seek it from him. In brief, he held strong to the most comprehensive rule of the convict code, which was to "do your own time."

Except for a single visit from Ruby, his only visitor through all his years inside was Charlie, who would every month visit him at whichever unit he was in, no matter how distant, though in the early years there would be periods when Axel was punished with the loss of visiting rights and they could not see each other for months.

He wrote to Ruby more often and at greater length than she wrote to him. During her only visit, early in his first year, she'd looked so desirable on the other side of the Plexiglas he'd nearly wept for want of her. She'd seemed unnerved by the surroundings and to be at some greater distance than the few feet between them. She promised to come again and they several times agreed on the date, but she each time made some excuse. He tried not to think about her so much, but couldn't help it, nor refrain from masturbating to the conjured images of her naked flesh. He once accepted a punk's offer to suck him off for a five-dollar credit at the commissary, but his pleasure in being fellated had always derived as much from watching the woman minister to him as from the actual sensation, and there was no such pleasure with a man. That first time was the last time, and he thereafter relied solely and glumly on his hand.

⌘

He had been inside a little more than a year when Charlie brought the news that Ruby had gone away and no one knew where. Ever since Axel's conviction, Harry Mack had of course continued to support her and Jessie and had often tried to persuade her to relocate to Brownsville, but she'd insisted on staying in Houston. Then one day the nanny, Mrs Adamson, showed up at Harry Mack's door with a suitcase in one hand and three-year-old Jessie in the other and told him Mrs Wolfe had said she was leaving town and had paid her to bring the child to the family in Brownsville. She had not said where she was going or why or if she would ever come back. Jessie would thereafter reside with Harry Mack and his housekeeper, Mrs Smith, but Axel specifically asked Charlie to watch out for her, and at least twice a week without fail, through all the years until she finished high school and left for UT Austin, he would take her to a movie and then someplace to eat and they would chat for hours.

By no other means could Ruby have severed Axel's love for her so utterly as by abandoning Jessica Juliet, deserting her to go . . . where? Why? With somebody? How could he have misjudged the low-down bitch so badly?

⌘

None of them would ever know that Ruby met a man named Donnie Weathers in New Orleans during Mardi Gras two weeks before she closed her bank account, paid Mrs Adamson to take Jessie to Brownsville, and went with Donnie to Los Angeles, where he had an ocean-view penthouse and kept a cabin cruiser moored at a marina. He also owned a condominium in San Francisco and a house on eighty wooded acres in the northern part of the state. He was a tall, handsome, physically fit man of fifty-one, twelve years a widower, without a living relative, and enjoying the benefits of a colossal inheritance. He liked to have fun and was what he laughingly called "a sex addict." She had laughed in turn and said that made two of them.

Until she'd met Donnie, she had been weighing a future in which the most money she would ever possess was Harry Mack's twice-a-month apportionment to her. Donnie's entrance into her life had considerably brightened her prospects. He lavished her with gifts, said pretty things to her, and before they'd known each other three weeks he professed his love. His major failing, as she saw it, was in the sort of sex he was "addicted" to—rough bondage games he liked to record on videotape and which usually pained and sometimes bruised her. Yet she readily obliged him, sensing marriage in the cards and already contriving toward the day she would divorce him on grounds of mental and physical cruelty, with the sex tapes as evidence, plus whatever other basis a lawyer might suggest. Once the community-property state of California granted her a lavish settlement, she could at last begin living the life she was meant for.

What she could not have foreseen was the night she and Donnie went cruising far off the coast and he initiated yet another of his games, this one involving, among other things, a technique he assured her would intensify her climax. She agreed to it with a lascivious grin, saying it sounded fun. They were well into the diversion when she found herself unable to breathe and tried to tell him that she was choking, that he was killing her. And he was. She died without knowing she was not the first of Donnie Weathers' sex mates to meet her end in the course of an outré libidinous game out at sea. Nor the first he cut open from belly to breast-bone to assure that the corpse would not surface, then dumped overboard, perhaps to sink all the way down to the bottom feeders, perhaps to be disposed of by sharks as it sank.

5

Shaved and showered, dressed in a fresh set of inmate whites, Axel lingers in his open cell. For the past weeks he and Cacho have made it a point to wait until the last half hour of the breakfast period before meeting in the dining hall. By then most of the cons have eaten and left the hall and it's easier to have a degree of conversational privacy. Already gone to breakfast is his cellmate, a beefy, silver-haired man named Duke Jameson doing seventeen years for robbery plus an eight-year jolt on top of that for bigamy. Jameson thought the bigamy sentence both unwarranted and severely excessive, and has said so to Axel on more than one occasion. "As if I hadn't already punished my *own* ass enough by bein married to two never-shut-the-fuck-up women at the same time and both of em spendin my money fastern I could steal it!"

He's been thinking hard since the block lights came on, especially about something Cacho said during supper last night, after they'd reviewed the plan yet again. "Hey, man, what's to sweat? The worse that can happen is they kill us." He had chuckled along with the kid, but the thought had stayed with him.

Because, as he saw it, getting killed wasn't the worst that could happen. Getting caught and having years added to his sentence—*that* was the worst. He had of course considered that risk from the start and had even emphasized it to the kid at the very beginning, wanting Cacho to understand clearly what they stood to lose if the plan went to hell and they were caught and not killed. He had pointed out that if Cacho kept his nose clean he'd be eligible for parole in less than five years. He'd still be a young man with his whole life ahead of him. But the kid had said, *"Five years?"* like it was eternity. He wanted out *now* and would run any risk to get free, even the risk of lengthening his sentence. But not until the first of his multiple wakings last night had Axel suddenly realized that it's a risk he himself cannot afford. What had ever made him think he could? Better to play it safe and serve out the eleven years he's got left.

Just tell the kid first thing, he thinks, *as soon as you see him . . . count you out. You can't do it, you can't risk more time. He's young and has a life waiting for him out there and can afford the risk and has good reason to take it. You're not so young and you've got nobody waiting but your little brother, but better to go out to nobody but Charlie in eleven years for sure than in however the hell many more years it'll be if you get caught. And it's not like you're queering the thing for him, because the plan doesn't require more than one guy. He doesn't need you. You'll wish him all the luck in the world and tell him if he makes it you'll be happy for him and kicking yourself in the ass for not sticking. But if you stick and get caught you'll be kicking yourself a lot longer. So . . . count you out.*

The kid will call him a pussy, a scared old man. That's okay, let him. There's really no way to tell him the truth about why he can't chance the added time. He's never told him about Jessie, never spoken about her to anybody inside the walls. She's never been to see him or ever written to him and that's her choice and there's nothing to be done about it. He wrote to her once, when she was fourteen. A letter of three pages in which he told her he was sorry he'd been a bad father and knew he didn't deserve her love but he wanted her to know he loved her very much and always would.

On his next visit, Charlie sadly informed him that she said she had burned the letter and did not want him to write to her again, and if he did she would burn the letter without even opening it. Still, not a day passes that he doesn't think of her. He has seen her grow up in the photographs Charlie has brought him over the years—pictures he now regrets having cut up and flushed away a few days ago rather than leave them behind for his cellmate and the COs to gawk at—but he aches to truly *see* her. See her in person. Even if she won't speak to him. Even if all he can do is look at her from a distance. He wants to see the woman she's become. There isn't much he wants anymore, and nothing he wants more than that. And eleven more years is long enough to wait for it without taking a chance of catching even more time. Never mind the chance of getting killed.

So count him out.

6

He would not join a gang. Gangs ruled the prisons, all of them bound tightly to themselves by race—white gangs, black gangs, Latino gangs— and the convict who did not belong to one was a loner without allies. But he would not obligate himself to anyone, not even to a gang that would have sided with him against all others. At every unit he was on his own. The first seven years were the roughest. Each time he was transferred to another unit, he was put to the test as soon as he arrived, forced to choose between backing down or fighting, and of course he always fought. He knew how, and though he was bloodied in every contest, he more often inflicted greater damage than he received. But, together with his antagonist, he was every time punished by the loss of privileges and visiting rights for weeks or months.

❦

His ruminations about Billy Capp were at times so infuriating he considered ratting him out. See if Harry Mack could still work a deal with the state, get his sentence cut in trade for Billy's name. He'd throw in Duro, too, if they cut it even more. But he couldn't do it. Not because ratting was against the convict way but because it was against his way. Against the

Wolfe way, actually, although some in the family—his father a prime case in point—believed that Wolfe loyalty was requisite only to Wolfe blood.

There were anyhow other possibilities about Billy. Maybe he was dead. Maybe he and Duro had been found by hirelings of the people whose bonds they stole. Maybe they had a falling-out and Duro killed him. Maybe they got caught by the cops, or just Billy did, and he was now back in prison, maybe somewhere in Texas, maybe in some other state. Or maybe not. Maybe he was settled down somewhere. Maybe married, had kids. Was maybe living off the accumulated fruits of his labor, had solid investments, spent his days watching ball games on a big-screen TV, grilling steaks and chugging beers with buddies. Maybe. . . . But if that's the way it was, then the son of a bitch damn well owed him. No maybe about it.

❧

He was in his sixth year when Charlie told him that their cousin Henry James and his wife Sally had gone sailing out on the Gulf and disappeared. The Coast Guard had searched for days but not a trace of them or the boat was found, and they'd been presumed dead. Shortly thereafter Charlie—a graduate of Texas A&M with a degree in history—had been made Henry James's replacement as chief of the shade trade. "By the way, I been promoted to superintendent of the export department," was how he said it on the visitor's phone on his side of the glass. "Long as I'm there, you know you got a job waiting when you get out. We don't discriminate against applicants of advanced years."

Axel grinned back and gave him the finger.

❧

The sameness of his days made it hard to retain a clear chronological perspective. His best record of time's passing was in the photos of Jessie that Charlie brought him every few months. Every picture had to be approved by the admin office, but once it was cleared and passed on to

him, Axel added it to the others of her in a small album, a collection that
would eventually grow into a photographic chronicle of her maturation
from child to girl to young woman.

He was in his eighth year inside and Jessie had just turned ten when
Charlie wrote that he had finally been able to persuade her to come with
him on his next visit. Axel was elated and counted the days. But when
the guard towers and high fence and razor wire came into view, Jessie
burst into tears and refused to leave the car. There was nothing Charlie
could do but go in and tell Axel, who said he understood and told him
to go back out to her right away and not chide her for it, just comfort her
the best he could on the way home.

In the exercise yard after dinner the next day he got into a fight
with an inmate for no reason he could name. He was in a frenzy when
the COs came shoving through the crowd to break it up. When one of
the guards grabbed him from behind to pull him away, Axel spun around
and punched him hard in the face several times, breaking the man's jaw,
before he was clubbed into submission by the other COs.

He was convicted of assaulting a corrections officer and sentenced
to an additional five years.

7

At a quarter to five he joins the last bunch of inmates headed for breakfast. They file down the tier stairs to the ground floor and then turn onto a broad corridor, staying inside the one-way lane defined by a yellow line about three feet from the wall on their right. In a similar lane on the other side of the corridor the inmate traffic moves in the opposite direction. Only prison staff and inmates in their custody are allowed in the corridor's wide central zone. After passing through connecting wings, the line of men arrives at the dining hall. It is now a little more than half full, droning low with conversations. Inmates are permitted to talk at meals but not to dawdle over them. Guards patrol the aisles between the long rows of tables, and the entire room is overseen by a guard on an elevated catwalk. Moving down the serving line, Axel sees Cacho seated at the end of a table near the far wall and occupied by only three other cons. He takes his tray over there and sits across from him.

"My man," Cacho says. His eyes are bright with excited anticipation. He is built much like Axel, lean and of medium height, but under his black, close-cropped hair his face is still a boy's, smoothly brown and yet to grow a whisker, flawed only by a pair of scars—a purple wither at the top of one ear and a shiny pink smudge at the corner of his chin. He has confessed to Axel that the pearly perfection of his teeth is the result of superior dental reconstruction occasioned a few years ago, like the chin scar, by a bottle hard-swung into his mouth.

He checks out Axel's breakfast and says, "Smart choice, the oatmeal. The powdered eggs usually taste like old rubber, right? Today they taste like old burnt rubber."

Axel trades a blank glance with one of the three cons seated at the table, mestizos yakking low in Spanish of Guatemalan intonations. About two thirds of the inmates at Zanco are Latinos, most of them Mexes, the rest primarily Central Americans of one kind or another, and Spanish is the prevalent language in the unit. Even half of the COs are Latin.

Having grown up in a bilingual family in a bilingual town, Axel speaks Spanish with exceptional fluency, but he has kept his knowledge of it a secret from everyone on the inside. Always better if they think you don't know what's being said. He has kept the secret even from Cacho. To retain his own competence with the language over the years, he has made a daily practice of speaking it to himself during his afternoon runs in the exercise yard, holding imaginary conversations requiring a complexity of ideas and denotations and a full range of grammatical inflections.

Cacho picks up a sausage link and bites off half of it. He scowls as he chews and drops the rest of the sausage back in the tray. He takes a slow look at the Guatemalans, then leans toward Axel and points down at his tray and whispers, "No more hog slop, old-timer. Not after today."

Axel spoons up some oatmeal. *Tell him,* he thinks.

Cacho looks about with studied indifference, checking for passing guards.

"Hear the weather?"

Axel shakes his head. The oatmeal is glutinous on his tongue. Laughing and gibing, the Guatemalans get up and leave.

"Gonna rain," Cacho says. "Heard a coupla COs saying. Probly real hard, they said, on account of some big-ass storm from the California Gulf or something. Rain be nothing but a great big help. Harder for them to see us, no? On the ground, from a chopper. Rain's a sign that God loves us and is smiling on us."

Tell him.

Cacho looks at his congealing food with distaste. "First thing I'm gonna have for breakfast back in the world? Chorizo con huevos." He spreads his thumb and forefinger. "With a stack of tortillas this high. Christ, I've missed that! Been *nine months,* man!"

Tell him!

Cacho taps his fingertips lightly along the table edge as if playing a piano and very softly and with the barest lip movement sings "La Valentina," a popular song dating to the Mexican Revolution. Axel is familiar with the song and its outlook of ready fatalism. It's a small wonder to him that although the kid is well aware he can die anytime he cannot conceive that he might someday be old. Can any kid? *He* couldn't when he was young.

Not that he's old now. You can't call forty-five young, but damn if it's *old,* no matter the kid's always calling him *"viejo"* or "old-timer." Even in another eleven years he won't really be *that* old. . . . *Oh man, cut the shit!* he thinks. The problem with playing it safe for the next eleven years is that no matter how safe he plays it there's no telling what might happen. He could get shanked in the heart, get his throat cut. Could trip on the stairs and break his neck. Could get cancer and die. He could fuck up royal and get more time added *anyway.* It happened once, could happen again.

And what if in those eleven years something happens to *her* again? What if next time she's not so lucky as she was in Mexico City last winter? What if Charlie can't help her next time? There's no knowing about next time, or even about goddamn tomorrow. All we ever have is right *now*—that's the plain and simple *duh* of it.

He's been bullshitting himself that more time is the worst that can happen. The worst that can happen is to just roll over and accept *at least* another eleven years of the same dead *now* he's been stuck in since the day they turned the key on him. Another eleven years of waiting for the chance to see her and during which time who-knows-what might happen to prevent it for good. Yeah, he can get killed trying this thing, and yeah, if he gets caught he'll be in for longer than another eleven. But if he says no to this and it ends up he doesn't get to see her *anyway,* he'll feel like a cowardly fool all the way to his last breath. If the thing goes to hell, it goes to hell, and if he gets killed, fuck it, no more troubles. And if he gets caught and catches more time, well, he'll just have to chew on that bitter bone when it happens. . . . *If* it happens. Because goddamnit, *if* can go the other way, too, and that's—

"Earth to Ax . . . Earth to Ax, over," Cacho says, holding a fist to his mouth like a microphone. He grins and turns the hand palm-up and says, "Where'd you go, old bro?"

"Was remembering this café in San Benito. Made the best eggs with chorizo I ever had."

Cacho smiles and pretends to strum a guitar and repeats a line of the "Valentina" song. *"Si me han de matar mañana, que me maten de una vez."*

Axel smiles at the line's audacious self-drama, translating it in his head—"If they're going to kill me tomorrow, let them kill me here and now."

"You two! Out! *Move!*"

They'd failed to notice the floor guard coming down the aisle. "Fist-face," the cons call him, for his chronic aspect of anger.

"Move your asses!"

They hasten to comply. Fist-face is one of those COs who'll write you up quick for so much as a smirk. Get you stripped of work privilege, restricted to your cell.

They take their trays across the room and slide them into the pass-through window to the kitchen. As they exit the hall, the PA crackles and announces the end of the breakfast period and orders all inmates back to the cells for head count.

8

Billy Capp was a senior-year transfer student from Fort Worth, but Axel didn't get to know him until they played baseball on the school team. With Axel at short and Billy at second, they were a formidable double-play combination. Billy's dad, an oil company pilot, was killed in a crash in the Gulf when Billy was three. His mother went to work as a waitress and they lived all over Texas before settling in Fort Worth when Billy was sixteen. When she died of a stroke at the end of his junior year, he moved to Brownsville to live with his widowed and childless aunt Jolene in her little house and finish high school.

The two boys soon became close friends, and Billy confessed to Axel that he'd had run-ins with the police since the age of thirteen. Breaking and entering, theft, possession of stolen property, such as that. It was a real rush, the night-prowling, even though he was caught twice, but his mother's tearful courtroom pleas and the character testaments of baseball coaches had both times saved him from juvenile detention. As a condition to living under his aunt's roof, he had promised her he would stay out of trouble. Axel had never committed a crime more serious than street fighting, but the rush Billy spoke of was the sort of sensation he associated with the shade trade, though he said nothing of it to Billy. One of the *strictest of Wolfe rules was that you never even hinted at the shade trade to anyone outside the family.*

❧

They often double-dated on weekends, Axel usually with a different girl each time but Billy always with Raquel Calderas, a Mexican beauty he'd met at a dance during the annual Charro Days festival. Her family lived on a large estate across the river, just outside of Matamoros, but she attended an elite Catholic school in Brownsville. In addition to the best education she could get close to home, her father wanted her to acquire American friends and further improve her English, so she was living with Brownsville relatives until graduation. Señor Calderas was a major partner in an investment company with branches all over northern Mexico, but it was whispered he had a hand in a number of illicit interests as well. Such rumors of course attached to a number of the most prosperous families along both sides of the Lower Rio Grande, including the Wolfes. Billy had recently confided to Axel that he was crazy about Raquel and believed she liked him a lot, too, even though she wouldn't let him do anything more than fondle her through her clothes and hadn't done anything more for him than give him a hand job through his swim trunks once when they were at Boca Chica Beach in water to their necks. He called her Rocky, and she delighted in the nickname, sometimes putting up her fists and making awkward feints and jabs at him. He took her to the graduation dance at the school gym, doubling with Axel and his date, and later that evening, after they took the girls home, they bought a six-pack and drank it on Aunt Jolene's porch, talking quietly about how great it was to be done with high school. They were down to the last two beers when Billy told him that during the dance he and Raquel had gone outside to do a little smooching and he'd told her he loved her and she said she loved him too, which was the greatest thing he'd ever heard. He asked her to marry him, but she said she couldn't. She had promised her father she would not get married or even engaged until after she graduated from college—she had already been accepted by St. Edward's University in Austin—and she had to honor the promise. They'd neither one said much on the way home, but when he walked her to her door she gave him the best kiss of his life.

"Aw, man," Axel said. "She's really beautiful and sweet and I know how special she is, but why would you want to get married? She's right. She's too young. So are you and me. We got a lot of beautiful girls to meet yet, bud, and we oughta sample as many as we can, don't you reckon? Before we settle down? If we ever do?"

Billy chuckled along with him. "You're right. What the hell was I thinking?"

They finished the beer and Billy went over to the car with him.

"It's on account of I got no money, I know that's why," he said at the driver's window as Axel started the engine. "I'll never have enough for her daddy. Never enough to satisfy him."

Before Axel could think of what to say, Billy slapped the car roof and said, "Take her easy, amigo," and headed back to the house.

He would not mention her to Axel again.

9

Half an hour after the postbreakfast head count, Axel arrives at the maintenance annex, where the work crews are mustering in the hallway. He joins the other three trusties waiting at the office door. The head maintenance officer, Mason, a lanky man with a fiery red pompadour, looks up from the papers on his desk and beckons the trusties into the room. He hands each one a printout of his crew's job list for the day. Axel looks at the last venue on his list and sees that it's the infirmary. As planned. He and Mason exchange a blank look.

Mason is one of the inside men. He's a longtime CO of good standing who has worked at a number of Texas units and has now been at Zanco for eight years. The word on him is that he has a gambling habit and has been married and divorced three times, the most recent split within the past year. It's said that he has on occasion sold a con an inside favor, always in a manner too sly to risk implicating himself. Axel hasn't known a convict who claimed to have personally done business with him, but he's long had a hunch Mason could be bought, and he had told Cacho so.

The trusties go into the storeroom, where under the eye of the supply officer they each load a utility cart with the equipment and supplies his crew will need for their morning labors. The mandatory forms are filled out and signed and the crews disperse to their assignments. Besides himself and Cacho, there are three other men in Axel's crew—an Okie kid doing four years for auto theft, a Mexican from Hermosillo doing fifteen for manslaughter, and a sixty-year-old Negro, as he insists on being called—he will bristle if called "black" and come at you swinging if referred to as "African-American"—who's been under a life sentence for murder since the age of eighteen.

Their first job is at the corrections officers' dining hall. They inspect a coffee urn reported to be malfunctioning, determine that it is, and a crewman loads it on the cart and takes it away to the maintenance shop. They sweep and mop the dining room floor, then run the buffer over it. They wash the windows, clean the hall bathroom, change the gasket on a leaky sink tap. They refill the paper towel dispensers and restock the bathroom shelves with towels, soap, toilet paper. They lug out the garbage cans and empty them in one of the Dumpsters that stand in long rows in full view of the tower guards.

All the while they're at work, Axel can't help thinking that this could be his last day alive. An alternate possibility, that he could be both alive and at large by tonight, seems more unreal to him by the hour. After so many years of caged regimentation in which nothing really changes except for your aging flesh, he finds it hard to visualize himself in the outside world and engaged with its countless and constant choices, its incessant changes. At the same time—and for the first time in more than two decades—he does not know where, if he's still alive, he will be tomorrow, what

he will be wearing, what he might choose to eat, what he might
see, whom he might talk to who's never been inside a prison.
Such uncertainty about his immediate future charges him with
a vibrant excitement he hasn't known for so long it seems an
alien sensation.

10

As the years passed, his embitterment about Billy Capp began to exhaust him. He came to see it as a sort of sickness that would make him old before his time—old and sour and maybe even loony—if he did not somehow surmount it. Wherever Billy was, dead or alive, it simply did not matter anymore. So did he tell himself.

❦

At the beginning of his fifteenth year of incarceration he was transferred to the Charles Zanco Unit in Terrell County. By then he had been able to stay out of trouble for more than seven years. No fights, no serious frictions of any sort. He was civil to the COs but never friendly, and, as always, he sought no friends among the inmates. He read copiously—histories, tech journals, newsmagazines. The Internet had come into being after he was imprisoned and he informed himself about its rudiments through magazines and Charlie's letters and listening in on discussions between some of the younger inmates. He kept fit with cell exercises and daily runs around the yard. He wrote to Charlie every two weeks and received a letter every other week in return. Though Zanco was much farther from Brownsville than were any of the other units where he'd done time, Charlie never failed to make his monthly visit.

Midway through his second year at Zanco he was permitted "contact visits" for the first time ever and could now greet Charlie with a hug in the outdoor visiting area, where they would sit at a table under an umbrella and chat while sipping soda pop. Their conversations no longer monitored, they could speak freely in low voice, and Axel was finally able to tell him who his partners had been. Charlie was outraged to learn that Billy Capp had deserted him, but Axel said he really didn't care anymore, that he'd exhausted his anger for Billy. It wasn't worth the toll it had been taking on him. Charlie said he was going to try to track him down anyway, the Duro guy, too, but Billy was his main ambition. Axel shrugged and said, "Whatever makes you happy, little brother."

⚬⚬⚬

Charlie continued to bring pictures of Jessie, including one taken at her high school graduation, and four years later, one of her receiving her BA in Journalism. There was a picture of her at her desk the first day on the job as a Brownsville newspaper reporter and one of her at the door of her new apartment. By then Charlie was allowed to bring a small camera to leave with the officer in charge at the Zanco visitors' entrance and with which the officer would take Charlie and Axel's picture at the end of the visit. Charlie had framed some of the better photos and put them on his living room wall, and on more than one occasion when Jessie came for supper, he had peeked out from the kitchen and seen her staring at them, though she never made mention of them. Still, Axel was pleased to hear it. Pleased that she knew what he looked like.

⚬⚬⚬

So well did he comport himself at Zanco that in his fifth year at the unit he was made a trusty. He proved worthy of the position, and he welcomed his responsibilities as a work crew leader as an additional distraction from his usual preoccupations. The X's on his calendar seemed to accumulate more quickly. The weeks passed. The months. The years . . .

And then last February, during his monthly visit, Charlie said he had a story to tell him, but began by assuring him that Jessie was at home and perfectly fine and unharmed.

"What? What happened?"

A few weeks earlier, Charlie told him, Jessie had gone to Mexico City to visit Wolfe relatives and serve as a bridesmaid at a college friend's nuptials, and the entire wedding party—bride and groom, four ushers, and four bridesmaids—had been abducted by a gang demanding five million dollars for all ten in the bunch from the wealthy parents of the wedding couple.

Charlie had gone down there with Rudy Wolfe, one of his best operatives, and with the help of their Mexico City relatives they extracted Jessie unharmed. "I wasn't going to tell you," Charlie said, "because why make you worry about something that worked out okay? But I knew it wouldn't be right to keep it from you. Believe me, though, Ax, she's absolutely fine; I wouldn't lie to you about that. Hell, man, I came out worse than her. Took a bullet in the side, but luckily no real damage. You oughta be damn proud of her, man, the way she handled herself. She's a Wolfe all the way to the ground."

One of their Mexican cousins, Jessie's longtime best friend, Rayo Luna Wolfe, had been a big help in getting her out of that jackpot, and she had come back to Texas with them. She and Jessie were renting the old beach house belonging to Harry Morgan Wolfe, an elder cousin of many younger Wolfes who call him "Uncle" in deference to his age. Axel wasn't pleased by the idea of the two of them living by themselves in that isolated place way back in the dunes, but Charlie said he didn't have to worry. In addition to being a stuntwoman in Mexican movies and TV shows, Rayo Luna had been a Jaguaro and was now working for him in the shade trade. "If you saw how that girl can use a gun and kick ass," Charlie said, "you'd know Jessie's got all the home security she needs."

Still, as Axel's yearning to see Jessie had grown keener over time, he had begun to fret that something might happen to him before he ever got the chance. Charlie's report of her abduction gave rise to another anxiety—that something might happen to her before he got the chance.

11

The next two jobs are plumbing problems, a common sort in these old cell blocks. The first one is easy enough to deal with, a sink trap plugged by a sludgy buildup of soap and hair. The second is a toilet stopped up with T-shirts jammed into the trapway by an aggrieved convict who had then copiously evacuated his bowels into it before wedging open the flush valve to keep the intake water coming. When the enraged guards sloshed into the cell through the foul overflow, the perpetrator laughed at their disgust and then made matters much the worse for himself by resisting his removal to the isolation block before at last being borne away unconscious.

By the time they clear the clog and mop up the reeking cell and the flanking corridor and clean off their shoes and rinse the mops in the outdoor spigots, it's nearing 10:30, the start of the lunch period and midday yard time.

They return the cart to the storeroom and get to the dining hall fast enough to be near the front of the line when the hall guards open its door. The hall is most crowded at the beginning of a feeding period, and especially so at lunch, the biggest meal of the day, when the guards are much quicker to eject any man lingering at a table or running his mouth instead of eating. Like most inmates who strive to be at the front of the chow line, Axel and his crew don't dally. Their usual mode is to eat in a hurry and then hustle away in order to have more time out in the yard before having to return to their cells for the next head count. Today Axel and Cacho cajole the servers into giving them a little extra of the mashed potatoes and gravy, and they take additional slices of bread as well. They clean off their trays to the last crumb because there's no telling when they will eat again, or even if ever again, as Axel anxiously reflects while mopping the last of his gravy with the last of his bread.

⚬✖⚬

Earlier that morning, when they crossed from the officers' hall to the cell block with the clogged drains, the sky was a cloudless blue but for a few sallow wisps above the mountains far to the west. "Rain, my ass," Cacho had said low-voiced. "Weathermen don't know dick. No big deal. Be a help, rain, but nothing depends on it."

But now, out in the yard after lunch, they're looking at a long, lean bank of bruise-colored clouds extending over the western ranges.

"Well now, lookee there," says Cacho.

"It's not much and a good ways off," says Axel, "but could turn into something."

"You feel it, bro? Feel God's big smile on us?"

12

After graduation, Billy put off looking for a job so that they could enjoy summer to the fullest before Axel left for the University of Houston. They often went fishing in Axel's little johnboat in the shallows of the Laguna Madre and always brought in some nice catches. One day Axel accidentally cut his hand cleaning a redfish on a dockside table, and Billy deliberately cut his own hand and placed his elbow on the table with the hand upraised. They grinned and clasped hands in the manner of arm wrestlers, and Billy cried, "Blood brothers!"

They loved to spend time in Wolfe Landing, a riverside village in the midst of a 450-acre palm grove about midway between Brownsville and the Gulf. Founded in the late nineteenth century by the first Wolfes to settle in Texas and duly chartered as a town in 1911, it has rarely had as many as a hundred residents, and the most recent census counted sixty-three. The only street not of dirt is tar-and-gravel Main, which contains a little town hall, Riverside Motors & Garage, Mario's Grocery, a secondhand-goods store, Get Screwed Hardware, and the Republic Arms gun shop. Where Main Street ends, a wide dirt trail branches northward and winds up into the slightly higher ground containing a cemetery and the mobile homes and wooden cabins of the main residential area. Opposite the Republic Arms is

*Gator Lane, which runs a short way down to the river, ending at Gringo's
Bait & Tackle and, just across the street from it, the Doghouse Cantina. The
Lower Rio Grande abounds with resacas— "resaca" being the local term for
an oxbow lake—and there are a number of them in Wolfe Landing. The
biggest of them, Resaca Mala, is in the perpetual shadows of the deepest part
of the grove and is inhabited by a colony of alligators, generations of which
have long served as an extremely effective mode for disposing of Doghouse
garbage as well as various other forms of organic remains.*

Billy loved the Landing and was tickled to learn that Axel's much
older cousin, Henry James Wolfe, HJ to everyone, was the mayor, the
police chief of a department consisting of only himself, and the owner
of the Doghouse. He would never know HJ was also chief of the Wolfe
shade trade operations. HJ was always glad to see the boys and always
let them stay for as long as they wished in one of the unoccupied rental
trailers.

On every visit, they would use up a box or two of cartridges at
the target range behind the Republic Arms. Billy had never before held
a loaded gun, and the first time he fired a round and felt the recoil and
saw the bullet's black hole in the white-paper target was a novel thrill.
He found he had a natural feel for handguns and was soon scoring tight-
group bull's-eyes at fifty feet. Axel's favorite pistol, a 1911 Army Colt
.45 semiautomatic, became Billy's, too. At the Doghouse Cantina they
would shoot pool and play the jukebox, flirt with whichever barmaid was
on duty, and gorge on the best barbecued ribs in the county. HJ would
let them have beer on the house, but never more than one an hour, his
prescription for avoiding getting drunk.

On Saturday afternoons they would visit the Arguello sisters, Rosa
and Ramona, who lived in a trailer far back in the trees. They were attractive, sweet-natured girls who worked at Mario's Grocery on weekdays
and liked a good time on weekends, and Axel and Billy always arrived
at their double-wide with steaks to grill and a cooler of beer. And always,

at some point during the night, the boys would give each other a grinning thumbs-up as they passed naked in the dim hallway, swapping bedrooms and giggling girls.

✧

Late that summer, Aunt Jolene had a fatal heart attack while making breakfast. She bequeathed the little house to Billy, who immediately sold it and then rented a furnished room. He told Axel he hoped to get hired as a charter boat mate and didn't want the responsibility of a house. The night before Axel departed for Houston, they had a few beers at the Doghouse and said they couldn't wait to get together when he came home for Thanksgiving. Nearly a month later, having received no answer to the two letters he'd written to Billy, Axel phoned the owner of the residence where he was rooming and was told that Billy had abruptly moved out one night almost three weeks before, without word to anyone and a week's rent in arrears.

13

After the postlunch head count they return to the maintenance shop to retrieve the cart, then get back to their job list. By 2:45 a breeze has sprung up, and the western horizon is a mass of swelling purple clouds. During the next hour the clouds begin to flicker with mute heat lightning as they rise toward the lowering sun and then consume it altogether.

Axel's crew is running a little behind schedule when it completes its work at the kennel, having rewired an outlet in the dog boy's quarters and rehinged a pen gate, the dogs whining and barking the whole while in agitation at the coming storm. Distant forks of pale lightning are trailed a few seconds later by muffled rolling rumbles. The wind builds, popping and snapping the big Stars and Stripes on its pole by the front gate. It carries the electric smell of rain into the prison with an effect as unsettling as the scent of a woman. It sets the convicts' nerves on edge, provokes abrupt scuffles that as hastily break up before the guards converge.

Now only the infirmary job is left on their list. At a quarter of four, they pack up their gear and set off to D Building—the

farthest-removed from the other admin buildings—pushing the
cart over a winding walkway under a leaden sky. The lightning
now branching more widely and coming in faster sequence. The
thunder gradually growing louder and crackling closer on the
heels of every flash.

14

Near the end of his first semester at Houston, he met Ruby Saint-Cyr at a street party. A drama major, more fun in bed than any girl he'd known, plus she had an aura of mystery, of a secret self, that made her all the more alluring. She was much on his mind during the Christmas break, and it occurred to him he might be in love.

Among the things he didn't know about Ruby was that, on learning he was from a family of lawyers, she researched the Wolfes in the library's Cameron County reference files, scrolling through microfilm and microfiche, reading newspaper accounts of Wolfe Associates' courtroom successes, of the sensational 1930s killing of César Wolfe by his wife, Catalina, of the acquittal of James Ryan Wolfe on charges of contraband smuggling some thirty years ago. She also learned of Wolfe ownership of other businesses, and of their substantial real estate holdings. In short, she learned they were rich.

She was aware of Axel's undeclared love for her and expertly nurtured it. One night after a party, as they lay in each other's arms, she murmured that she loved him, an avowal that kept him awake long after she'd fallen asleep. A month later they were living together. At the end of the spring term she told him she was two months pregnant. No, there

*had been nobody but him, and yes, she had been on the pill but even her
doctor said it was not foolproof. She said the biggest surprise to her was
that she wanted to have the baby. She assured him she would make no
demands for support of any kind and would raise the child herself.*

*They talked and talked and then he lay awake into the night,
considering the circumstances, and in the morning he asked her to marry
him. She wept as she hugged him. He telephoned his father and forth-
rightly explained the situation. Harry Mack intuited chicanery on the
part of the young woman but did not say so. Whether the pregnancy was
a consequence of carelessness or contrivance, he saw it as a fortunate turn.
He had always suspected subterfuge in Axel's early agreement to go to
law school and had anticipated his intention to default on it as soon as
he got his BA. But a family was the foremost of all responsibilities and
would be far more reliably provided for by a partner in Wolfe Associates
than by a shade trade operative, and Axel would surely see that. And if
the woman was gold-digging, well, there were simple legal measures to
thwart that.*

⚬≫⚬

*They were married in the Church of the Sacred Heart in Brownsville.
The reception was at Harry Mack's home, where Ruby was introduced
to so many Wolfe relatives she couldn't keep them straight. After a brief
honeymoon in Galveston they returned to Houston. Jessie Juliet was born
the following January, midway through Axel's sophomore year, and she
was attended by nannies night and day.*

*Axel maintained excellent grades to better preserve the fiction that
he was prepping for law school. In truth, college was an aching bore and
he could hardly wait for the day he would get his degree and enter the
shade trade. He dearly loved his wife and child but did not deem them
a sufficient reason to choose a lawyer's life over the one he truly wanted.
There was no sufficient reason. As for what Ruby would say when the*

day came that he informed her of the shade trade and his choice of it and all its risks, well, what could she say? She'd say if that's what you want, baby, that's what we'll do. She was smart and she was his partner. Until then, he simply had to bite the bullet, be a good student, and bide his time. But the wait was chafing.

᠁

One summer evening at the end of his junior year and a few weeks after he and Ruby and baby Jessie had been to Brownsville for Charlie's high school graduation, Axel walked home from the campus and was almost to the courtyard gate of his apartment complex when a car parked across the street tooted its horn and he looked over to see Billy Capp grinning at him from behind the wheel. Then they were in the street, hugging and pounding each other on the back, Axel calling him a lowlife bastard for not having been in touch in all this time and Billy saying yeah, yeah, he was a no-good friend and he knew it. He'd phoned Charlie, who told him Axel was married and a daddy and gave him his phone number and address in Houston.

Axel wanted him to come in and meet Ruby but Billy said he had things to tell him that it would be better his wife didn't hear. So they went to a nearby sports bar and Axel phoned Ruby to say he'd been roped into a few beers with some pals and would be a little late. She said to enjoy himself, he deserved a break.

They sat in a rear booth and toasted their reunion. "It's been, what, damn near three years," Axel said. "Where the hell you been?"

"Mostly in prison," Billy said. And told him about it.

15

Because of the infirmary's store of drugs, inmates may not work there except under the direct, on-site supervision of a senior corrections officer. When the crew presents itself at the door, CO Mason is seated in the waiting room and chatting with the doctor. The day's last ailing prisoner has been treated and discharged and the doctor has his coat on, prepared to leave. He takes up his bag and says he hopes to beat the rain home but won't take bets on it and says so long to Mason.

In addition to the waiting room, the infirmary comprises an examination room and a rear storeroom containing a large industrial desk and an assortment of high shelves and multiple-bin lockers. The job is a general cleanup plus stocking a load of medical supplies that were supposed to have been received that afternoon. But as Mason informs them, the delivery agent has phoned the main office to say he's running late. He'd had a flat tire just north of Fort Stockton and won't get to Zanco till about 4:30. No putting the delivery off, either: Zanco is the guy's last stop at the end of a two-hundred-mile, daylong route. If he doesn't make the drop today he won't be this way again for another two weeks, and the doc wouldn't be happy about that.

"Me and you and whatever guy you pick are gonna stay and stock the stuff," Mason tells Axel. "I'll cut the others loose soon as the cleanup's done."

The workday ends at four o'clock with another head count in the cell blocks before the inmates are released to supper and the last yard period of the day. However, if an inmate is working on an overtime job, the officer in charge can vouch for his presence at the work site by phoning the duty officer in lieu of sending him back to his cell for the count. Axel and Cacho know that Mason has already contacted the duty officer to apprise him that the infirmary tasks won't be completed until well after four, so he'll have the crew escorted to the mess hall from here, and that he and a pair of convicts—Wolfe and Ramirez, inmate numbers thus and such—will be staying at the infirmary to receive a delayed delivery, cartons of medical equipment that have to be handled carefully and sorted and stocked. The job will take till six o'clock, maybe longer, so he'll be late turning in the maintenance reports.

Shamming a doleful look at this extension of his duty day, Axel turns to the others to make his choice. They avert their eyes.

"Ramirez, you're it," he says, addressing Cacho.

"*Chingado,*" Cacho mutters through his teeth. And makes an "up yours" hand sign to the grinning others.

16

"Coupla weeks after you left for college," Billy said, "I got in a fight and hit the dude over the head with a beer mug and was afraid I'd killed him, so I quick split. Then in San Antonio this fella offered me a job shuttling hot cars from one part of Texas to another. Went real good for a few months before I got pulled over for a dead taillight on a five-year-old Mercedes Coupe. Did two years at Goree Unit before I got paroled. My last few months there I got to know a robber named Gary Duval who was getting out two weeks before me and needed a partner. Asked was I interested and I said yeah. When I got out we met up and he introduced me to the robbery trade. Near to five months ago. We hit nothing but bagmen who make daily collections from the street sellers and then deliver the week's take to the dealers. I tell you, bud, I never known juice like it. The gamblers got a saying, maybe you know it. They say won money is sweeter than earned money, and I guess it is. In gambling, though, the money's the only thing at stake and your biggest risk is going broke. But every time you go out to do a robbery you're staking your ass, and that risk beats just everything. It makes robbed money the sweetest kind there is, let me tell you. Anyhow, we worked out of Port Arthur, where Gary rented a house. He'd buy tips on bagmen—their pickup routes, where *they lived, all that—and we were doing two rips a month. By "we," I mean me and Gary and a driver named Bud. We always used a stolen car and Gary and I carried cut-off 12-gauge pumps. We'd hit them on the morning of delivery day. Wait down the street from where they live till they come out. Most of them got a bodyguard who usually does the driving. When they got in their car, Bud would zoom up and block them and Gary and me would jump out and poke the shorties in their faces on either side of the car and Gary'd strip the bagman of his piece and the money while I took the driver's gun and snatched the keys outta the ignition, then we'd jump back in the car and get gone. We were doing good till one night little more than two weeks ago when Bud starts coughing blood and we take him to the emergency room and two days later he dies. We still didn't have a driver when Gary goes to this bar in Bridge City with a redhead whose husband's on the road a lot, and they're drinking at the bar when hubby comes through the front door with a revolver in his hand. The way the bartender told it to the cops the hubby never said a word, just* bam-bam-bam-bam, *shot Gary four times. People screaming, running out the doors. Wifey tried to make a run for it and* bam-bam *he shoots her in the ass and down she goes. She's still crawling for the side door and he's walking toward her and reloading when the bartender pulls his own piece and shoots hubby in the brainpan and that was all she wrote. I heard about it on the radio the next day, and there I was with zero partners. That was two days ago. The kicker is, three days ago a fix-up guy Gary knows—one of those guys who for a price can fix you up with information, partners, buyers, whatever you need—he'd called Gary to ask were we interested in meeting a San Antone guy in need of two partners for some kinda major league score. Said the guy was Mexican but spoke good English. It'd cost us a grand for a meet, same as the Mex. Gary'd been wanting to move up from bagman rips, so he says yeah and goes and gives the fix-up the money and gets the time and place for the meet, which was at this fancy little café four nights from then."*

"*Meaning tomorrow,*" *Axel says.*

"*Meaning tomorrow. But my problem is—*"

"*You need a partner,*" *Axel says.* "*I'm in.*"

Billy gawked at him. "*Jesus, man! Just like that? I thought I'd have to talk and talk and you'd still say no on account you're—*"

"*I just want to know, why come to me?*"

Billy grinned. "*Well, hell, you never did lack for sand or, well . . . strike me as a toe-the-line sort. I've heard some of the stories they tell around Brownsville about those old-time Wolfe badasses and their outlaw ways. Always had a hunch you might have a touch of those ways in you.*"

Only now did Axel grasp how well Billy had come to know him. Quicker than I've come to know myself, *he thinks.* "Good hunch. *Like I said, I'm your huckleberry.*"

"*You're sure? I mean . . . you got a family, dude.*"

"*I know what I've got.*"

"*You can't say nothing to your wife. I ain't saying she can't be trusted, just that—*"

"*She'll never know a thing.*" *Axel put his elbow on the table and raised his hand as if challenging him to arm-wrestle.*

Billy laughed and clasped it. "*Amberlight Tavern, downtown,*" *he said.* "*Eight o'clock tomorrow night. I'm Billy Jones, you're Axel Smith. Wear a jacket.*"

17

The infirmary is a more orderly venue than most and its cleanup is quick and easy. They're just finishing up when the storm crashes over the prison. The rain pounding the roof, thunderclaps ripping and blasting across the sky, the detonations tinkling the glass containers in the cabinets. When the overhead lights flicker, the other Mexican, Santos, says, *"Ay, dios!"* and makes the sign of the cross. With his back to the others, Cacho looks at Axel and silently mouths, *"God loves us."*

Now there's only the storeroom to attend to. It's at the back of the infirmary, its rear door abutting a circular driveway where convicts requiring hospitalization are picked up and where medical shipments are delivered. The room's sole window overlooks the driveway and glows with every lightning flash. Wind gusts fling the rain against it like gravel. Axel tells the crew to set the big trash bags next to the back door and he and Cacho will take them out to the Dumpster after they unload the coming delivery. "We're anyway gonna get wet unloading, so what the hell," he says. He glances at the digital clock on the wall. It's ten after four.

Mason ushers the other three men of Axel's crew back out
to the waiting room, where he phones for a CO to come and
provide the mandatory escort for them through the administration annex. Axel and Cacho stand at the storeroom window and
stare out at the storm, the panes framing a rain-streaked view of
the main fence about forty yards away and the high guard tower
alongside it—Number Four Tower—its square booth bordered
by an outer walkway. A narrow access lane connects the infirmary
driveway to an inner perimeter road that runs all the way around
the prison.

The lights are on in the tower booth and the guard inside is a
vague figure. From his vantage he has a clear view of the infirmary
door. One of his duties is to keep a close eye on every vehicle that
makes a delivery there. He is another of the inside men.

18

Cacho arrived at Zanco in the early spring under the name of Carlos Ramirez, the name on his Texas driver's license, and three weeks later was assigned to Axel's maintenance crew. They sat next to each other at the midday meal and the kid said to call him Cacho, which Axel knew was a common nickname for Carlos. There was nothing of the toady about him, and Axel liked his sense of humor, and when they finished eating they went out to the yard together. The kid already knew the rules of convict life well enough not to pry beyond the permissible limits of asking what Axel was in for and for how long. When Axel told him he was doing thirty for armed robbery plus another five for assault of a CO, Cacho said, "Damn, old-timer, you're hardcore." On learning he had been at Zanco for ten years, the kid said, "No shit? Man, I guess you know this joint pretty good by now."

"Like a zoo monkey knows its cage."

Cacho scratched at his ribs like a monkey and said, "Uh-uh-uh," and they both laughed.

They continued to converse through the afternoon maintenance jobs, shutting up whenever a CO or even another con was within earshot. At the end of that first workday together, when Axel said he was going to take a jog before supper, Cacho asked if he could join him. He considered for a moment and had to admit to himself he liked the kid. And so said, "Why not?"

Thus did he accept the first friend he'd ever had inside the walls.

⚬✦⚬

Cacho told him he had been born in Monterrey and lived in Mexico all his life, mostly on the border, but was familiar with a lot of Texas border towns, plus San Antonio. He was orphaned at twelve when the bus his parents were taking to visit Sabinas went off a bridge and into a river. He then went to live with his much older half-brother, Joaquín, who had grown up in the riverside border town of Nuevo Laredo and now owned a real estate company there. Joaquín spoke English fluently and Cacho had learned it from him and from watching gringo TV shows.

Before coming to Zanco, he'd been in two processing units at the start of a ten-year sentence for a fight he got into in San Antonio. He was standing outside a nightclub with his date when some dude grabbed her ass, so he went at him with both fists. Next thing he knew somebody was whacking him from behind with a club and so he tore into him, too, and fucked him up pretty bad—facial fractures, damage to one eye. Turned out the guy was a security guard. From jail he called his brother, who got him a lawyer who couldn't do much against a dozen witnesses who'd seen him pounding the guard. He drew ten years for aggravated assault. The lawyer told him that as soon as he was processed into the system and assigned to a regular unit, another lawyer would go to see him and handle his appeal. Cacho had been at Zanco a week when an El Paso attorney named Somoza came to visit and promised he would visit on every Saturday to come.

From the start, the kid was impressed by Axel's store of knowledge and wanted to know how he'd acquired it. "I read, you oughta try it," Axel said, but soon after admitted that he'd gone to college for three years.

"You were in college and got jammed for armed robbery?" Cacho said. "How does that happen?"

"I fell in with wayward companions."

"Yeah, right. I hear that happens to a lot of college guys, making friends with robbers and falling into the life. You got some strange ways, old-timer, you know that?"

"So I've been told."

Other than the facts of having gone to college and of his prison record, Axel told Cacho no other truth about his past. He claimed to be an orphan, too, to have no living kin at all. The only visitor he got, he told Cacho, was an old college buddy named Charlie. It wasn't so much that he didn't trust the kid with the truth but that all his convict years had made it second nature to lie, to hide things about himself. The unknown truths about you are among the few things you can truly possess in prison, that you can refuse to relinquish. So he did.

❦

He had known the kid only six weeks on the day they were walking in the yard after the midday meal and Cacho said, "Hey, old man, what say we bust out of this zoo?"

19

At 4:20, Axel says, "Where is he?"

Cacho shrugs. "Storm's probly slowed him."

The escort guard having collected the other three crew members, CO Mason returns to the storeroom. He has locked the front door and flung the ring of keys into a corner of the waiting room. His face is drawn tight. Axel knows he isn't looking forward to what he's in for. Who would be?

"What, he ain't *here* yet?" Mason says.

Cacho keeps his gaze out the window and says nothing. Axel doesn't know whether to admire the kid's cool or be irked by it.

At 4:25, Axel whispers to Cacho, "Flare's in twenty minutes."

"I know it," the kid says, without taking his eyes from the window.

"This thing's fucked!" Mason says, pacing on the other side of the room. "You shitbirds got no idea what the hell you're—"

"He's here," Cacho says.

A pair of blurred yellow headlights has appeared on the perimeter road. And now they can see the small white vehicle that
always makes the twice-monthly delivery of medical supplies, a
Chevy panel van of a sort widely used by florists. It turns onto
the access lane and bears toward them.

20

The Amberlight Tavern was a low-tempo place catering to young business types. Soft music, hanging plants, booths all along a side wall opposite the bar. Billy had arrived ahead of him, and it took Axel a moment to spot them in the rearmost booth. As he made his way toward them, Billy saw him and gave a passing waitress a three-finger signal.

He slid in on Billy's side. He and Billy wore sport jackets, the Mexican a glossy blue suit. He was thickly black-haired, big-shouldered, with a brush mustache. Late thirties, was Axel's guess. Billy introduced him as Duro Cisneros and they exchanged nods.

"Smith and Jones," Cisneros said with a smile, his voice a deep rasp.

A tall blonde in a black pantsuit and red bowtie brought three large drafts and set them on the table. As she collected the two empties, Cisneros reached up with one hand to adjust her tie, eliciting a stiff smile from her, and Axel glimpsed a small red crescent on the man's inner wrist.

"So, Mister Cisneros," Axel said after the waitress left. "Who are you?"

"A guy in the same business as you boys, Mister Smith, only a better-paying end of it. I'm good enough at it I'm here and not in some cell, same as you. My favorite color's blue and I like Pacino movies. Enough of the get-to-know-you?"

"Fine by me. What've you got?"

Cisneros leaned forward. "Bearer bonds. I told your buddy while we were waiting, but he doesn't know what that is. You?"

"Interest-bearing instruments. They're not registered to the people who buy them. Not registered to anybody. Whoever holds a bearer bond can collect the interest on it to maturity or redeem it anytime, no ID required. But they make it too easy to evade taxes, launder money, all that, and the feds stopped issuing them more than a year ago. There's a lot of them still in circulation, though, and you can still buy them in Europe."

"Your buddy said you're smart. College guy."

"That's me. How much is the rip?" Axel said.

"Seven fifty K."

"Jesus," Billy said. "No shit?"

Cisneros smiled. "No shit."

"What's the play?" Axel said.

"Jewelry store, but fuck the jewels. Pain in the ass to fence and too easy to get cheated. The thing is, the store's also a laundry and a drop for an investment company does all sorts of illegit shit. It's got no ties to any outfit, of that I'm sure. If it did I wouldn't touch it. The store's run by an old man, got a guard. Around ten o'clock on a morning not very long from now, somebody's gonna stop by that store to drop off the bonds and collect some jewels. Then just before noon, somebody else is coming by to pick up the bonds. Only the bonds won't be there anymore because we'll have them. There's a security camera that wouldn't help the cops much even if they saw it, but the company's not about to call them. They won't want to discuss bearer bonds with them or the IRS."

"Your guy knows all this?" Axel said.

"He does. That's why he gets seventy-five. He buys the paper from us for six seven-five, I get two seventy-five, you each get two. If it's not enough, we're done talking."

Axel and Billy exchanged a look.

"*Why not we cash them?*" Billy said. "*Get another twenty-five apiece?*"

"*Listen to you. Be the most you ever had in your hand and already you wanna bump it. The guy's a pal. Him and me play straight with each other. He gave me the lead, he gets his cut.*"

"*Who is he?*" Axel said.

"*My business.*"

"*How's he know about all this?*" Billy said.

"*His business.*"

"*Yeah, all right,*" Axel says. "*But I take it the carriers are pros, which is why you aren't doing the job by yourself, why you're talking to us.*"

"*Nothing gets by a college guy.*"

"*Pro carriers can make it hairy,*" Billy said.

"*It can always get hairy. But odds are not this one. The investment people been using this laundry for a lot of years, using the same carriers. Never had a problem. The carriers are good, but they've been doing this for so long without trouble they'll probably be sleepwalking it and we won't break a sweat. Still, you never know, and the take is worth a three-man team. I already scouted the scene, mapped the thing out. I'll take you there, show you how it lays. We can run through it all except for the inside stuff, and I can draw that for you on paper. We'll be ready is what I'm telling you. So . . . what do you say? In or out?*"

"*You ain't said when or even where,*" Billy said. "*Here in Houston?*"

"*You boys ain't said in or out.*"

Axel and Billy looked at each other.

"*In,*" Axel said. "*And we ain't boys, we're just not old as you.*"

Cisneros laughed. "*Three weeks. Third of July. Dallas.*"

21

Cacho goes to the rollup back door and raises it head-high, the door rattling on its roller tracks and folding under the ceiling. The rain blows in and soaks him. The little medical supplies van comes around the driveway, its panel doors windowless and without outside door handles, its side emblazoned with a triangular logo of three small red crosses over the name "Tri-Cross Medical Supplies, Big Spring, Texas." It follows the paved circle partway past the infirmary door and then backs up and stops with its hatchback some six feet from it. By prison regulation—and without exception even in bad weather—no vehicle may park within five feet of a building doorway, assuring that the nearest tower guard can observe everything that passes between vehicle and door. Keeping the engine idling and the windshield wipers going, the driver releases the lock on the hatchback door and Cacho darts into the rain and raises it. Zanco is the biggest delivery of the driver's day and half the compact cargo area still holds small cartons of medical goods, over the tops of which Cacho meets the driver's wide jumpy eyes. His name is Balestro, and he's the civilian insider. Bushy-haired and thinly mustached, he's been making the Tri-Cross deliveries to Zanco Unit for years, but this is Cacho's first time in the infirmary and hence the first time they've ever seen each other.

"Sorry I'm a little late," the driver says. "Took longer than I thought it would to change the flat, and this *rain,* man, I—"

"Shut up," Cacho says. He nods at Axel and starts taking cartons out of the van and chucking them into the room.

Mason has already handed Axel the two pairs of plastic flex cuffs off his belt, and at Cacho's nod that all is in order, Axel stuffs one pair into his waistband and cuffs Mason's hands behind him with the other, then turns him back around. "How's that, Matthew? Not too tight?" He has never before addressed Mason by his first name.

"Cut the shit and get to it."

"Right," Axel says. He snatches Mason's shirtfront with both hands and yanks hard, snapping away buttons and pulling the shirt partway out of his pants, then tears open the neck of his white T-shirt. He puts a hand to his pompadour and musses it. He looks off to the side and says, "What's that?" and when Mason turns to look, he digs his fingernails into his cheek and claws four scratches into it.

"Jesus!" Mason says, glowering at him.

"Gotta look good, Mattie," Axel says. "You put up a fight but it was two against one and we had a blade. You're lucky we didn't kill you. You'll be a hero just for trying." He's feeling the old adrenaline rush.

Cacho comes over to them. They could have saved time by dealing with Mason while waiting for the van, but if for some reason it didn't show up or not in time and the plan had to be scrapped they would've had the problem of Mason explaining his beat-up state. "You can bet we'd sock you," Axel says. "So, shiner on the other cheek and we're done."

"Just watch the teeth and nose," Mason says, turning his head as Axel gets set to hit him—but Cacho pushes Axel aside and wallops the CO squarely in the face with a roundhouse that knocks him sprawling. As Mason struggles vainly to sit up, hindered by the cuffs, blood gushing from his broken nose, Cacho kicks him in the ribs and then the mouth.

"Ya, enough!" Axel says, pulling Cacho back.

"Watch the teeth and nose," Cacho sneers at Mason. Then says to Axel, "Never liked this shitheel."

Mason chokes and coughs as they drag him over to the big desk. He works his tongue and spits out a front tooth. "Mother . . . *fuckers,"* he gasps, reflexive tears mingling with blood and mucus.

While Cacho goes to the door and lowers it to waist level, Axel cuffs Mason's ankle to the leg of the heavy desk and then rips a long strip off his torn T-shirt, rolls it, and uses it to gag him, tying it so the gag holds down his tongue yet permits him to breathe through his mouth. He regards Mason's battered face and dull red-eyed stare and marvels at the shit some men will eat for money.

"Let's go!" Cacho calls.

⤜∞⤛

They duck under the rollup door and into the rain and Axel crawls into the cargo space as Cacho lowers the infirmary door the rest of the way and then dives in after him and pulls down the hatchback.

"All set? *Go?"* the driver says in a strained voice.

"I'll tell you when," Cacho says.

The storm is still gaining strength, and the afternoon has darkened under a solid gray cloud cover. Because the panel doors lack windows, Axel and Cacho have to scrooch up to the folded-down front passenger seat and look out the driver's window to see the guard tower and the slate sky behind it. A cylindrical compass mounted on the dashboard reads due east. Axel has seen the driver on previous infirmary assignments, but the man seems not to recognize him. Few visitors to a prison ever really look at the convicts.

"What are we waiting for?" the driver says.

"What time is it?" Cacho asks him. "Exactly?"

The driver raises his wristwatch and pushes a button to illuminate its face. "It's exactly four forty-fi—"

"*There!*" Cacho says as a red flare bursts in the high sky beyond the guard tower—a parachute emergency flare that even in broad daylight would have attracted the notice of every tower guard and is even brighter in the gloom of the storm and reeling on the wind.

"What the hell's *that*?" the driver says.

"Get moving," Cacho says.

The nervous driver almost goes off the driveway in getting back on the access lane and Cacho says, "Easy, man!"

"Sorry," the driver says. "I'm okay." They turn off the access lane onto the perimeter road and head south toward the fore of the prison. The posted speed limit is 20 and Cacho tells the driver to hold to it. Then says, "You got something for me?"

"What? Oh yeah ... *yeah*." He fumbles at his shirt pocket and withdraws a small black cell phone and hands it to him.

Axel has never used or even held a cell phone, but he knows enough about them to recognize this one as a cheap sort, what's called a burner. Cacho will use it to let the men waiting in Fort Stockton know when the van has passed through Sanderson, and then again to alert them when the van's within a few minutes of the rendezvous point. Cacho presses a button and the phone face comes alight. Then presses another and looks at the little screen, smiles, dims the screen, and puts the phone in his shirt pocket.

Now visible in the hatchback window, the flare is slowly descending by fits and starts, whipping about erratically in the wind gusts. Axel shifts his attention between the back window and the windshield, scanning for any sign that they've been found out.

"Quit worrying, old man, we're cool," Cacho says, leaning forward over the folded front seat and probing under it. "It'll be an hour before they even wonder where Mason's at, and then a while more before they go looking for him. By the time they find him we'll be way up in the sky and chugging cold beers. Nothing now but the gate."

From under the seat, he pulls out what looks like a small cloth handbag and sits up. The driver gives it an anxious look. As instructed, he had made a restroom stop at a specified minimart gas station in Midland that morning, during which respite the bag had been placed in the van, as he had been told it would be, though on returning to the van he had not dared even to feel under the seat for it. Cacho unzips it and takes something out and holds it up for Axel to see—a crude shiv fashioned by filing a plastic toothbrush handle on the concrete floor to shape its sharp point and hone both sides to keen edges. In the story Mason and the driver will tell investigators, it's the weapon against which Mason dared to resist and with which Cacho threatened to slash the driver's throat if he gave the gate guard any indication of the convicts' presence in the van. Cacho chucks it aside to be found by police investigators, then takes something else out of the bag. A pistol.

Axel's shock is such that he says, "What's that?" before he can check the stupid question.

"Glock," Cacho says, thinking he was asked about the make. "A seventeen."

Although the Glock did not come into prominence until after he was imprisoned, Axel has read and heard a great deal about it. This is the first one he's seen other than in photos. There isn't enough light in the cargo space for Cacho to see if there's a round in the chamber by drawing the slide back a little and taking a look, but Axel sees him feeling for the jut of the ejector with his forefinger to assure himself a bullet's chambered. "You never said anything about a gun," he says. For the first time it occurs to him that Cacho may have withheld some details of the plan.

The driver, too, seems unnerved by the pistol. The kid catches his look and says, "Just drive." Then says to Axel, "Why add to your worries? Think of it as Plan B. If there's a problem at the gate, I put this to the hack's head and he gives the tower the open-up sign."

"They don't open up for hostages. Any hostages."

"So they say. Let's hope we don't have to see if it's true."

Axel feels his pulse in the palms of his fists, in the soles of his feet. His tongue tastes of copper. It's the old euphoric fear.

On their right the passing buildings' windows are aglow. As the road nears the end of the side fence, it curves westward until they're driving parallel to the front fence. Ahead and off to their left is the front gate, brightly lighted in the stormy dusk. A guard tower looms over it. As they approach the intersecting road that leads to the gate, they can distinguish the guard's small dark form at the tower booth window. They turn at the intersection and head for the gate, the dash compass rotating to SSW.

Cacho crouches behind the driver's seat, pistol in hand. Axel up close behind him.

"All right, my man," Cacho says to the driver. "Nice and cool."

22

Not until after the escort CO has conducted the three members of Axel's work crew through the administration annex, released them to go to the chow hall, and then returned to the duty office to finish up some minor paperwork in the last hour of his shift—first sidetracking to assist a female CO in breaking up a trash-talking, finger-jabbing confrontation between an Aryan Brother and a pair of Texas Syndicate Chicanos, then pausing for a chat with a fellow Houston Astros fan who works in data processing—does he realize he is minus his favorite pen, a big-barreled orange ballpoint topped with a smiling bust of the cartoon charac-ter Yogi Bear. The CO's name is Jeffrey Berra and the pen was a stocking gift last Christmas from his bride of three months, a joke present inspired by his nickname among his coworkers. Her giggling delight in giving it to him had made the silly pen special. The thought that he may have lost it upsets Berra until he remembers having handed it to Mason in the waiting room to cosign the release form for the inmates. Heading back to the infirmary, he hopes that if Mason put the pen in his pocket he hasn't yet finished with the late delivery job and already gone back to the maintenance office, which is way the hell over in a separate building and would oblige a hike through the storm. No problem if Mason left it on the desk, because Berra has an infirmary key. He finds the door locked though its frosted glass shows there's a light on inside, suggesting someone's still in there or that Mason forgot to cut the lights when he left. He raps on the door, waits a few seconds, then uses his key. The waiting room is deserted and the pen's not on the desk and he lacks a key for the locked drawers. He goes to the storeroom and sees no one there and is puzzled by the jumble of supply cartons near the rear door. Then he hears a strained snarling and turns to see Mason squirming on the floor—hands behind him, foot cuffed to the desk, eyes bulging in his bloody face, teeth bared in a white-gagged grimace.

Berra grabs for the phone on his belt.

PART II

FUGITIVES

23

The prison's front gate is in fact a pair of gates, one at either end of a large cagelike sally port made of ironwork and chain link, a structure that affords visibility into it from every side as well as from up in the adjoining tower, where an armed guard operates both gates electronically. When entering or leaving the prison, a vehicle must first be cleared by a gate guard on the ground who checks the identification of everyone in the vehicle and, if he so decides, searches it. However, vehicles of regional companies under long-standing contract with the prison and whose drivers are well-known to the gate guards are rarely searched, a detail Axel has many times observed over the years of front-fence cleanup jobs. One such vehicle was the Tri-Cross Medical Supplies van, which came twice a month. It was one of the many aspects of Zanco operations he had passed on to Cacho in their Q&A sessions. In either case, once the vehicle is cleared by the guard on the ground, the tower guard opens the first gate to admit the vehicle into the sally port and then shuts the gate behind it. The second gate is then opened and the vehicle enters or exits the prison.

Axel feels the van slow down and then stop in the amber cast of the gate lights. The driver lowers his window, which is leeward of the blowing rain. From his position behind Cacho and the driver, Axel can't see the guard who has come out to the van, but he knows that he is the third prison insider.

He sees the guard's hand at the window to receive the driver's Zanco pass and ID card. Rain sprays into the van on a swirl of wind, the storm gusting in thick sheets, the lightning and thunder unremitting.

The guard returns the driver's ID and goes back into his booth to clear the vehicle with the tower guy. The driver shuts his window and they wait. Axel forces himself to take slow deep breaths. He smells the cleaning solvent on Cacho's pistol, and the scent conjures a flash memory of the Republic Arms gun shop at Wolfe Landing.

A loud buzzer sounds and then there's the whir of the gate as it draws open laterally. The van advances into the sally port and again halts and there's another buzz. Through the back window Axel watches the gate draw shut behind them.

Seconds pass and nothing happens.

They *know*, Axel thinks. They wanted to get us in this cage. They'll be on us in—

The buzzer blats.

The outer gate opens.

The van starts moving.

As he watches the gate slide shut behind them, Axel is profoundly aware of being free and wants to howl his elation. He knows of course that anything can happen in the next crucial hour between here and the transfer vehicle in Fort Stockton that's waiting to take them to a private airfield outside of town and a ready plane to Nuevo Laredo, but right *now*, right this minute, he's by God, no-question-about-it *free*.

Cacho grins and slaps him on the arm. He slips the pistol into his waistband and says to the driver, "Okay, dude. Don't speed. Next stop, Stockton."

⌒∞⌐

They're only a hundred yards from the prison and still in blurry sight of it—and less than a mile from where the road ahead curves west and out of sight behind a range of hills—when, through the pounding of the rain, they hear the rising wail of Zanco's lockdown sirens.

"They're on to us!" Axel says.

"*Go!* Hit it!" says Cacho.

As the van gains speed, there's a *thunk-pock* of a bullet piercing the roof and forming a starburst near the bottom of the windshield an instant before they hear the rifle shot.

"*Floor it!*" Cacho shouts.

"It's *floored!*" the driver says. "It's four-cylinder."

The tower guard is armed with a semiautomatic Ruger and its reports come in quick succession. It is hard to stop a fleeing vehicle when shooting at it from the rear and at an elevated angle, but the shooter is an able rifleman and his bullets punch through the rooftop, through the hatchback door and window, *whang* off the metal framework, and lodge in the windshield, in the center console, in the padding of the seats.

"Holy *Mother!*" Cacho says, his forearms clasped on top of his head.

"Cut the lights! Weave!" Axel yells, crouched behind Cacho, pressed against the panel door.

With its lights off, the van's a tougher target, and the driver shrugs low over the steering wheel, wipers flapping at full tempo, tires *whumping* through puddles, the driver weaving through the rain haze but only slightly for fear of skidding off the road. Then the gate tower's spotlight comes ablaze and its beam races up the road through the glittering rain and finds the hatchback door and the rifle shots come faster, the bullets *thunking* through the roof, *pocking* through the glass, ricochets *chinging* off the chassis under the floorboards. One hits the heel on Axel's shoe and bats his foot aside.

The driver grunts and slumps over the wheel and the van veers to the right and off the road and out of the spotlight. It tears into the scrub brush, rocking and bouncing as Cacho crawls over the console and grabs the wheel with one hand and reaches across with the other to unlatch the driver's door and shoulders the man hard against it, tumbling him out of the slowing vehicle—whether dead or alive, Axel can't say—and slides onto the driver's seat. They pitch and sway over the rugged ground, the spotlight beam flicking all around the van, unable to settle on it. They slew into a mud pocket and the drive wheels lose traction and for a sinking second Axel thinks they've mired, but then the wheels grip and the van heaves out of the muck and Cacho gets it back on the road.

Axel scrabbles over the passenger seat and unfolds its back and hunches behind it as the spotlight fixes on them again, though less brightly. The riflefire continues but now fewer rounds hit the van, and then the shooting stops.

"*Wooo!* Out of the fucker's range!" Cacho says, and turns on the headlights. Through the beating wipers they see the road bend just ahead. The back window's an opaque mesh of starbursts.

"Not for long," Axel says. In the side mirrors they see the headlights of vehicles emerging from the prison. Coming after them.

Then the van's into the road bend and out of the pursuers' view.

24

They talk fast. The little van's no match for the prison vehicles that will come around the bend in a minute and barrel up to them shooting from the windows and maybe blowing out their tires and maybe their brains and the road runs west for about a mile before turning north to Sanderson where for goddamn sure there's gonna be cop cars parked across the road and cops waiting with shotguns but the Rio Grande's only four or five miles south and the whole region's full of little ranch roads and horse trails and the thing to do is take one of those to the river or close enough to it to get out and hotfoot it the rest of the way and cross over to Mexico and if a tire gives out before then they'll just have to hoof it farther to the Rio and . . . *there's* a side road going north . . . but they need one to southward and need it right fucking now before the chasers see them make the turn and there's nothing showing up ahead and . . . *there's a south turn!*

Cacho hits the brakes and Axel braces himself against the dashboard as the van loses traction, its rear wheels drifting to the left, and Cacho cuts the front wheels into the slide and the van's back end swings the other way. They skid across the road and

past the side road junction and off the pavement and go bucking over rough ground and then fishtailing in mud. Through the
driver's window Axel sees headlights starting to come around
the bend—and then the lights vanish as Cacho gets the van on
the ranch road and into the flanking cover of creosote brush and
mesquite trees.

It's one of those common ranch byways that are less road
than old stock trail, most of them so narrow that whenever oncoming vehicles meet one of them has to pull over partway into
the scrub to grant the other passage. On roads like this thirty
miles an hour can feel like sixty, and like so many such roads used
chiefly by ponderous vehicles with all-terrain tires it has been
permanently rutted to a washboard surface. The van jars without
pause as it winds through the mesquites and around one stony
outcrop after another, raising small wakes in the water sheeting
the rigid ruts, the steering wheel reverberating and jerking from
side to side under Cacho's tight grip. They keep checking their
side mirrors for chasers.

"Even if they didn't see us make the turn they'll know we
took it when they don't spot us ahead of them on the main road,"
Axel says, still breathless. "At least one of them'll come behind us,
the others'll probably try to cut us off by other trails. Whatever
they're driving's a lot faster than this thing and can handle these
roads better, and a lot of the hacks know this country pretty good."

"Yeah, yeah," Cacho says. "But whatever they're driving's
way bigger than this and can't take the curves as good. The river's
anyway only two, three miles now, skip, hop, and jump. We'll get
there and cross over before they catch up."

"Cross over how?"

"*Somehow.* Hell, there's ferries and shit, ain't there? There's
ferries all up and down the Rio, everybody knows that."

"Yeah, right. You know where any of them are? I don't know where any are!"

"*Somewhere,* that's where! We'll find one! We don't, we'll swim it."

"*Swim* it? *Tarzan* couldn't swim it in this storm!"

"We'll get across somehow, man. God loves us!"

Axel feels a tremor in his hands, suddenly conscious of being scared in a way only a free man can be.

Cacho gets the phone out of his shirt and says, "Take the wheel!"

Axel leans over and grips the wheel with both hands and it's like taking hold of a small angry beast by its horns. The van jerks left and right and Cacho says, "Damn, man, don't crash us!!" He presses a button and stares at the phone. Then presses another, stares again, and says, "Fuck!"

"Nothing?" Axel says.

"Nothing!" He turns the phone off and stuffs it back in his breast pocket and takes the wheel again.

They turn off the headlights to be harder to detect. In this dimmer light of looming mesquites it's also harder to see the trail but they can see it well enough, and the continuing lightning helps. Axel doubts the little van can take such a bashing for long before breaking down. It's a wonder the tires have held up. Cacho turns on the dashboard light, and its low glow allows them to read the compass, which rotates one way and the other, eastward, then westward as the trail snakes, but holds on a generally southbound heading.

They round another curve and now the trail runs straight and they pick up speed, shuddering, rattling, splashing. Cacho looks at his side mirror and says, "Here they come."

Axel's mirror shows a watery glare of the high-standing headlights of some large bulky vehicle moving up behind them.

Now the trail curves to the right and through a rock passage and the chaser's lights disappear from the mirror. Cacho turns on the headlights and they glare against another rock wall less than ten yards ahead and just past a leftward curve. Cacho taps the brakes and cuts the wheel and they skim into the turn and hit the rock— Axel bonking his head on the window, the panel door buckling inward. They carom across the trail and the left-side wheels slip into a shallow ditch and the van tilts leftward even as it keeps going forward and it feels like they're going to capsize but then the ditch ends and they bump upright and roll on.

Cacho whoops and says, "God *damn,* this thing can take a lick!"

"Lucky we didn't bust a wheel."

"That's us, old-timer—lucky up the ass!" He lets out a maniacal *grito.*

Because the chasers are running with their lights, Axel figures they'll see that last turn sooner than Cacho did and be able to keep from hitting the rock, but it'll still slow them down a bit.

They pass through two more sets of tight weaves around rocky outcrops and then the mesquite growth on their right gives way to a rail fence and a breadth of open land with the dark shapes of cattle standing in the gray rain. But it's another straight stretch here and the trail is still rutted and the chaser's going to cut the distance on them pretty quick. The compass is reading due south. The lightning is still forking bright, the thunder still explosive.

Ahead and off to the right behind the ongoing fence is a two-story building with lighted windows. The rancher's house. The front door light comes on, illuminating a covered porch that runs the length of the house. A pair of dogs that had been sheltering on it bound down the steps and come yowling toward the fence. The front door opens and a man steps out.

Their back window brightens with the chaser's headlights and Cacho again switches off theirs. They're coming fast. The trail ahead bends rightward at the end of the fence.

They hear gunshots.

"They can't hit nothing, bouncing on this road," Cacho says. But they both hunker lower.

They skid into the turn, stones clattering on the van's underside, and again lose the chaser's lights and Cacho once more turns on the van's. The trail again straightens and the fence still runs beside them. They're looking for the next southward turn. Then see it just ahead where the scrub line bends.

"*Yes!*" Cacho says. "We make that turn and if the road keeps winding we can keep our distance from them till we get to—"

"If it's a straightaway they'll catch up."

"No. We'll pull off into the scrub and plow through it as far as this heap'll take us, then hop out and run for the river. They come after us with flashlights they'll be easy targets. I'll pop them all."

Axel cuts a look at him. In the dashboard light the kid's profile seems carved of black stone. Then he looks to his right and in the side glow of the porch light sees the man running toward the fence, waving his arms. He barely hears the man's rain-muted shouts and can't make out what he's saying.

The chaser's lights reappear. Cacho cuts off the van's. The shooter fires twice without hitting them.

Cacho makes the south turn, the van's bumper whacking aside a small wooden sign, and loses sight of the chaser once more. The road now runs straight ahead and is vaguely visible and he leaves the lights off.

"What'd it say?" Axel says. "Something Creek Bridge?"

"*What?*"

"The *sign*," Axel says. "There's a *bridge* ahead . . . a creek!"

"*Creek?* Man, we best cross it before we bail! Good thing you saw it."

The chaser comes around the turn and again begins gaining on them. The shooter fires and fires, the reports getting louder, most of the rounds now hitting the hatchback. A round comes through the back window and ricochets off the frame of Axel's seat and *whunks* into the dashboard.

"They're gonna be up our ass in a minute!" he says.

They see an upcoming bend around a rock rise to the right. Cacho taps the brakes and goes into the turn and behind the rock cover. They're midway into the bend when the chaser vehicle rounds back into view, its lights swelling.

"Fuck it," Cacho says, and turns on the headlights. He speeds up as the curve begins to straighten. "Where's the *bridge?*"

And there it is, not twenty feet ahead . . . what's left of it. A few feet of guard railing and planked deck projecting over a surging current of black water that has overrun its banks and torn away the rest of the bridge.

Cacho stomps the brakes and the van slides into a quarter-turn and smashes through the remnant railing and hits the water at a nose-first, sideways tilt, the windshield going under and the headlight glow presenting an eerie green vision of the stony bottom passing under them—and then the van surfaces and rolls upright and the current whisks it away in a slow spin as the engine spasms and dies and the headlights quit.

Behind them an oversized pickup truck slews off the wrecked bridge in a half-spin and plunges rearward into the water. Its front end swings toward them and wobbles from side to side, but the truck seems held fast, its rear half entirely submerged and the front end sinking forward, the water already halfway up the cab windows, the headlight beams wavering, then shorting out.

"*Die,* fuckers!" Cacho yells as the van is swept around a bend and they lose sight of the truck. Then he says to Axel, "This ain't no *creek*! It's a river! The *Rio*! We're there, man! That's Mexico! All we—"

"No it's not," Axel says. "Nearest bridge to Mexico's a hundred miles off at Del Rio. It's a *creek*!"

"*This* big-ass?"

"Flash flood like this, they can swell up big as rivers. Besides, we were heading south, and this water's running to the right. Rio Grande runs the other way. This creek'll take us to it, though, if we stay afloat."

Water trickles in through torn seals in the buckled panel door, through bullet holes in the sides and rear glass. But with the windows shut the van remains buoyant, revolving slowly as the current speeds it into the rainy twilight, and Axel has a fleet remembrance of riding an inner tube down the Guadalupe River when he was a boy.

25

The thunder and lightning begin to lessen but the rain persists, drilling on the van roof, its runoff cascading from banks fifty feet apart in some places and hardly more than fifteen in others. The heavy air smells of creosote. The van swishes through a series of meanders, slinging from one side of the creek to the other, here and there skimming past piles of brushy debris bunched and bobbing along the creek sides. Now they enter a tighter progression of bends where the water runs even faster. They twirl from bank to bank, scraping on its rocky washouts and mowing through inundated brush, rebounding off rows of exposed tree roots where bank sides have been washed away.

"You *sure* we're headed for the river?" Cacho says.

"All creeks run to it. We'll get—"

The hatchback window bursts inward in a spray of glass and the van is arrested so abruptly it snaps their heads back—the window pierced by a fallen tree limb that has jammed up into the headliner and stuffs the cargo space with a crush of smaller, leafy branches. With its other end wedged tight in a tangle of tree roots extending a few feet into the water from the base of a collapsed bank, the limb keeps its hold on the van even as the current wrenches the skewered vehicle around to face mostly downstream and rocks the van up and down, its left rear side scraping the row of roots.

"Out your door!" Axel yells. "Climb up to higher ground!" His own side of the van is at an upstream angle and he knows he wouldn't be able to open the door against the force of the current if he tried.

Cacho shoulders open his lee-side door and water swamps the floor to their seats. He steps out onto the row of roots and starts treading carefully toward the largest knots of them where the base of the limb is caught and the root growth can be scaled to the top of the six- or seven-foot bank wall lined with leaning trees. Axel scrambles over the console and follows him.

But then Cacho stops and turns, stepping around Axel and sidling back to the van, saying something Axel doesn't catch over the noise of the current and the splattering rain.

"What?" Axel says.

"The *gun*! Fell out!"

Cacho hunches into the half-sunken van and begins probing the water all around the driver's side. The jouncing limb is creaking louder under the vehicle's increasing water weight.

"Forget it!" Axel shouts. "Come on!"

He hears yells from upstream.

He turns and scans the upstream creek bend and in the next flash of lightning sees somebody clinging to a float of some sort. A man, crying for help. He lets out a long yowl as the meander's current bears him very fast toward the pinioned van.

The man slams into the hatchback door, losing the piece of planking he'd been holding to but able to grab onto the limb where it's joined to the window. There's only about six feet of limb between him and its attachment to the bank roots, but he's on the outward side of the limb and the current has his legs and he can't pull himself out of its tow, he can only hold fast.

"*Help me!* Jesus! *Hellllp!*"

Axel hurries to the limb and uses the smaller branches for handholds as he wades to within reach of the man's hands. Even though the water is only up to his hips and he's only in the current's periphery, he can feel its proximate strength and he's afraid to get any closer. Another step forward and the water might pull his legs out and trap him under the limb or haul him away.

"Take hold!" he says, reaching out to grip the man's wrist.

The man locks onto his with both hands. "Don't let go!" the man pleads. "Don't let me *go!*"

Rain running into his eyes, Axel leans backward and tugs hard on the man's arm, dragging him against the creek's tow. In slow gradations he backs up along the limb and into shallower water, having to stoop more and more as he does, the man working his arms around the lesser branches without letting go of Axel's wrist. It's a matter of only a few feet, but the effort is strenuous. Axel is in water almost down to his knees when the man manages to extricate his legs from the current and get his footing. Then roughly breaks free of Axel's hold.

Off balance, Axel stumbles backward but stays upright. He sees the man putting a hand to his pocket and then apprehends that it's not a pocket, it's a hip holster, and the man's drawing a gun. *Chaser,* he thinks. *Made it out of the truck.* A shimmer of lightning exposes the man's CO uniform as he points a revolver at Axel with both hands, cocks the hammer, and wheezes, "*Got* you . . . dickwad."

A gun blasts and the man staggers sideways and fires a round into the brush at the same time that another gunshot swats his head aside and he spins halfway around and pitches face-first into the water. The splash heaves him outward and the current takes him under.

Crouched beside the half-submerged van door, Cacho lowers the Glock and stands up. He comes over beside Axel and turns the pistol in his hand as if to offer him a better look at it. "Forget this, you said?"

"Cancel that request," Axel says. He has twice seen men stabbed dead, has seen a man beaten to death by fists and feet and has seen one throttled, but this was his first witness to a killing by firearm. It crosses his mind this was not the kid's first kill.

"Heard the hollering and talk and I'm looking and looking for this and finally find it and I see the dude pointing a piece at you and looking like he meant to use it. Nice shooting, huh? I mean, hardly no time to aim, this lousy light and all?"

"Very commendable."

Cacho tucks the pistol in his waistband, his grin vivid in the dimness. "Yeah, that's it. *Commendable!*"

At which moment and with a loud tearing sound, the anchoring limb rips free of the roots and—still jammed in the hatchback, and before they can even think to react—swings around on the van's outward veer into the current and rakes both of them into the creek.

26

Underwater and face up beneath the limb, clinging to it as it tows him behind the van, Axel is sure he'll drown if he lets go and sure he'll drown if he doesn't. Then the limb rises with a roll of the van and his head surfaces and he's gulping air.

"Oh man . . . thought we . . . !" Cacho says, gasping hard, clinging to the limb, not an arm's length from him. "Oh *man* . . ."

The van's riding the current nose-down with only the upper rear part of its body above water, the embedded limb trailing from the back window.

Water billows into Axel's face and he inhales some and coughs. "Hang on!" he says.

"No *shit*, hang on!" Cacho says. "And don't breathe the water . . . Ah *goddamnit* . . . lost the gun!"

"Wanna go back . . . hunt for it?"

"Eat your mother!"

Every rightward roll of the van dunks them again. Each bang against a bank drives the limb into their chests or nearly yanks it from their grasp, depending on the direction of their spin. They keep their legs drawn up to avoid hitting them on

rocks in the shallower parts of the creek. The van ships water at
every jolt and is soon sunken almost to the limb's juncture with
the broken window.

"It's gonna go under," Cacho says. "Gotta get to ground."

"Let go the limb we'll drown."

"It goes *down* we drown! . . . Gotta try."

"No! Current's too—"

"Watch it!" Cacho hollers.

The van rams into a bank-side boulder with an impact
Axel feels to the roots of his eyes, and the limb snaps off at the
hatchback window with a sound like a whip crack. They twirl
away on its truncated five-foot length as the van sinks between
the boulder and the bank and holds there.

Loosed of the van, the limb fragment flies. They careen
through the shadows, swaying through curve after curve, snort-
ing water, hacking. Then the meanders lengthen and the limb no
longer runs into the banks, which are now rising on both sides.
The current's flow now discernibly downward and faster yet.

There's a growing rumble somewhere ahead.

The creek sweeps into another wide bend and begins a
series of short dips as they head into the deeper forward shadows.

"Oh man," Cacho says. "You think the river's—"

They cry out as they fly past the creek mouth and into the
rage of the Rio Grande.

27

They're in a narrow canyon—a steep gorge that amplifies the Rio's roar as they whoosh downriver, hugging to the limb for their lives. There is no other thunder now, no longer lightning, only the torrential river under the teeming rain. The surrounding world now delineated in shades of black and gray to either side of them, the odor of mud now woven with a strong smell of iron.

It's hard for Axel to believe this is the same river that so placidly winds through the flatlands of South Texas and past his hometown to its mouth at the Gulf of Mexico, some five hundred miles downstream. He fears they're going to be crushed against a gorge wall or knocked off the limb and drowned, and then perceives that the river is now running mostly straight, its bends here few and of wide arc. The limb is cleaving to the current's main channel and no longer whirling. He's read and heard about this untamed portion of the Rio Grande that runs from the upriver Big Bend wild country to somewhere down here—a stretch of narrow canyons and intermittent white-water rapids and pool drops. It's a big attraction to thrill-seekers in canoes or kayaks or inflatable rafts, but it can be hard going even for an expert river-man when the rapids deepen and surge even faster with runoff from a storm.

The question is whether they entered the river at a point past the last of the rapids or if there are still some up ahead. Axel figures it's best to assume there are, and so they'd better get aground before they reach them. But the vertical rock bluffs offer no exit from the river and they're anyway moving too fast to even try to make it to a bank. There's nothing they can do but hold to the limb in terrified exhilaration and let the current take them where it will.

"*Fuck!*" Cacho says. "Mexico's right *there* and we can't get on it." Then says, "*Look!* Up ahead! One o'clock!"

Axel sees it. A glow. A light. Not much more than a yellow pinpoint in the rain. It seems to be at river level, though it's hard to say. Slightly to their right and at some distance, but they're approaching it fast.

"What is it? " Cacho says.

"Don't know! Lantern? Gotta be a lantern! Camp lantern under some kind of cover!" They have to holler to hear each other above the river roar.

"*Camp* lantern? Who'd be *camping* here? *How?*"

"I don't know! Some . . . *sportsman! Hiker!* . . . Some canoe guy didn't expect a storm! But that light's on flat ground! River beach of some kind!"

"Well, if he got off there, so can we!"

"Coulda got off before the storm hit and river got bad!"

"It's on the right, in *Mexico,* man! That's where we want!"

But as they close in on the light its position shifts, moving slowly to a point a little to their left—and they realize they've been deceived by an illusion in the dim light. Fooled by a long straight length of gorge facing a distant but gradual rightward bend, so that not until they're into the bend do they see that the light, which had appeared to be on the right side of the river, is actually on the left.

"It's in *Texas!*" Cacho says. "What if that light's whaddaya-call-'em, those park guys?" He catches a faceful of water and coughs.

"Park rangers? Hell no! Nearest park's Big Bend, way upriver!"

"I don't want back in Texas!"

"Maybe no choice! Other side's nothing but straight-up rock! That light's on the only flat bank we seen! We're heading for *rapids,* man! We hit those, we've had it!"

"How you know there's rapids?"

"I *know!*"

"Guys ride rapids all the time!"

"In *boats,* on *rafts,* not on fucking tree limbs!"

"Ah man, you . . . Goddamnit! . . . *So? How* we get off?"

Axel has no idea. They'll be abreast of the light any second now, and it's obvious they'll come no closer to the riverbank than seven or eight feet. It won't look far off, but to try to swim to it would be suicidal.

They watch as the little light comes rushing up on their left.

"HEYYYYYYY!" Cacho shouts. *"HELLLLLLPPP!"*

"Never hear you in this boom! Even if he *did,* what can he do except wave when we go by?"

And then they're past it, speeding on.

"*Now* what're—"

"Dead ahead!" Axel says.

A dark shapeless structure has materialized downstream, a few feet above the waterline and extending from the left bank to midway across the river.

"Rocks!" Cacho says. "It's *rocks!*"

Axel thinks so too. Maybe a shattered segment of fallen gorge wall. The current is deflecting around it at mid-river but it's going to ram them into it. They'll break their bones, their skulls.

They hurtle toward it, bracing for the impact, Cacho letting out a long holler and Axel having a flash-impression of the river taking his mangled, bloated corpse all the way to Wolfe Landing, the turtles and garfish feeding on him until some kid with a cane pole hooks into his clothes. Nobody will recognize what's left of him.

They plow into the barrier with a yielding crunch, Axel's cheek gashed by something that just misses his eye. The limb halts, arrested in place but joggling on the current. For a baffled few seconds they don't know what's happened . . . and then comprehend that they're partially burrowed into a massive mound of vegetal debris—broken tree limbs and saplings, uprooted scrub brush and cactus and foliage—all of it borne here on the current and caught in a growing cluster on a bank bend, the river pressing them into it and ripping through the porous accumulation like a strainer even as it adds to it.

"Holy *fuck*!" Cacho yells. "You alive?" The river is even louder here.

"Yeah! Let's get to ground!"

Fighting the push of the river and the dense netting of brush and branches, they pull themselves out of the cluster, the current tugging at their legs, their pants. The gorge now so murky they can barely tell where its wall joins the darker bank at its foot. But they can see each other, and can see that they're only about ten feet from the solid blackness of the bank, the river swirling over its rim, the mound scraping up and down on it.

The current's deflected outward flow is too strong for them to pull themselves to shore, and they have to climb atop the

mound, pausing to pull up their pants, then start crawling toward
the bank, Cacho closer to it and leading the way. Careful of each
handhold and foothold as they push through the branches of the
bucking mass, cursing each prick of spine and stab of sliver, they
edge ahead on all fours. Where it abuts the bank, the mound looms
a few feet above it, jouncing on the current. It's hard to judge
the bobbing, vertical distance between them and the indistinct
ground. The cluster suddenly jerks more forcefully and they're
nearly thrown off.

"It's gonna break away!" Cacho says. "We musta loosened
it when we hit!"

"Jump!" Axel yells.

Cacho rises to a half-crouch and jumps into the darkness
and lands with a cry of pain.

Axel can't see him. "You okay?"

"Yeah, *shit*! Busted my assbone is all!"

Now he sees him. A hunched dark figure on the ground
just ahead and a little below the mound. Axel raises himself on
all fours and hops forward, landing awkwardly and bonking the
back of his head on the hard ground.

"Whoo, I *heard* that!" Cacho says, helping him to his feet.
"You're a hard-headed old bastard, I'll say that for you!"

Axel fingers the knot on his head. He tests his legs and arms,
relieved not to have suffered worse harm.

The mound is now quaking even more roughly, and they
back away from it. It begins to pivot outward with a low ripping
sound as it tears away from the bank, then lunges away into the
current and vanishes into the darkness like a ragged phantom
vessel.

"*Jesucristo!*" Cacho says. "Little sooner and we'da still been
on it! Who knows how far it woulda taken us.... God *damn* it!"

"What?"

"The phone!" Cacho's patting his shirt pockets, his pants. "Lost the *phone*!"

Axel stares at him. "Oh, no! How we gonna call a cab?"

"Real fucking funny!" Cacho says. "Was gonna use it to call my guys once we get outta here!" Then looks around and says, "So . . . *how* do we get outta here?"

Shielding his eyes against the rain, Axel stares upstream. "You know . . . could be this beach runs back to where the light is!"

"If it's flat all the way back, where's the light? We oughta be able to see it, no?"

Axel shuffles a few yards farther in from the riverbank and stops.

"Over here!" he says.

Cacho comes up next to him.

"Straight ahead and a hair to the right!" Axel says.

Cacho searches. "I see it!" It's a tiny speck, but no question it's the light.

"Boulder or something up the way was blocking our view from over there!" Axel says.

"Well, hell, man, let's get on over to it! If it's some guy hiked in here, he can show us the way out! Or if he got here by way of the river—"

"Hold your horses, kid! No telling how far off it is, and just because we can see it doesn't mean we can get to it! Could be there's a break in the beach between here and the light, or someplace up ahead that's solid wall to the water! That'd be as far as we can go!"

"Or could be it *doesn't* hit no dead end! If it *does,* we'll just have to come back this way, and so what? Gonna make us late to the party?"

Axel has to grin. "I was just pointing out a possibility!"

"Yeah? Well, here's a possibility for you. We can stand here blah-blah–blahing till we starve to fucking death, or we can get moving! So let's cut the horseshit and—"

"Hey, junior," Axel says, starting upriver, "if you're waiting on me, you're way behind!"

28

As they move upriver, the stone beach narrows in places, widens in others. It is strewn with fallen boulders and piles of flotsam—scraps of brush and tree, sections of wooden fencing with lengths of wire still attached. They at times lose sight of the light before spying it again. The wind has kicked up and chills them through their sodden clothes. They have no means of estimating their distance from the light, but they seem to be gaining no ground on it, its minute glow not noticeably brightening. Axel wonders if it's another illusion of some sort.

They couldn't have said how long they've been moving toward it when they're startled by a loud repetitive sound whose source or even direction they can't immediately identify.

"What's *that* now?" Cacho says.

It's coming from somewhere above. A *thwuck-thwuck-thwuck* sound.

"Chopper!" Axel says.

They scurry to the thick brush at the base of the gorge and hunker in it, shielding their eyes from the rain as they search the lesser darkness of the band of sky between the canyon's walls.

They can now hear the whine of the helicopter's engine as well as the *thwucking* of the rotors. The chopper grows louder as it approaches along the lay of the gorge, and now they see its rain-blurred spotlight.

"They'll see us!" Cacho says.

"No!" Axel says. "Too much rain reflection! Stay small!"

They hunch deeper into the brush as the aircraft closes in, its light swiveling from one foot of the gorge to the other. The light flashes past them, the noise of the engine and rotors mixing with the river's resonance in a deafening din, the rain swirling madly.

The light and the *thwucking* fade into the darkness.

"What if they saw the light on the bank?" Cacho says.

"If they did they'd be hovering over it right now, calling in coordinates. *We* can hardly see the light. It's gotta be harder to see from up there, with all the rain glare."

"You *hope*!"

"You better too!"

"What *you* better hope is your old ass can keep up with me!"

The kid moves off and Axel hustles at his heels.

29

The beach widens as they advance, wending past debris and boulders, but staying hard by the river. The driving rain gradually relents to a drizzle, ceasing its clatter, and now the only noise is the river's rumbling. After a while they come to the widest part of the beach yet, marked by scattered rockfall and bench elevations between the river and the bluff—and there the light is. Shining within a small, blue nylon pop-up tent about forty or forty-five yards from the riverbank and a few yards from the foot of the bluff, facing downriver with the wind. Axel figures the light for a battery lantern, since only a fool would use gas or kerosene in a tent, especially such a small one, and whoever positioned the tent so sensibly is no camping fool.

They move in closer, easing up to a low outcrop about fifteen yards from the tent and affording a good view of it. Now something in the tent blocks the light—a distorted silhouette of somebody shifting around. Then the dark shape settles, seems to lie down, and most of the tent side is bright again.

"One guy, looks like," Cacho says, just loud enough for Axel to hear him. "Don't see no boat. You?" He hugs himself against the chilling wind.

"Could be stashed the other side of the tent."

"What for? Hide it from all the thieves on the loose around here? If there's no boat, he had to've hiked in on some trail, and *that's* our way out."

"Right. Except we don't know where the trail is, and we sure as hell can't just walk up and ask him. Guy could be armed, and everybody in Texas knows who wears these state-issue whites. Might shoot us on the spot, turn our dead asses in for a reward. The thing to do is lay low, wait till he packs up and heads out, then follow him at a distance."

"And what if he sticks around a while?" Cacho says. "No telling how long he might. Another day? A week? We can't hide here, hoping he won't spot us. No, man, we gotta jump his ass. We move up close as we can, hide good but so we can keep an eye on the door. Soon as he comes out, take a piss, whatever, we come down on him. Make him show us the way out."

"Could be a hard case. Say fuck us."

"He won't say it more than once."

The kid's right, and Axel knows it. "Okay," he says. Then points to their right at an outcrop forming a rock wall at the top of a gradual slope and running all the way to the bluff. "Up there's good cover, and we can position ourselves behind it for a straight look at the tent door. When he comes out in the morning, first chance we get we'll take him down."

"Now you're talking."

With Cacho following closely, Axel leads the way up the slope, cutting looks at the tent as they advance in a semicircle to get behind the outcrop wall. But now the wall blocks the tent glow, casting the ground on this side of it in near-total blackness, and they have to move more carefully still. Feeling his way along the wall and over the uneven footing, Axel sidesteps into something knee-high and almost falls over it.

"*What?*" Cacho whispers. They can barely make each other out.

Axel eases himself down beside the ill-defined structure obstructing their way.

"What *is* it?" Cacho says.

"Oh *baaby,*" Axel croons.

Cacho crouches and puts a hand to the thing, amazed to feel some sort of hard, canvaslike material. "What the *hell* . . . ?"

"Got us a boat, junior."

Axel crawls around in it, gauging its measure by feel, running his hands over it, its fittings and equipment. He grew up with boats of all kinds and recognizes this as one of the most basic. "Inflatable dinghy," he says. "Horseshoe design, about eight by four, maybe a little bigger. Polyester fabric with PVC coating, I'd say. Thing probably doesn't weigh fifty pounds. Separate air chambers, two each side, feels like. Braced deck, grab ropes all the way around. Transom for an outboard but there's no motor, or else he's got it in the tent. Pair of paddles. Aluminum."

"All I understand you saying is it's small and got paddles. And big enough for two, right?"

"Yeah. Some people think these things are no more than a fancy inner tube, but this one's pretty well made. Dude was smart to put it way up here in case the river overran the bank so much he wouldn't be able to get to it. Tied it down, weighed it with rocks. No seat, unless it's in the tent."

"Well, let's get the thing in the water and *go.*"

They remove the hold-down rocks and Axel detaches the bowline from a small boulder and drops it in the boat. He takes hold of the bow and hoists it to waist level and Cacho picks up the stern end and they begin sidestepping cautiously down the mild incline. The boat's not much heavier than Axel guessed, but it's a cumbersome load, and together with the darkness and unsure ground it's tricky work to lug the thing between them. The tent light is still on. The guy isn't asleep yet. He wouldn't waste the battery while he slept.

Then they're back on the flat rock beach and making their clumsy way toward the river. They're more than halfway to the river, stepping sidelong, huffing hard, when Cacho's foot gives way and he falls with a yelp.

"Damn, man, come *on!*" Axel says in low voice. He looks at the tent, sees a black shape rising inside it. The guy's sitting up. He heard.

Cacho gets to his feet, hissing, "Fucking ankle!" He picks up his end of the boat and they start moving again, but he's limping and can't match Axel's pace.

The man is scrabbling out of the tent on hands and knees.

Axel moves around ahead of Cacho so that the bow is facing the river. "Put it down and get in!" he says.

"What?"

"Get in the boat! *Do it!*" Axel shouts, stealth no longer necessary.

Cacho sets down the stern and crawls into the boat as Axel wraps the bowline around his hands and starts scuttling backward, pulling the boat toward the river.

"*HEY! . . . Hey, you bastards!* Stop right there! . . . *Stop!*" The man is hurrying toward them, a shadowy figure.

Axel drags the boat with all the strength and speed he can marshal, leaning back on the bowline, digging in with his heels, at times slipping and nearly falling, the bowline chafing his palms. The boat rasps over the gravelly ground, Cacho chanting, *"Go! Go! Go!"*

"Stop!" the man yells.

A gunshot cracks through the river roar.

"Carajo!" Cacho says. He huddles lower in the boat and hollers, *"Move it! Move!"*

Axel pulls harder, faster, laboring for breath. They have the advantage of being able to see the man against the lighted tent behind him better than he can see them against the dark canyon wall on the other side of the river, though it doesn't help that they're wearing white. Glancing over his shoulder, Axel sees that they're almost to the river, then looks back at the man, who has fallen and is getting back up. Axel sees the flash of his gunshot, and the round buzzes just over his head.

They reach the river's edge and Axel flings the bowline into the boat and darts around to the stern, hearing the man yelling, shooting again, the round striking to Axel's left and sparking off the rock beach with a whine. He pushes the boat forward until the bow juts over the low lip of the bank and the swashing current is thumping on its underside, the boat teetering. But before he can get in, the next shot punctures the hull's hindmost left chamber with a loud burst of air and knocks the boat forward, and it slides off the bank. In sheer reflex Axel dives after it, catching the transom with both hands as he smacks into the churning water and the boat veers away on the current, slinging him outward in a half-submerged and rolling twist that wrenches his left hand loose of the transom. Through the crashings of the river he hears another gunshot.

Clinging one-handed to the boat, he's stretched out behind it, rolling from side to side, being dragged with such force he's unable to pull himself forward or even reach up far enough with his other arm to grab on with both hands. It's hard to keep his face out of the water. He doesn't see Cacho and thinks he's gone overboard. His clutching hand aches and is beginning to lose its grip.

Then hands clamp around his wrist, and Cacho's hunched form looms over him, swaying in the tossing boat, shouting, "I got you! Let go! I'll pull you in! . . . Let *go*!"

He's afraid to release his hold on the boat, afraid he'll slip from Cacho's hands or pull him into the water too. But lacking other choice, he lets go.

Cacho fights the river for possession of him, both hands locked around Axel's wrist, his good foot planted against the skewed transom for leverage. He lugs him up against the sagged corner of the boat. Axel's shoulder feels like its arm is unrooting. He grabs the transom with his left hand and helps to pull himself up over it, submerging it under his weight, water pouring in as he fumbles into the swirling boat. Cacho releases his arm but still holds tightly to his shirt. Axel rises on his elbows and spews a great gush of water.

"You hit?" Cacho says. "You shot?"

He doesn't know, doesn't think so. He feels a variety of pains, but none of bullet severity. He knows what a gunshot wound feels like. "I'm okay! You?"

"Not a scratch! God loves us! We're clear, bro, we're on the *move*!"

The boat is awash and listing hard to its left rear side, but the other three chambers keep it afloat well enough.

Cacho shakes him by the shirt and yells near his ear, "Look up! Up there!"

The band of sky between the looming canyon walls has broken into ragged, scudding clouds brightly lit by a moon still out of their view, patches of its light playing in the higher shadows on one wall of the canyon.

30

They hold to the safety lines affixed along the top of each side of the boat—the grab ropes—and discuss their options in shouts as they rise and fall, bobbing and wheeling on the swift current's undulations. They can't guess where they are or how fast they're moving or how much time has passed, but they reckon it's still a few hours till daybreak. They have to get off the river before then or risk being spotted by a riverside search party or a helicopter. The canyon walls are getting lower, the visible sky is widening, though they still can't see the moon. They're hoping that when the banks flatten again the boat will get swept into another accumulation of debris, but on the Mexican side this time, and they'll be able to achieve the beach as before.

Even if they don't run into any brush, Axel says, as soon as the river's calmer they can paddle to the bank. Once they're on Mexican ground they'll find a road and hitch a ride or walk if they must to the nearest pueblo and from there somehow get in touch with Cacho's people.

What about the rapids he mentioned, Cacho wants to know. What if they hit those first? Axel says he isn't absolutely sure there *are* any bad rapids ahead. Could be they entered the river below the last of them. He tells the kid not to worry, they're not riding a tree limb anymore.

"Even with an air chamber blown, look how good we're doing! This thing's like a big life vest! What the hell, we hit white water we'll just ride it out till the current eases again and then we paddle over to the first flat bank!"

"Yeah, right, nothing to it!"

Which is when they discover they've lost one of their paddles. But Axel is confident he can get them ashore with the remaining one.

The canyon walls soon shrink into short, fragmented bluffs, exposing a gibbous moon, the river agleam with its light. And then the meanders begin to contract, their bends following more closely on one another and tightening the current into greater rigor and the boat moves faster and faster. The river loudens as they round a sharp bend and the boat sways on the current's flow over a wide rock and they plunge off a sudden short drop, both of them yelling in fright, holding tight to the grab ropes, and the boat hits with a jarring splash and leaps forward on a raging white-water rapid.

◦✖◦

They rocket downriver, pitching, yawing, whirling, gripping the ropes, flopping about on the flooded deck, gulping the sodden air, their shouts lost in the white water's boom. The current lashes them through the wider rock passages, the boat caroming off the larger boulders and wobbling over the smaller ones, now almost capsizing, now momentarily aloft before smacking down again. They run up against a high rock that tilts them precipitously and Axel falls hard against Cacho and the kid tumbles overboard with

a yelp. Then the boat is upright again and all Axel sees of him is a
fist still tight on the grab rope and faintly hears his gasping cries.
Cacho's head bobs up over the hull for a second as he tries to
pull himself aboard, then drops from sight again.

Axel lunges to the right-side grab rope and holds to it with
one hand and reaches down with the other and snatches a fistful
of the kid's shirt at the shoulder and leans back, pulling hard, the
boat reeling every which way and parting his ass from the deck
with every buck, each time nearly tossing him out. Cacho's head
again comes up, hair plastered, eyes wild. He works his arms into
the boat, Axel still pulling on his shirt, and he's got one leg over
the hull when the boat plunges over another drop, a long fall that
feels like they've gone off the edge of the earth. The boat hits the
water nose-first with its rear still arcing forward in the manner of
someone launching into a handstand, and the kid is flung away.

Axel feels himself parting from the deck and for a second
sees his feet against the moonlit sky, the airborne boat ahead of
him, and then he's in the water too and shielding his head with his
arms, bouncing off rocks and only dully conscious of the impacts.
The overturned boat precedes him through a series of passages and
then vanishes and he follows it over another steep drop, and then
he's underwater, tumbling in the current, not knowing up from
down, wild with panic and sure that he's about to drown . . . and
then he's at the surface again, gasping and spinning, glimpsing
the bright moon, flailing to no effect against the river's force, the
muddy water mashing into his mouth as the rapid carries him as
easily as a leaf. It whips him in an outward arc and he flashes past
a stretch of open bank and then tears through a stand of reeds
that lash his face and dim the moonlight. His collar snags around
his neck and arrests him, cutting off his breath and holding him
faceup and outstretched on the river's pull, legs flapping.

Thrashing like a hooked fish and clawing at his collar, he's strangling even as he's looking at silver fragments of sky above him through a mesh of leafy tree branches.

"Stop *fighting* me! Reach up! Reach *up* and grab my wrist!"

Cacho!

Heart banging, his eyes feeling about to pop from their sockets, Axel puts a hand behind his head, finds the kid's hand locked on his collar, and grasps his wrist. The collar eases on his neck and he sucks deep breaths broken by hard coughing.

"Hang onto me till you can reach up to the tree!" Cacho yells.

As the kid slowly draws him rearward against the river's drag, Axel is able to crane his head enough to see him holding by one hand to a low branch of an overhanging tree, struggling to keep his feet against the rushing current at his waist, the black bank but a few feet past him. Snarling like a weight lifter at every tug, groaning in pain whenever he puts too much pressure on his bad foot, Cacho pulls him within arm's length of a low branch and Axel seizes it. "Got it!" he cries in cracked voice. He lets go of Cacho's wrist and grabs onto the branch with that hand too. A dipping swirl in the current yanks his feet down and bumps them on a hard bottom and then slaps them out again. The water here is only about thigh-high, but the current is far too strong to permit footing.

They have to work their way to shore by arm strength from handhold to handhold along the branch. Then Cacho's up on the bank and reaching back for him and they lock hands and he drags Axel out of the river and into a dark stand of trees. Coughing and gasping, they crawl out onto the open bank, fall on their bellies, and roll onto their backs, chests heaving, relishing the feel of solid earth under them. The moon blazes on them from a sky now almost cloudless, the flat bank whitewashed in its light.

"Hey?" Cacho says.

"Huh?"

"We're on the right . . . *right*?"

Axel can hardly hear him through the rapid's rumble and is so dazed with exhaustion he doesn't grasp what the kid's asking. He coughs and turns to look at him. "Are we . . . on the *right*?"

"What? . . . That's what . . . I'm asking *you*! . . . We got off on the *right,* didn't we? Not, maybe, you know . . . the *wrong* side?"

"The *wrong* . . . ? Oh, man, you . . ." It's a labor to talk. *"What?"*

"Listen! . . . We got off on the . . . *right-hand* side . . . *correct* side . . . *Mexican* side. . . . We're in *Mexico.*"

"Oh, man, that's good! . . . Because, you know . . . if we were in Texas again . . . I think I'd rather be caught . . . than go back . . . in that fucking river."

The kid says something more in a tired slur and Axel doesn't catch it but doesn't care. It feels *so* grand to lie still, eyes closed, do nothing but breathe.

Through the sound of the river comes the high yipping of a nearby coyote, and then the cries of a pack of them in high chorus. He thrills to the sound, which he hasn't heard in over ten years. There are lots of coyotes in Terrell County, of course, but people shoot them for fun, so they tend to silence except at night, when you're in the cell block and can't hear them. This is the first one he's heard since his transfer ride to the Zanco Unit in a TDCJ bus with the window glass raised outside the steel mesh, a late-night drive during which they heard the madhouse yowlings of coyotes off and on for most of the trip. A gray-whiskered con sitting next to him had said it was the freest sound in the world. "Except for a wolf," the con added. "Wolf howl is *kick-your-ass* free."

He wonders how long they've been lying here. "Hey?" he says. "We gotta get moving at first light. . . . find a road . . . pueblo."

Cacho's asleep.

Then he's asleep, too.

❧

He's awakened by the swelling sound of a helicopter. He scrambles over to the trees, Cacho crawling up beside him. They crouch in the cottonwood shadows as the chopper approaches, its racket swelling. It passes close to the trees, a spotlight flashing against the tree cover but not penetrating it. And then it's gone.

"*Madre mia,*" Cacho says. "I about had a heart attack. No more under the stars for me." He crawls about in the shadows, testing the earth with his hand, finds a satisfactory site, and lies down.

Axel stays put, too. It takes a while for his pulse to settle. After a time he says, "Hey?" just to see if Cacho's still awake, and gets no answer. He wonders how the kid could drift off again so easily. And a minute later is once again asleep.

31

He wakes in the deeper night, curled up on his side, arms folded to his chest, hands in fists, cheek to the hard ground, his ear numb against it. His neck hurts. It's a torment to unclench his fists and work the fingers.

Then he senses it wasn't pain that woke him.

He stops flexing his hands and lies motionless. Listens hard. Bits of moonlight filter through the trees. Close by, Cacho lies with his back to him. And then from somewhere behind him he hears it, the sound that roused him.

A low, reverberant growl.

His scalp tightens and his bladder feels a sudden urgency.

He knows with an instinct as old as that of the first men to walk the earth that he's in the presence of something against which he stands not a chance. Only in movies has he heard a lion growl, and now knows it bears no comparison to the real thing. The growl comes again, and he feels its resonance in his bones. His hand closes around a large rock and draws it close. You do what you can.

He waits, motionless, chest aching for the deeper breath he dares not risk lest his fear be heard in it, even though he's sure the thing can sense his fear anyway, can probably *smell* it. He waits. And waits. Then hears the growl again, but only barely. At greater distance. Moving away. He waits a long time before he very slowly turns over onto his other side, suppressing a groan, and looks in the direction from which the growl came.

In the near distance is a low rise running roughly parallel to the river, its sloped, moonlit face scooped and deeply shadowed. He hadn't noticed it when they crawled out of the river, but then he hadn't been focused on much of anything at the time except the fact of still being alive. He rolls over again and looks at Cacho, who hasn't stirred. He stares at the glow of the moon behind the lower leaves, certain he will sleep no more tonight, not with that growl still sounding in his mind. And then is once again asleep.

His next waking will be to a reddening dawn.

32

Within minutes of the duty officer's receipt of CO Berra's frantic phone call from the infirmary storeroom where he has found Mason battered, bound, and gagged, the Zanco Unit is in lockdown, sirens wailing. A pursuit party of two-man teams draws weapons from the armory, vehicles from the motor pool, sets out in chase of the van. A state alert is issued, and Texas Rangers unite with a half-dozen sheriff's departments in a region-wide manhunt. Roadblocks are set up at Alpine and at the western boundary of Val Verde County, sealing off a 125-mile stretch of Highway 90. Others are placed at the juncture of every road connecting to the south side of I-10 out of Jeff Davis, Reeves, Pecos, and Crockett Counties. Helicopters are deployed from Fort Stockton and Del Rio.

One of the Zanco pursuit vehicles, a Ford 250 pickup truck, loses radio contact with the others and is not heard from again, its whereabouts unknown until a rancher assisting in the search for the convicts finds it that evening in Lonely Woman Creek where the storm has washed out the old bridge. He calls the sheriff's office, which sends out deputies and a tow truck. Only the fore part of the pickup's roof is above water, and the tow crew ascertains that the truck has been held in place against the current by its rear axle, caught on a creek bottom undercut.

When the truck is finally hauled out, the drowned driver is still in his seat, but missing is his partner, CO Tillis Moore. The passenger-side window is down, and the deputies infer that Moore got out before the cab was swamped, then was taken away on the current. Scattered through the truck is a litter of .38 cartridges and spent shells, indicative that they'd had the van in sight and that Moore fired his revolver at it repeatedly from the open window and reloaded more than once. But the gun is not in the truck and so was either lost in the creek or was still in Moore's possession when he exited the vehicle.

Because the van must also have gone into the water, a downstream search is initiated along both of the creek's rugged banks, but the search progresses slowly in its early hours, severely hampered by the storm. And because the driver died in direct consequence of their escape from custody, the fugitives now stand charged with felony murder.

❦

The storm is still driving hard when a ground team searching the outer perimeter of the Zanco Unit with flashlights finds a dead man in the muck some thirty feet off the entrance road. His uniform confirms him as the van driver. The body is taken to the prison infirmary and identified as Juan Balestro, age thirty-two, eight years employed by Tri-Cross Medical Supplies in Big Spring, where he lives, eleven years married, father of four daughters, ages eleven, ten, nine, and six. The Terrell County sheriff relays the information to the sheriff in Big Spring, the seat of Howard County, who personally delivers the sorrowful news to Mrs Balestro at her home. Shortly after, the Terrell sheriff makes the van driver's identity known to the press.

In days to come, the medical examiner's report will affirm that Balestro was inadvertently and fatally wounded by a round discharged by the front gate tower guard in his attempt to halt the fugitives. The specific cause of death will be attributed to trauma to the right subclavian artery caused by a .223 bullet that entered the torso at an upward angle under the right scapula and embedded near the top of the sternum, just below the clavicular notch, the round's deformed shape clear indication that it was a ricochet. The fled convicts will then be charged with a second count of felony murder.

❧

By 10:45 that night, the storm has abated to fitful gusts and a misty rain, though it will be days before the local creeks subside to normal levels, and CO Matthew Mason, sitting before a summarily assembled fact-finding team chaired by the warden, has concluded his detailed account of the escapees' actions in the infirmary storeroom. Also on the team are an assistant to the executive director of the TDCJ, a Texas Ranger captain, the county sheriff, and two other Zanco administrators. Mason's bruised face, missing front tooth, cuff-abraded wrists, and torn clothes all attest to his valiant attempt to prevent the breakout.

In keeping with his statement, the team's report will maintain that the van driver Balestro was compelled under mortal threat to abet the convicts Wolfe and Ramirez in their escape. The team members thank Mason for his thorough answers to their questions as well as for his fortitude and willingness to remain at Zanco and be interviewed prior to being taken to a hospital for treatment. The warden grants him an indefinite leave of recuperation, and the TDCJ assistant says he is going to nominate him for a commendation for valorous service. Mason thanks them but says he was only doing his job. He is then conducted to a county patrol car that makes its way past the glaring cameras and clamoring reporters outside the front gate and conveys him to the hospital in Fort Stockton, a deputy following in Mason's Jeep Wrangler.

The team next summons CO Marco Baker-Gómez, who has been waiting in the hall. During the escape, Baker-Gómez was manning Number Four Tower, whose purview includes the loading zone for the infirmary. Like the other tower guards, he was diverted by the emergency flare that was launched within view of the prison, which the team suspects may have been a constituent of the escape, specifically designed to distract the Number Four Tower guard from the infirmary's loading door long enough for the offenders to board the supply van unseen.

Although Officer Baker-Gómez—again, like the other tower guards—had at once reported his sighting of the flare to the duty officer, the warden asserts that had Baker-Gómez also reported the diversion of his attention from a delivery in progress, the information might have prompted the office to call the front gate guard and direct him to make a meticulous search of the delivery vehicle. Baker-Gómez admits this oversight but adds that in all the excitement of the flare it did not cross his mind that the diversion might have been a ruse linked to an escape attempt. He respectfully points out that it did not cross the mind of anyone else, either, not at the time, or, if it did, that person said nothing about it. All the same, he agrees he should have informed the duty officer that the delivery van was still at the infirmary door when the flare distracted him.

The warden expresses appreciation for his forthrightness and sense of responsibility, but his lapse of professional judgment in this critical instance cannot go undisciplined. Owing to Baker-Gómez's heretofore exemplary record, his punishment is relatively light—a three-day suspension without pay, and a letter of reprimand in his personnel jacket, the letter to be expunged in two years' time if Baker-Gómez incurs no other disciplinary action in the interim. Baker-Gómez is dismissed from the interview room and CO Roland Wiley is called in.

His interview is a comparatively brief affair. The front gate guard at the time of the escape, CO Wiley admits to the investigation team that he did not search the delivery van before signaling the tower guard to let it pass. He cites Zanco's long-standing custom of forgoing a search if the vehicle and driver are well-known to the gate guard and are of established reputation with the prison. Tri-Cross has been the medical supplier to Zanco for nearly thirty years, or so he's been told. The driver, Balestro, is known to all the gate guards and has been making the Tri-Cross deliveries since before Wiley came to Zanco. In the four years Wiley has been here, the gate guards have always given Balestro a recognition pass-through. The TDCJ executive assistant narrows his eyes at these remarks and scribbles in a small notebook. Casting a nervous glance at the assistant, the warden says that, in any event, the unequivocal fact of the matter is that the escape succeeded because Officer Wiley made a unilateral decision not to search the van, an act of gross incompetence for which he must be held fully accountable. Effective immediately, Officer Wiley is placed on indefinite and unpaid suspension from duty until the process for his termination of employment is completed. The sheriff adds that he will want to question Wiley further as his own investigation proceeds. "Don't go wanderin' off anywhere, boy, you hear?"

Wiley is dismissed and the interviews conclude. The panel confers privately regarding its public statements, then the warden and the sheriff go out to address the assembly of reporters waiting at the gate.

33

On the drizzly drive home to Sanderson following his session with the investigation team—the short drive heavily trafficked by vehicles with flashing rooftops—CO Marco Baker-Gómez sings along with a CD of Los Tigres del Norte. He gets a cigarette from the open pack in the console and lights up, exhaling with great satisfaction after a long shift on a job where smoking is prohibited, and especially satisfying at the end of *this* workday. Three days without pay and a jacket reprimand. BFD, as the onliners say. What's three days of a CO's salary to a man of his means? He loves the sound of that—"a man of his means." Never had he thought he might someday come into so much money all at one time, never mind with so little effort.

"The flare will be your exculpation, you see. Every tower man's attention will be drawn to it. When you report it to the duty office, if they ask about the delivery, you say you have not seen anything unusual about it. If they don't ask about the delivery, you don't say anything about it, either. That is all we require of you. What could be easier? Even if they get caught, you will have committed no crime. Why should you have thought the flare was intended as a deliberate distraction to you or in any

way related to an escape? At most you might be accused of negligence for failing to include in your report that the delivery was still in progress at the time. Whatever penalty you may receive will be minor."

The Mex dandy had called it exactly right.

The light rain is still falling when he reaches Sanderson, where only a few other COs live, the majority of Zanco employees preferring to live amid the larger population and range of amenities to be found in Fort Stockton, notwithstanding that it's a commute of more than an hour each way. A state patrol car comes down the central street, roof light flicking. Lots of cop cars at the eateries, most of which would normally be closed at this hour, but this was hardly a normal night.

Near the end of town he wheels into a trailer park where his double-wide stands on the far side, where there is more space between neighbors, a site he deliberately selected for its measure of privacy. The park's tall pole lamps are the only lights on at this hour, the mobile homes still dark with sleep.

Except, he now sees, for his own. The windows of the living room and kitchen are brightly lit, though it isn't his habit to leave lights on when he goes to work. He parks beside the Dumpster at the end of his street and scans for an unfamiliar vehicle but doesn't see one. He takes a .44 Magnum three-inch revolver from the glove compartment and checks the loaded cylinder, then untucks his shirt and gets out of the truck. He holds the gun under his shirt hem as he walks slowly to the house, watching his windows for movement within, the nearest neighbors' windows for sudden light. He eases up the low set of steps to the front door and finds it unlocked. Neatly picked.

The living room is in chaos. Furniture overturned. Sofa and chair pads slashed open, stuffing pulled out. All the cabinets in the adjoining kitchen are open, so too the refrigerator door, the floor littered with foodstuff and melting ice cubes, the plastic ice bin lying in the corner. He stands motionless and listens intently but hears nothing other than his own breath. *Wasn't them,* he tells himself. *Some random housebreaker is all.* The notion is so ridiculous he almost laughs. Then almost cries, thinking that if they hadn't found what they were after, they'd still be here. He moves down the hall to the bedroom and finds the room undisturbed. The search stopped before they got this far.

No, no, no, he thinks. *God, no.* Then commands himself to stay calm. It could've been some other reason they quit and left.

He tucks the gun in his pants and goes out on the front steps, stands in the darkness and soft rain, looks all about. Nothing astir. No lights showing in other windows. He goes around to the back of the house, which faces a stony hillside clumped with mesquites, and again stops to look around. Then gets down in the gravelly mud on his hands and knees and ducks his head and crawls under the house a short way and then rolls over on his back and stares up into the blackness of the mobile home's underside. *A really good flashlight by the bed and did you think to bring it, dumb-ass?* He digs a butane cigarette lighter out of his pocket and flicks it aflame, thinking, *Set your house afire now, why don't you?*

He reaches up through the rows of pipes and bundled wiring and into the floor-beam hidey-hole and feels around for the bag. It's not there. His hand darts around faster, as if the bag might be trying to evade it. He tells himself not to panic, he must've moved it over a little the last time he was down here checking on it. *Stay cool, it's here somewhere.* He wriggles about on his back, searching every adjacent recess, and again returns to the niche where he'd last put it, as if this time it might be there. He keeps at this pattern, searching the same places over and over, before he finally accepts the truth.

When he crawls out from under the house the rain has stopped altogether and a few breaks show in the cloud cover. He feels sick to his stomach. He goes back inside and sees that they took the unopened twelve-pack of Shiner bottles he'd had on a fridge shelf but left the four cans in the door rack. The bottle of Johnnie Red is still in the well-ordered pantry, which they obviously hadn't got to before finding the bag. Team search—an inside guy or two and one or more under the house at the same time. He sits at the kitchen table, sipping from the bottle and chasing it with beer, staring at the mess around him. Double-crossing spick bastards.

"You see how we trust you? How you can trust us? We do not pay you half now, half after, no. You get all of it now. Up in the front, as you say. Right here. Count it if you wish. Why should we not fully pay you beforehand? Will you cheat us? Will you accept the money and then not do your part of the agreement? Of course not. It would not be in your best interest to do that. We must trust each other because it is in our mutual best interest to do so. I must, however, insert an important caution. One hundred thousand dollars in cash that cannot be legally accounted for is not a simple thing to accommodate. This is especially true—and I mean no disrespect—for a man of your minor means. You must not spend any of the money right away. You do not want anyone to even suspect you are in possession of such a sum. There are too many dangerous thieves in the world. And you must not put the money in a bank right away, or ever all at once. As you may know, your banks must report to federal authorities all cash deposits of more than ten thousand dollars. As you may not know, they must also report any sequence of cash deposits of smaller sums, because such a sequence may indicate an intent to evade the requisite report. You see how it is? They have you, how do you say, going and coming back, no? If you put any of the money in a bank before the completion of the project, you might attract attention from officials and

perhaps put the project at risk. Then you would have trouble with us.
*And that is something you do not want to happen. Once the project is
completed, you may of course do as you wish, but until then you must
hold on to the money and not spend any of it. That is not a suggestion.
Hide it with care."*

Yeah, right, Baker-Gómez thinks. *Hide it with care. Keep it
around here somewhere, fool. So we can steal it all back from you while
the project's going on. And who you gonna complain to about it? The
cops? A lawyer? Chamber of Commerce?*

He hadn't spent a dollar of it. Had planned on buying himself
a cabin in East Texas, where he was from. On a nice lake. Maybe
on the Neches.

Bastards stole my future.

The windows are pale gray with dawn light and he is thor-
oughly soused when he recalls that he'd got the idea for hiding
the bag under the house from a crime movie he'd seen last year.
A movie set in this very part of Texas. Very popular flick, as he
recalls. He thinks it won an Academy Award. His visitors, it now
occurs to him, probably saw it too.

◦∞◦

"Scapegoat" is not a word CO Roland Wiley has ever used in
conversation or in writing but he knows what it means and he
knows it's what they needed and that's exactly what they're making him. A fucking scapegoat.

Well, hell with them, he thinks on the rainy way home to
Fort Stockton. *They can shove the job all the way up their ass till it's
stuck in their throat. Worse job in the world, anyway, a CO. And fuck
you too, Sheriff, and your* Don't go wanderin' off. *Just watch me,
mister. Investigate all you want, but you ain't gonna be asking me any
more questions. Gonna grab up my money and hightail it to . . . where?*

He's been giving it plenty of thought and all he's decided is that it ain't gonna be Mexico. *Land of the fucking locos. Canada's way more like it. And Gretchel? His engaged-to-be-engaged girlfriend of . . . how long's it been? Four years? Ask her to come along? What for? Why even bother? She ain't about to want to go anywhere, not her. Thirty-seven years old and still living with momma and daddy. Night manager at La Quinta and loves the job. She's anyway lost a goodly share in the looks department these last coupla years. Good titties still, give her that, but she's getting a belly, and that ass is got way out of hand. Really, guy, where's the loss? Bound to be more good-looking Canadian girls than you can shake a dick at who'll take interest in a dude with an ever-ready roll of greenbacks. American buck's worth more in Canada too. Yessir, Canada's it. You're a man with a plan, Stan.*

A half-mile south of Fort Stockton he comes upon the most serious roadblock he's ever seen. Cop cars of every kind—state, county, city—all with roof lights going. Cops in SWAT gear and with automatic weapons. He opens his window and presents his ID. A flashlight fixes on it, then on his face, plays over his uniform, and he's waved through.

His rented one-bedroom house is in a small neighborhood near the city park. As soon as he walks in and sees the place turned upside down his gut knots and he bolts to the bedroom and starts toward the corner where he keeps the little stool and then sees it's not there, it's already standing in the closet. Lying beside it on the floor is the nine-inch-square section he'd cut out of the rearmost part of the closet's plasterboard ceiling, above the shelf over the clothes rack, a part of the ceiling you couldn't see just standing in front of the closet. He had put the money up in there and then put the square piece back in place, so evenly cut it hardly showed a seam. How could they know to look there?

How you think, *dickhead? By being a fuck of a lot better at this sorta thing than you.*

He stands on the stool and reaches up into the opening and feels all around in the emptied spot. He can't accept this. Can *not* believe it. He goes out into the hall where closet stuff has been tossed on the floor and gets his softball bat and goes back in the room and rams the crown of the bat again and again into the closet ceiling until he's broken it all up and brought it down in chalk-dusty pieces. No bag. Then he's kneeling over the toilet, being sick. After a while he gets up and rinses his mouth and paces around the house, eyes hot with enraged dejection, a sour taste still on his tongue. *Fucking greaser pricks! What'd that fancy-suit beaner say? All that cash could be hard to* "accommodate." *Bastard son of a skanky whore!*

"*You understand correctly,*" the guy had told him. "*You need to do nothing but to follow the same procedure as always with this vehicle and its driver. You check his identification. You give the signal to the tower to open the gate. The vehicle passes through as it always does. That is all. In your happiest dreams you will never receive so much money for such a routine service of no risk at all to yourself. For simply doing what you always do.*"

Showing you them pearly teeth. Patting you on the shoulder like a old pal.

His stomach roils again and he rushes back to the john and for a while remains kneeled there, staring into the ruin of his life. He cannot believe his circumstance. Thirty-two years old and nothing ahead for him now but an empty road to nowheresville. Everybody knows things can change awful damn sudden in this life, and there's no place on earth you'll hear more stories about that than in a prison. But *this?*

Last month he was nothing but a low-pay prison hack and likely to stay one the rest of his working life, and then until a half hour ago he was a rich man planning a move to Canada! And *now*? No money, no job, nothing. No family. Never no wife. Neighbors just to wave to. No real friend since Lucas Jonesbury at Coffield Unit back when. Been five years at Zanco and living in Fort Stockton and still nobody's pal, never nobody's guest to supper. Even when there's a party where the whole staff's invited, he's always on the outside of the talk and joking, just standing there with a beer and smiling at nothing like a goddamn ass. And that *sheriff*! Giving him the stink-eye and practically accusing him of having something to do with the break!

Good God almighty, what if he *does* get found out? Talk about how things can change! Go from CO to inmate in a blink and even that wouldn't be the worst of it because everybody knows what cons do to ex-cops and ex-hacks.

He goes over and lies on the bed, steeped in self-pitying misery. Then it's daybreak and he knows she's up and is making breakfast for her daddy and momma as usual and any minute now they're gonna see the news on TV or in the paper.

A few minutes later his cell rings. He doesn't answer. After another twenty minutes he hears her car pull into the driveway, then her key in his front door, then "Dear Lord!" when she sees the mess. Then she's in the bedroom and looking at him curled up in bed in all his clothes, hugging a pillow to his chest. "Oh, sweetie, what *is* it?" she says.

She lies down with him and holds him close and he tells her all about the prison break and losing his job for not searching the van and how the sheriff threatened him, and if all that wasn't bad enough, he comes home and finds the place tore up, the cash he kept hid in the sock drawer gone, same with some money he kept in the freezer. Most likely some shitkicker Mex kids having a high old time playing at being bandidos.

She pets him and coos to him and tells him to just lie there and relax, and then makes a call to her cousin Buddy Joe up in Midland who's been a paralegal for nearly four years. She catches him before he leaves for work. He's heard about the prison break on the news, and she tells him about the trouble Ronnie's in on account of it. Buddy Joe tells her that the TDCJ can fire Ronnie for the dumb-ass mistake of not searching the van, which it surely was, but no way was it a crime, and if they try to make it one without solid evidence they're dumb-ass themselves because it'll never stick.

"So there, you see?" Gretchel tells Roland Wiley after the call. Worse they can do is fire him and who cares about that stupid old job, anyway? There are lots of other jobs, better jobs where he won't have to be around a bunch of criminals every day. Heck, she just bets she can get him on at the motel, no problem at all. She thinks they may be looking to hire a new handyman, and he's real good at that sort of stuff. "Don't you worry, sweetie pie," she says, hugging him close. "Everything's gonna be fine." He slips his hand under her shirt and she smiles and they fumble out of most of their clothes and have sex. He will never tell her the truth about the break and the brief time he was rich.

Later she will make breakfast for him and afterward they will clean up the mess and then go shopping for groceries to replace what had to be thrown away. By that time he will have understood that things might have been very much worse.

Because those old boys might've still been there when he came home.

34

Matthew Mason, too, lives in Fort Stockton, where the Terrell County deputy has driven him to the hospital. X-rays show that one of his ribs is fractured, and the doctor says nothing can be done about that except to take pain relievers as needed and avoid stressing the rib; it will repair on its own. Another physician tends to his facial injuries and makes an appointment for him with a dental surgeon the following month, after his face is sufficiently healed. The attending doctor wants to keep him in the hospital overnight for observation but Mason refuses. He tells the waiting deputies he can drive himself home, it's only a short way, but they say no, the doc told them he's too full of painkillers to get behind the wheel. One of them drives him in the Wrangler, the other follows in the Terrell squad car. It's half past midnight and the rain has quit.

❧

He lives in a neighborhood of big homes, though the house has seemed even bigger since Linda Jean left. A note on the kitchen counter said she'd gone to her sister's and not to call because she was all done with talking. When the papers came he signed them and sent them back and that was that. Made him an official three-time loser at marriage, and the third time the shortest. *Well, good riddance and up yours, Linda, you sorry bitch. And thank you so very much for cutting yourself out of my good fortune, which I never woulda told you about nohow.*

First thing he'd done was take one of the hundred-dollar bills to the bank to have it checked. He told them he won it in a poker game and just wanted to make sure it wasn't counterfeit before he used it. He was gonna spend his recuperation leave watching ball games and movies on the TV, eating T-bones, drinking Jim Beam and Shiner Bock, planning a trip for his next vacation. Vegas, by God, where he's been wanting to go. A fella at Chuckie Sewell's poker barn in Odessa told him of a Vegas escort service he swore can't be beat. Said it's expensive but you can arrange a visit there ahead of time over the Internet and they definitely will not cheat you and they got pictures of so many great-looking girls to choose from you'll near go crazy just trying to decide which one you want. Might buy himself a brand-new vehicle up there, too. Truck, maybe. Tell everybody back here he won it in a drawing.

❧

The deputy parks the Wrangler in the driveway of the dark-windowed house and they get out. The young officer starts toward the door with him but Mason assures him he can make it into his own house without help. He ain't crippled, for Chrissake, just a little beat up, no big deal. The deputy joins his partner in the idling county car and they wait while Mason fumbles with the door key before managing the lock. He reaches in and turns on the porch light and waves at them. They give him a horn toot, wheel around, and head back to Terrell County.

He goes inside and clicks a wall switch that turns on the table lamps at either end of the sofa. He's already closing the door behind him before his mind registers the sofa's ripped-open disarray and then he sees the man hunched low at the far end of the table in the dining room and holding a firearm much larger than a handgun pointed squarely at him. In druggy alarm, Mason turns toward the door but a man standing beside it with his back against the wall steps forward and punches him in the side of the head, dropping him to his knees, the blow inflaming the pains of his mouth and nose wounds.

All is confusion to him as he's jerked to his feet, squealing at the agony of his broken rib, at the rough pressings into it as hands search him, relieve him of wallet, keys, phone, his assail-ants addressing each other in Spanish. A dining chair is dragged over and he's shoved down onto it. He thinks there are three of them now but isn't sure. His hands are bound behind the chair back with what feels to him like a belt. He chokes and coughs. The low light of the table lamps is the room's only illumina-tion, and tears blur his vision, but he now sees there are only two of them. Mexicans. They talk in whispers a few feet away. The windows are closed, their drapes drawn, the air conditioner cranked up high and humming.

He knows they're here for the money. There's no other reason. And he tells himself he won't give it up. Whatever they do, he'll live through it. Bust his bones, his teeth, okay, it'll hurt, but bones heal and teeth can be replaced. He can take a stomping and they don't want a murder rap. Wouldn't do them any good to kill him. Just lay a good dodge on them and man up. That's the trick. It won't last forever.

The one with the big firearm—a submachine gun, Mason now sees, with a forward-curved magazine jutting from its underside—comes around the table and lays the weapon on it and pulls up a dining chair and sits directly in front of him, their knees almost touching. He is short and stocky, thick of hair and mustache, and is absent a left ear. Under his open windbreaker of light nylon, the butt of a shoulder-holstered pistol is visible.

"*Hablas español?*" the man asks.

"No," Mason says, "I'm . . . I no—"

The man flicks a hand. "Is okay. I have English. No so very good like this one"—he gestures at the other man—"but good for talk with you, I think. First I say is very good luck for all of everybody the two policemans don't come in this house. If they was come in this house everything is then very bad. Much shooting, much blood, you know, then we have to make the fast, ah . . . " He looks at the other one. "*Escapada?*"

"Escape," the other one says. He is as short as the one-eared guy but leaner and sinewy, dressed in jeans and a blue-and-white Dallas Cowboys T-shirt, a rolled blue bandanna around his head, his mustache neater, nattier. A blued pistol is tucked in his waistband at his belly.

Even as Mason listens, he's concocting a dodge.

"*Ah, si, claro* . . . 'escape,'" the one-ear says. "We have to make the very fast escape, and then . . . *Ay, Chihuahua!*" He flaps a hand upward to suggest some great catastrophic consequence. Then looks past Mason and says, "*Pues? Nada?*"

A man emerges from the hallway. "No," he says, and comes over to stand where he can see Mason's face. He is unusually tall for a mestizo, over six feet by Mason's guess. Buzz cut, clean-shaven. Also in jeans and T-shirt, this one reading, "What If the Hokey Pokey Really IS What It's All About?" Like the other man, he has a pistol in his waistband, and in his hand is a Taurus 9-millimeter semiautomatic that Mason recognizes as his own. Bastard took it from the bedroom dresser.

The one-ear glances at his watch and fixes Mason with a mildly tired look. "Okay, my friend," he says. "We have wait for you much time. Enough the, how you say, shit-shat, eh? Where is the money?"

"The *money*?"

The man sighs. "The money was give you, where is it?"

"Hey, man, we had a *deal*! Me and . . . your guys, your boss, whoever the fuck," Mason says, high-voiced. "I carried out my end, didn't I? I'm the one who got them out! I *earned* that money! Man, just look at my fucking *face*!" He feels he's playing it well—a wronged but very scared pussy who's easily enough going to give it up. That's the image he has to project here.

The man stares at him. "Don't be a stupid. I have not very much time for you. You want *deal*? Here is deal. You don't tell us where is the money, we give you very much bad pain. To stop *more* very much bad pain you will give us the money, and then you don't have the money no more but you still have the bad pain. You see? Is not smart for you, hombre. Don't have the pain. Be smart. *Ahora* . . . one more. Where is the money?"

Mason works his face into a desperate display of fear and interior struggle. "Okay, okay," he says. "I ain't no brave guy, I ain't no hero, I admit it. But *goddamnit*, listen . . . how about you leave me with . . . thirty thousand? That's fair, ain't it? We had a deal but, all right, yeah, I get it, this is how it's gonna be and what the fuck can I do about it? But thirty's fair, ain't it? After what I done for you guys, the *beating* I took from those fucks?"

The one-eared man studies him. Mason wants him to believe he will do anything, give up anything, to avoid any further pain, but wants also to convey a burning desire to come away from all this with *something* in his pocket. Greed is always real, always believable. He is counting on that truth to pull off his ploy. He wouldn't be asking for a cut of money he didn't have, would he? Money he's ready to turn over?

"All right, all right . . . *twenty*!" Mason says. "Jesus, man, just leave me with *twenty*!"

The one-eared man purses his lips. "Twenny towsands, eh?" He smiles. "Okay. Is a deal."

"*Yeah?* We got a deal?"

"Chure. You give us the money, we give you the twenny towsands for your helping, and we go. So . . . where?"

"The bedroom," Mason says. "Under the mattress, up near the head of the bed. People always look under a mattress but never right at the head of it, did you know that?" He simpers. "You oughta let me have another five grand for teaching you something."

The man looks up at the tall Hokey Pokey one, who shakes his head.

"No," the one-eared man says. "He look. Is no there."

"*What?*" Mason blurts this with all the raw confusion he can simulate. "*Bullshit! It's there! I put it there!* What the *fuck's* going on? Look again! Near the head of the mattress! Look again!"

The three men look at him blankly.

"Oh Jesus *fuck*! Somebody . . . somebody musta come here! Somebody *had* to've come and stole it! Oh, fuck me, they *stole my money*!"

Doing good, he thinks, *doing good.*

The man asks the other two something in Spanish. The tall one replies and goes into the hallway. Mason hears him rummaging in the closet.

"I'm *telling* you, man," he says, weeping, raspy voice breaking. "It was there! I *swear* to you it was there this morning! It's been there ever since I got it. I check it every fucking day before I leave for work! If it wasn't *your* guys came and took it . . . shit, man, I don't know *who* the hell's got it! Son of a *bitches!*"

"*La televisión,*" the one-ear says. The Dallas Cowboy picks up the remote control and examines it, then turns on the TV. A game show. He clicks through the channels and finds a music video station, then raises the volume and sways in place to the beat. Whatever they're going to do, Mason knows, it'll likely make him holler a goodly bit, and they don't want to take a chance of him being heard by anybody who might pass by out on the sidewalk. But that's okay, that's okay. They won't kill him. They don't need *that* kinda trouble. Anything else, bring it on, he can take it. For a *hundred grand?* Damn straight he can take it. After a while he'll be okay again, and then it's good life here he comes!

The tall man returns with a claw hammer and hands it to the one-ear.

Mason's gut stirs at his sight of it. *Hold tight, man,* he thinks, just *hold tight.* The tall guy squats and pulls the shoe and sock off Mason's right foot.

"No, man, don't, *don't,*" Mason says. "I don't *know* where it is, I swear to fucking *God!*"

"*Mordaza,*" the one-ear says.

The Cowboy takes the bandanna off his head and wads it and stuffs it into Mason's mouth. Then the one-ear whips the hammer down and converts Mason's big toe to a scarlet crush of flesh and bone.

The pain surpasses any Mason has ever before known and instantly eradicates his resolve not to tell where the money is, though he cannot immediately say so because he's screaming into the balled bandanna. The one-ear doesn't even look up at him before swinging the hammer again, this time driving its face into the upper arch of the same foot, the bone-crack audible above the TV and stoppered shrieks. Mason writhes in such frenzy that both of the other men have to hold the chair to keep it from tipping over.

The one-ear looks up and says, "*Shush,* mister, *shush.* Is no so very bad. No yet. *Shush,* hombre! Listen to me."

Mason is able to restrain his cries to a stuttering low wail. Mucus runs from his nose and he is choking on the bandanna. The one-ear turns the hammer in his hand to better display its claw head to Mason. "This part is for . . . *la rodilla?*"

"The knee," another says.

Mason's wail rises.

"For the knee," the one-ear says. "But maybe no. Maybe you want to say where is the money."

Shrilling into the gag, Mason nods and nods, struggling for breath, his streaming eyes wild. The handkerchief is yanked from his mouth and he throws up on himself.

A minute later, the Cowboy goes outside and gets in the Wrangler and starts it up, opens the garage door with the remote, then drives in and cuts the motor off and lowers the door again. The tall one is there, holding a plastic grocery bag from the kitchen, and waits until the door comes down before he turns on the garage lights. The Cowboy gets out and unlocks the gas cap, then removes it. One end of a length of fishing line is looped around the top of the gas filler neck, and the rest of the line runs down into the tank. The Cowboy slowly pulls the line up hand under hand, withdrawing an attached length of flexible plastic tubing like a long black snake, and with it a pervasive odor of gasoline. They lay the tube on the floor in a wide spiral, then the Cowboy slits it open as carefully as a surgeon and they remove the end-to-end rolls of cash. They make a scan count of it and put it all in the grocery bag, seal it with a twist tie, and head back to the living room.

Mason is slumped forward in the chair, his hands still belted behind its back. The room is frigid with conditioned air laced with the reek of his vomit. All his other pains are overwhelmed by that of his misshapen foot, which in its bloody-purple bloat looks to him through his tears like a foul discard from a butcher shop. The one-ear is now standing before the television, absorbed by a video of a tall man in top hat and tuxedo dancing with a trio of young women in scanty dress who seductively strip him of his tie and cummerbund, seemingly intent on disrobing him.

When the other two men enter from the garage, one of them turns up a thumb and the one-ear smiles. The three converse in whispers, then the two men go over and stand by the front door, and the one-ear returns to Mason, who stares up at him, unable to suppress his low keening despite his fear that it might anger the man into harming him further.

"Very good, mister," the one-ear says. "Is there like you say. The truth is good, no? Always more better, the truth." Then adds with a comradely grin, "But maybe sometime no with the womens, eh?"

Mason's attempt at an acquiescent smile is grotesque, so stark is his terror.

"Ay, hombre, don't be so very afraid," the man says. "You have no more trouble of us. No more pain. You don't have no twenny towsands but you are still alife, no? Now we go and you never see us no more again, eh?"

Mason manages to bob his head. The man smiles and pats him on the shoulder and steps around him, and even as Mason hears a distinct *snick* sound, the man's fingers close on his hair and his head is pulled back and he feels the incisive draw of the blade across his throat, at once icy and searing, and his blood jets. His attempted scream emerges as a thick gargle and he falls forward in the chair as far as his bound arms permit. He sees the blood cascading onto his shirtfront, spreading darkly on his pants, dripping down between his feet. Then everything goes black and he thinks he's dead—not understanding that the men have turned off all the lights before quickly slipping out the front door and closing it again—and as he marvels at the revelation that there is consciousness after death, and wonders what other awesome surprises await him . . . he dies.

35

The three men move rapidly down a dark street lined with dripping trees. Their eyes cutting everywhere for signs of possible confrontation. The one-eared man carries the bag of money in one hand, and in the other—in a black trash bag he holds against his chest—the H&K submachine gun, his finger on the trigger guard. The other two men hold pistols under their shirts. They go around the corner and then down a long block to the convenience store where their SUV is parked in the side lot.

While the Dallas Cowboy goes into the store to buy a twelve-pack of Corona and packets of beef jerky, the one-ear snugs the bag of money under the rear passenger seat, the tall one keeping watch for anyone who might show interest in them. The one-ear then sits up front in the shotgun seat, the H&K down between his legs, and the tall one gets behind the wheel. The Cowboy comes out with his purchases and settles himself in the backseat and they're off, the tall one working the SUV's radio tuner in search of local news reports, the Cowboy manning the scanner in the backseat with a set of earphones, monitoring police activity in the area.

Earlier that day, in the midst of the late-afternoon storm, they had been listening to the scanner while parked in the rear lot of a motel at the east end of Fort Stockton, waiting for the Tri-Cross van to bring Cacho and his gringo friend to them for transport to the airfield at the nearby ranch. In addition to his own three-man team, the one-eared man is in command of three other teams, each with two men and each team assigned to repossess one or another of the bribe payments.

Two of the other teams had already reported their success in recovering the cash from the homes of Wiley and Baker-Gómez without any trouble and were on the way back to Nuevo Laredo, but the one-ear and his team had failed to find any money at Mason's house, and he intended to return there after taking Cacho to the plane. He knew Mason would have to undergo interrogation at the prison and likely require medical treatment and would be late getting home.

As for the van driver, Balestro, on arriving at the motel lot he was expecting to get tied up and gagged and left in his vehicle to be found by whoever and then questioned by police. Such was the plan as it had been explained to him. He would tell the cops the same thing the guard Mason would—that the convicts had threatened to kill him if he didn't do as they said—and that they had promised to let him go in Fort Stockton. When the cops were done with him, he'd reclaim the van and go home.

In fact, however, the fourth of the one-eared man's teams had also been waiting behind the motel, assigned to get back Balestro's bribe money. Their intention was to put him in their SUV and take him home to Big Spring, 150 miles north, advising him en route that if he did not produce the cash they would kill everyone in his family in front of his eyes and then blind him, cut out his tongue, pierce his eardrums, and destroy his knees. They would of course do those things if necessary but didn't think it would be. They knew Balestro was a devoted husband and father who had joined in this risky proposition mainly because his youngest daughter has a heart disorder and his job-provided bare-bones medical insurance had reached its cap. They had no doubt he would make the wiser choice of returning the money rather than lose his family and be reduced to a crippled, sightless, deaf and dumb state.

As the two teams had waited in the motel lot, the scanner's hiss in the one-ear's vehicle was occasionally interrupted by a dispatcher's voice directing a patrol car to intervene in some public disturbance or domestic altercation. But just about the time they expected the van to be departing the prison, the scanner suddenly began to emit a steady series of strident calls pertaining to a breakout from the Zanco Unit and they learned of the prison's premature discovery of the escape and that the van was being pursued south over nameless ranch roads.

The one-ear knew that whatever Cacho Capote now had in mind, it wasn't to try to get to Fort Stockton. The kid had to know he'd never make it. And because there was no telling what might become of the van driver, the one-ear ordered the two men in the other SUV to leave for Big Spring at once and keep a round-the-clock watch on Balestro's home until they received word about what to do next. He then called his chief and informed him of the breakdown in the plan. Reasoning that Cacho would likely try to cross the river somewhere along the Terrell County border, the chief said he would begin a search for him on the

Mexican side, and he okayed the one-ear's request for him and his team to go back to Mason's house and wait for him and get back the money.

And so they had.

⟨∞⟩

The one-eared man is Francisco Arroyo, known to his associates as Sinoreja—the one without an ear—more often simply as Sino. Wearing the Dallas Cowboy shirt is Enrique Fortas, called Vaquero for his love of the Texas footballers. Vicente López—El Alto, the high one—is the tall young man with the Hokey Pokey shirt. In addition to a Texas driver's license, a Social Security card, and a voter registration certificate affirming residency in Laredo, Texas, directly across the river from Nuevo Laredo, they all three possess state permits to carry a gun. All these documents are of valid issue to counterfeit identities. And although none of these men has ever set foot on any of the four Laredo branches of So-Tex Motors Sales & Service, they are on the company's personnel roster as auto mechanics and twice a month receive paychecks by direct deposit into their bank accounts. A So-Tex accountant files their federal income tax returns. None of them has a police record anywhere in the United States.

⟨∞⟩

They take a northside ramp onto I-10 East and see the scores of flashing lights at the roadblock on the south side of the interstate. The SUV's radio is full of excited chatter about the prison break and they learn that the kidnapped van driver was earlier found dead alongside the Zanco road. Sino calls the chief with this information and they confer for a minute. Then he phones the two men he sent to Big Spring and gives them further instructions.

For the next one hundred miles they see roadblocks at every southside ramp, and then no more of them after they pass through Ozona. Another hundred miles farther on, they turn south at the town of Junction and head for the border, a cloudless red daybreak heralding a scorcher that is predicted to exceed one hundred degrees.

36

Shortly after the red sunrise, a rancher's twelve-year-old son, eager to get a look at the flooded creek, finds the body of Zanco Unit CO Tillis Moore snared in bank brush two hundred yards above the creek's junction with the Rio Grande, the upturned face missing much of its left side, its ruin being fed upon by small eels. The boy runs home to tell his father, who telephones the sheriff.

The autopsy report will cite the cause of death as either of the victim's two gunshot wounds, both inflicted by the same nine-millimeter weapon, one round penetrating the victim's right side at a slight upward angle, fracturing the number eight false rib and passing through liver, stomach, and abdominal aortas before lodging between the fourth and fifth left-side true ribs, the other round entering the cranium just below the right zygomatic and inflicting fatal trauma to the brain before exiting through the left-side temporal. Investigators will presume he was killed by the fugitives—though they will be unable to explain how Moore encountered them or how they acquired a nine-millimeter handgun—and capital murder will be added to the charges against them.

❦

Almost three hours after Moore is found, one of the crews searching along the creek comes upon the sunken Tri-Cross van jammed
between the bank and a boulder. It takes more than another hour
for a tow truck to make its rough passage to the site and winch
the van ashore, its cargo space crammed with a fragment of leafy
limb. There is no one in the vehicle, but a search of it turns up the
shiv CO Mason referred to in his account of the escape. Lacking
evidence that anyone debarked from the van at this point, and
because summoned trackers and their dogs find no trace of the
convicts within a mile of the site, the search team can only assume that they tried to achieve the bank here, or had maybe tried
to do it somewhere farther upstream, but were overcome by the
current and carried away on it. The creek-side search for them
is intensified and reaches the Rio Grande shortly after midday
without turning up the body of either man. It can only be supposed they were borne out into the booming river and drowned,
if they weren't already dead before then.

❦

That afternoon a Texas Ranger helicopter searching along the
river detects a plume of smoke from a narrow canyon and tracks
it to a fire on a rock beach where a man is waving a shirt above
his head. Near him is a small blue tent. Hovering above the gorge
rim, the chopper lowers a rescue line and the man straps himself
into it and is hoisted up. "Sweet baby Jesus, that's one hairy ride!"
he says when he's pulled aboard. "Near shit my britches thinking I was gonna fall off!" The Ranger crewman takes a revolver
from the man's waistband, saying, "I'll just hold this for you, sir."
As they head back to the operations center at Fort Stockton he

tells them he is Gaston Bonheur and thanks them profusely for
saving him and says it took hours for him to find enough burnable
wood to get a fire going but at least it raised pretty good smoke.
He tells of his inflatable boat being stolen by a pair of thieves in
the night. "God alone knows how they even *got* to where I was!
River blasting like that and them with no boat? *How,* I ask you?
And they couldn't just ask me for help, no sir, didn't say word
one, just snuck up and took my boat and left me for dead in the
wild. No way I coulda got outta that canyon *except* by boat. If
you boys hadn't come along, I'da been a goner sure, starved to
damn death. Oh, them no-goods had some brass balls, let me tell
you! I fired warning shots—you know, way up over their heads,
not wanting to really shoot nobody and maybe get in a jackpot
with the law—but they didn't slow down even a little bit. Then
I shot the boat and had to've deflated at least one chamber but
they shove off in it anyways, and I don't care how good they
can paddle, there's no way in hell they could make it past the
downriver rapids. The *both* of them in that little boat with a air
chamber out? No way, José. You boys go have a look-see below
the rapids, you'll find them fellers floating asses-up, you can put
money on it." Did he see how they were dressed? Not really, it
was so damn dark. Kinda light-colored clothes, about the best he
can recall. Both of them.

    After interviewing Gaston Bonheur, investigators believe
it possible but improbable that the men who stole his boat were
the escapees. It defies credulity they could have made it down
the stormy river canyon without a boat or a life vest all the way
to where Bonheur was camped and not have drowned or even
been separated. The helicopter resumes its river search and late
that afternoon sights a capsized inflatable boat caught in strainer
brush almost thirty miles downriver from where Bonheur had

made camp. The pilot radios the coordinates to the operations center, and a pair of vehicle teams are sent out. They arrive at the site in the last hour of daylight and confirm that the boat is Bonheur's, but there is no evidence that anyone had been in it when it got there.

The consensual surmise is that the boat capsized in the up-river rapids and the two men who thieved it drowned. Perhaps they were the fugitives, perhaps somebody else, but in any case, either in the creek or in the river, the escaped convicts had surely drowned. Their bodies may eventually turn up along one bank or the other, but given the many isolate stretches of this section of the Rio Grande, the remains may go unfound for a long time, and if they should be hung up in bottom roots or wedged in an undercut, they may never surface. Moreover, for lack of the bodies, the fugitives cannot officially be declared dead, and the state posts a ten-thousand-dollar reward on each of them for any information leading to him, dead or alive.

❧

Earlier that day, both the Zanco Unit doctor and Mason's physician at the Fort Stockton hospital had tried to contact him by phone but were able to access only his voice mail. Because of his heavy prescription of pain medication, they anticipated that he would be sleeping much of the day, and they opted to let him rest undisturbed. Both of them left the same message—they simply wanted to check on his condition. But when he will again fail to reach Mason by phone the next day, the Zanco doctor, who also resides in Fort Stockton, will drive over to Mason's house that evening and find it completely darkened, the drapes drawn on all the windows, the air-conditioning unit alongside the house whirring at full function. He will ring the front door bell, to no avail, then peer in the little garage window and see Mason's Wrangler, then again call the CO's mobile and again get only voice mail.

After banging hard at the back door and rapping loudly at all the windows and still raising no response, he will call the police. On arrival, they will repeat all the doctor's attempts to rouse Mason, then at last jimmy the front door and find his bloody and waxen-faced corpse bound to the chair. The subsequent investigation will discount the possibility that his killing had any connection with the prison escape. If anyone involved with the break had wanted him dead, the escapees could have done it when they jumped him in the infirmary, or they could have taken him as a possible hostage and killed him elsewhere, but would have had no reason to bring him home first, nor to search his house. The police will give greater credence to the idea that he may have been killed by a former convict seeking revenge for some prison grievance. He had tortured Mason before killing him and decided to rob the house before he left. It will also be conjectured that Mason may have been the victim of a random home invasion, like the unfortunate old couple murdered by home invaders just ten months earlier at their house a few miles outside the city limits. That premise, too, would account for Mason's searched house and mutilated foot. In the months to come, every convict released from Zanco in the last five years will be sought out and interrogated, but nothing will come of that line of investigation. As with the home invasion killings of the old couple, the murder of Corrections Officer Matthew L Mason will remain unsolved.

◦≈◦

When COs Marco Baker-Gómez and Roland Wiley hear of Mason's murder and that his home was ransacked, they will each wonder if Mason had been part of the plan. But each of them had believed himself the only CO involved, and even now they have no concrete basis for believing that Mason or anyone else besides the driver was in it, too, or to disbelieve that he was a victim of a vengeful ex-con or a random home invasion, as investigators have speculated. They will of course wonder about each other, both of them having been disciplined for duty infractions associated with the escape. But wondering will be as far as it ever goes, because neither of them can take the chance of confessing himself to the other, and after another few weeks they will neither one even wonder anymore.

37

The Balestro residence is in a pleasant neighborhood near the state psychiatric hospital, a mix of single-family homes and small apartment houses. After a long night of keeping an eye on the house from their SUV in the parking lot of an apartment building a half-block away, the two men Sino sent to Big Spring rented a second-floor apartment in the building and have since maintained surveillance of the Tri-Cross van driver's house from a street window.

The neighborhood has been in gloom since the sheriff and a medical technician came last night and notified Mrs Balestro of her husband's death, and the word along the block is that she is under sedation. Neighbors have been taking covered-dish meals to the house and looking after the widow and her four girls.

Sino's men will get their first look at her three days later when she leaves for the funeral. Through careful eavesdropping and solicitous conversational gambits at the corner washateria, the two men will learn that the couple who accompanied her and her children to the cemetery were her brother and his wife, who live in Castroville. They will learn, too, of the widow's plan to go stay at her brother's house for a week or so, wanting to be with family for a while.

The two men will phone this information to Sino and discuss the possibility that Balestro told his wife of the money and she might know where it is. If she knows, and if they don't find it while she's visiting her brother, they can extract it from her easily enough when she returns. But if she doesn't know, then their interrogation of her would both be fruitless and become a police matter, which would then make it much harder to ever find the money.

Sino will agree with their thinking but tell them they're getting ahead of themselves. First see if it's in the house.

❧

The following day the bereaved family will depart for Castroville in the brother's station wagon, and late that night, the neighborhood in deep sleep, the two men will slip the back-door lock and enter the house and secure the drapes and blinds against any leakage of light and search the place. It will prove a short job, the house only a small two-bedroom. In the closet of the parental bedroom they will find a locked carrying case for a rifle or shotgun, a hand-printed notice taped to it—"DANGER. DO NOT TOUCH. ORDER OF DADDY." They'll break its lock and see that the case holds a bolt-action .30-06 hunting rifle and, tightly packed with it, three plastic bags containing a sum of twenty-five thousand dollars.

Finding no other money in the house, they will turn off the lights and then cross the backyard to a large shed secured with a heavy but uncomplicated padlock which they easily open. They'll shut the shed door and by the glow of a butane lighter find the switch for the overhead bulb and begin their search among the

clutter of toolboxes and disordered shelves, cursing the owner for
his untidiness that makes their own work more difficult. When
they push aside a large heavy tool cabinet they will uncover a
square of four juxtaposed floor bricks, under which is packed a
plastic bag holding another twenty-five thousand dollars.

To exit the shed, they'll have to push the big cabinet back
over the hidey-hole. They will return to the house and sift through
a small ring of keys they earlier noted on a little hook next to the
kitchen door and find the one they need and remove it from the
ring, then turn off the lights and go out and around to the side of
the house where Balestro's old Chevy Lumina is parked. One of
them will get in it and wait until the other has walked away and
is almost back to the apartment, then start the car and drive off.
A short time later he will pay a seventeen-year-old member of a
street gang called Los Fuerzos to drive the car to a certain garage
in San Antonio. The man will then take a taxi to the state hospital
and from there walk to the apartment. His partner will by then
have reported to Sino their recovery of half of the Balestro money.
Before noon the next day the Lumina will lie strewn in dozens
of parts over the floor of the San Antonio garage, and the owner
of the place, a member of the same organization to which Sino
belongs, will notify him by phone that the only money found in
the car amounted to a dollar and forty-two cents in coins recovered from the floorboards and under the seats. Sino will then go
to his chief and apprise him of the situation, and the chief will ask
if the van driver was the one with a little girl who has a medical
problem. After their meeting, Sino will phone his two men in Big
Spring and tell them the job is finished and to come home with
the fifty thousand.

❧

On her return from Castroville the first thing Mrs Balestro will
notice when her brother pulls up in front of the house is that
the family sedan is gone. She will be perplexed, but her husband
had often let friends borrow it, and her first thought will be that
one of them has done that. But when they find the front door
unlocked and the house rummaged, her brother will immediately
call the police while Mrs Balestro calms her alarmed daughters.
A careful probe of the house will establish that nothing has been
stolen, not the television nor any of the kitchen appliances or
the hunting rifle whose case was broken open. Though the shed
will be found to be lacking its padlock, the widow will not note
anything missing from its cluttered contents, either, though she is
not really familiar with them and can't be sure that everything's
there. The police will commiserate with the widow over the
violation of her home, especially so soon after the death of her
husband, but will have no reason to suppose a tie between the
two events. They will guess that the intruders were in search of
something specific, most likely a drug stash, but had been misin-
formed about the address where they would find it. Such errors
were not uncommon among their kind. When they'd come across
the car keys, it had been a no-brainer to take the old Lumina and
get a few hundred dollars from a chop shop for their evening's
work. The police will encourage everyone in the neighborhood
to call 911 at any sign of suspicious activity, and will promise a
more pervasive street patrol in the evenings.

Over the next few weeks, the grieving Mrs Balestro will
bit by bit resume a daily routine. She will tend to the house,
visit with neighbors, help her daughters with their homework,
light a weekly candle for her husband's soul, and pray daily
to the Holy Mother to ease the younger girl's affliction. Balestro's employer-provided life insurance will suffice to meet the

family's basic financial needs for the present, but she will have
to rely on the free clinic for the minor treatments and generic
medicines it can provide her daughter, will grudgingly accept
the small monetary contributions her brother presses on her to
help with expenses, and will despair about the girl's future care.
To try to distract herself, she will resume puttering with her
long-neglected potted plants along the rear wall of the house,
deriving emotional respite from the perfunctory acts of ridding
the pots of their old dirt and desiccated contents and refilling
them with fresh soil and rooting them with new cuttings. One
late afternoon she will empty an oversized clay pot and find in
the encrusted dirt a tightly packed black plastic bag sealed with
duct tape which she'll cut open with a pair of shears to reveal a
jumble of packets of one-hundred-dollar bills. For a long minute
she will stare at the money, confused and feeling a sickly turn in
her stomach. Then carefully look around and see that no one is
in sight and scoop up the bag and take it into the house. And
there learn that the contents amount to fifty thousand dollars.
She will mull the matter through the long night, will several
times pick up the phone before once again putting it down, not
knowing who to call or what to say. She is not a stupid woman
and will know that the money has something to do with the
break-in of her house and almost certainly something to do with
her husband. She will slowly accept the frightening explanation
that he must have received it for abetting the escape and was
paid beforehand and hid the money in the potted dirt. Of all
the questions that will beset her, the easiest to answer will be
whether to notify the police—of course not.

   The next morning, after feeding the girls breakfast and waiting with them at the corner for the school bus, she will go back
to her kitchen, brew a pot of tea, and decide on a course of action.

Then she'll go back to bed and sleep more soundly for the next few hours than she has since becoming a widow. That evening she will phone her brother to share the happy news of the life insurance payment she's to receive on a private policy she hadn't known her husband had purchased. In less than three months she will have sold the house in Big Spring and be residing in San Antonio, only a short drive from her brother in Castroville. And she will be working on the maintenance staff of a large hospital, a job that includes excellent medical benefits for her and her family.

38

Axel wakes up under the trees, in the gray shadow of imminent daybreak, the sun still behind the faraway hills that stand black against the reddening lower sky.

"Free" is his first thought. Pain his first sensation. He lies supine and unmoving, but everything hurts—head, hands, every muscle and joint. To swallow is an ordeal.

Just before waking he'd had a brief dream. All his life most of his dreams have been unsettling, and early in his prison years he had trained himself to give them no thought, to eliminate them from memory as soon as his eyes opened. He'd grown so adept at it that for a long time now he has seemed not to dream at all. But this short one was of his daughter, and for some reason, perhaps his weariness, he'd lapsed in his habit of direct dismissal and remembers it clearly.

He was standing in the outer dark and watching her through a window. She looked exactly as she had in the most recent photo Charlie had brought him, with reddish blonde hair to just below her shoulders. She was standing in a brightly lighted room, appearing to be deep in thought, and then suddenly looked up, as if sensing she was being watched. She glanced all about until her gaze came to the window where he stood and . . . he woke.

Goddamn dreams. Then he remembers the lion and its fearsome growl and feels a rush of inexplicable pleasure. He makes a promise to himself that he will not be taken again, never again imprisoned. He dies, he dies free.

He suddenly grows aware that the river isn't as loud as before.

With a grunt of pain he sits up and peers at the Rio through the ragged bank-side foliage and sees that it's still running strong but not as riotously as last night. He guesses they're at the tail end of the rapids and the storm runoff has subsided. There isn't a stir of breeze. The trees droop. In the dawn light the nearby rocky rise is bigger than he had thought last night, an escarpment maybe forty feet high, and stretches off into the upriver shadows. A few yards away a ring of blackened rocks marks a campfire site littered with emptied food tins and plastic bottles. The sight of the bean cans makes him hungry. Cacho is still lying on his side and facing the other way and seems not to have moved at all in the night. Axel eyes him closely but cannot tell if he's breathing.

His chest hollows at the thought that the kid might be dead.

He doesn't know Cacho's people and anyway wouldn't know how to contact them. Who could he call except Charlie? But call him how? From where? He doesn't even—

Cacho stirs, moaning low. Then haltingly sits up. He puts his hands to the small of his back and carefully twists his torso from side to side, wincing. He sees Axel looking at him. "Christ almighty. Feel like I been thrown off a cliff!"

Axel is surprised by the size of his relief that the kid's alive. "Hurting a little, eh, junior?" He has an impulse to tell him about the lion, then decides against it without knowing why.

"Don't tell me *you* ain't hurting," Cacho says. "You look like roadkill! Look like somebody ran a can punch across your cheek there!"

"I might have an ache or two. Why you yelling?"

Cacho stares at him. Then looks out at the river and smiles. "About time it shut up some." He catches sight of the campfire ring, the empty cans and bottles. "Wetback hotel, looks like."

It does, Axel says in Spanish. We're obviously not the first travelers ever to spend the night here.

Cacho gapes at him. *"What?"* Then in Spanish, says, Are you . . . you speak *Spanish*?

I'm fairly confident that's the language in which I'm addressing you, yes.

You tricky *fuck*! Where'd you learn it? *When*? And so . . . *proper*?

Axel shrugs. I acquired it from some Mexican pals when I was a child.

You lying prick. No Mex kid taught to you to speak like that. *Acquired*. But why didn't . . . ah! You didn't want anybody to know so that *you* could know without *them* knowing you knew. But why not tell *me*? You didn't trust *me*?

You kidding? You were a *convict*. Now you're not.

He can see that Cacho's injured look is more simulated than genuine. Then the kid grins too. Jesus Christ, you kept it a secret from *everybody* all those years?

Till now.

You really got some funny ways, man.

So you've told me.

So what're *we* gonna talk, English or Spanish?

Whatever suits you. How about a mix? "We start a sentence in English like this" and switch to Spanish in the middle of it, like this, "and maybe finish it in English again like this."

Cacho laughs. "My brother and I do that all the time. But look, man, it's gonna take me a while to get used to talking Spanish to you. What do you say we stick with English for now?"

"Okay by me."

Both of them are lacerated of face and limbs, their palms scored raw by the grab ropes, their prison whites torn and filthy. Axel gingerly fingers the cheek gash, which runs from under his eye to his ear and is still bleeding a bit. His left forearm throbs with the puncture wound. They get to their feet, and he notes Cacho's limp and remembers his injured ankle. The kid sees how he's looking at him and says, "Don't sweat it, old man. I'll get me a walking pole and do just fine. Probly outrun *you*." He inspects a few of the lower and smaller tree limbs, finds a suitable one, and says, "Gimme a hand." Pulling together, they break it off, and Cacho starts stripping it of smaller branches and twigs.

The upper rim of the sun breaks over the hills, and they see that in the upstream distance the low rise bends northward with the river and out of view. About forty yards downstream, however, the rise either ends or curves out of sight to the south—it's hard to know which from where they're standing—and past that point, the riverbanks lie flat and bare but for wide swaths of low scrub brush.

"We gotta get moving, *viejo*," Cacho says, testing his six-foot staff, his limp lessened by it. "If we stay by the river, we got plenty of water. Hit a road eventually."

"Let me have a look first what's on the other side of this rise," Axel says, heading for it. "Could be a road's not far off."

"Yeah, maybe a Greyhound station. *Train* depot."

Axel clambers up the slope, gasping and hurting, his raw palms burning. The crest he achieves is flat and wide and over-looks an immense plain of ground shadow receding toward the eastern hills in a dark tide as the sun rises from behind them. Downriver, the rise curves to the south and runs straight out into the plain for maybe a mile before coming to an end. Peppered with scrub brush and studded with outcrops, the plain spreads southward all the way to a horizon of long purple mesas and blunt brown buttes. Given the slight elevation of his vantage, Axel estimates the horizon to be less than five miles distant. And now a plume of dust takes shape shy of the horizon and begins moving west. A vehicle on a dirt road? What else? There isn't enough wind to raise that dust on its own. The road cannot be even four miles away.

He goes back down and describes to Cacho what he's seen and says they should follow the rise all the way around to its end point and keep going to the road, that it's a better choice than following the river. If they stick by the river, there's no telling how far they might have to go before coming to a road, and once they pass the bend in the rise there's no place to hide along the bank, not in that open scrub that's no higher than their knees. They'd be easy to spot by some posse patrolling on the other side, and if a chopper caught them in the open they'd be sitting ducks for a shooter. But if they hold to the rise and a helicopter comes, they can hide in hollows in the wall or behind rocks before it sees them. They can carry water in some of these plastic bottles. If they cover just one mile an hour they can make the road well before noon, then flag down the first vehicle to come along. He asks if Cacho thinks he can walk a mile an hour on that ankle. The kid says hell, yeah. He thinks it's pretty chancy to head farther into the desert without knowing if there's a road out there, but he concedes Axel's points about the riskiness of holding to the river.

They sort through the empty bottles. Many of them are cracked and useless, but three quart-sized bottles are intact and six pint-sized ones. More than enough, they figure, to take them five miles and last them till a vehicle comes along.

They're filling bottles at the bank when Cacho says, "I just wish we had hats."

"Wish? You *wish*? Well, *I* wish I was in an air-conditioned bar in Galveston, drinking beer and eating shrimp . . . with Scarlett Johansson . . . *and* she's whispering to me she's not wearing underwear."

"Well, *hell,* you wanna have a fucking wishing contest, *I* wish—"

"Damn it!" says Axel, looking upriver at the sound of an oncoming helicopter.

They scuttle to the cover of the trees as the craft's small form hovers into view over the escarpment's upriver bend.

"Think they seen us?" Cacho says.

"No. Lot easier to see them than them us."

The aircraft comes fast, its rotors beating above the roaring engine. It's following the river and it passes directly overhead, its downdraft flailing the tree limbs and flinging leaves.

They stay under the trees until they can't hear it anymore, then return to the bank and finish filling bottles and then drink from the river till their bellies are full, hoping they don't get sick and thinking it unlikely from water that's running so fast. They each put three of the smaller bottles inside their tucked-in shirts. Axel will hand-carry two of the bigger bottles, and Cacho, needing one hand for the staff, will carry the other liter bottle.

Then they set out, holding close to the escarpment, the sun now clear of the hills, the day's heat building fast.

39

Now they're dying.

The sun is past its meridian and they are several miles into Mexico. The rise is far behind them, a small dark projection in the shimmering heat. They are out of water. They walk like old drunks, and one of them lame. Axel has known many days of one hundred degrees or more at Zanco, and this one is a match for any of them. But at Zanco there had been water, shade, hats, food. . . .

⌒∞⌒

From the outset, Cacho's ankle had rapidly worsened, slowing them more and more. And although they had been sparing with their water, taking sips only every now and again, the heat grew monstrous and had them sipping more and more frequently as they went, and they'd finished two of the quart bottles before they reached the southern end of the rock rise. By then they had twice had to hide from helicopters, both times hunkering in shadowy scoops in the rock wall until the choppers passed by to the north of them, holding to the river.

They had just arrived at the end of the rise, telling each other they had to go easier on the water, when yet another helicopter came in sight, this one out of the south, out of deeper Mexico and probably a unit of the Mexican Federal Police, maybe state cops. Its engine sound was distinctly different from the others, of a higher whine, but in the blinding sunlight the chopper was no more than a loud black entity whose markings they couldn't distinguish. It came faster than the others had and at lower altitude, and in their haste to hide under a low shelf at the foot of the rise they flung themselves prone beneath it, cracking some of the bottles in their shirts and feeling the water draining into the sand under them.

The helicopter made a low pass parallel to the escarpment face and then turned around and bore away to the west. They came out from under the shelf and found only two of their shirt bottles still intact, the others emptied. They considered returning to the river but then agreed that if they were careful with the remaining water—a full quart and two pints—they could still make it to the road up ahead with some to spare. Several more brief sightings of raised dust had suggested that the road was regularly traveled and they would not have to wait long to meet with a vehicle.

So they had kept going forward under the heightening sun, trudging deeper into a pale wasteland of visibly wavering heat, Cacho hobbling on his staff. They intermittently sipped from the smaller bottles but at times could not help taking a gulp, and in another hour both of those bottles lay behind them. They cautioned each other to take only a single small sip at each turn with the remaining quart, and vowed to enforce the resolution that one of them would hold the bottle to the other's mouth.

The sun was at its apex and the bottle held but two inches of water when another cloud of dust rose in the near distance. It began coming toward them, forming into a plume, then veered slightly to westward, to their right. "This way!" Cacho said, heading in that direction, limping fast on his staff. "The road must be over here! Come on!" They were gasping, laughing, Axel saying he hoped to hell whoever it was had some water in the car, Cacho saying cold beer would be better but he just hoped they weren't cops.

Then the plume swerved directly toward them and they stopped and watched it approach, heightening and broadening as it came their way. Coming from where they knew there was no road. And then they knew what it was. *"Carajo!"* Cacho said, and tried vainly to spit. The climbing spiral hove up over a low outcrop and swooped onto the open ground before them—a dust devil, a whirlwind generated of the heat. They were both from the Rio Grande flatlands and had seen dust devils before, and that they could have mistaken this one and the others before it for the dust of road traffic was evidence not only of the visual pranks of the desert heat but of their exhaustion and desperate hope. . . . Axel felt a fool for having inferred that just because there had been no wind where he stood on the rise, there wasn't any out on the plain to raise the dust he had taken for that of a moving vehicle's.

The dust devil whirled past them, stinging their eyes, and they watched it go, gyrating like some antic specter. Again, their inclination was to head back to the river, but they knew they'd never make it. They had come too far. The only thing to do was push on in hope of coming across a road, however primitive. They told each other that maybe some of the dust clouds they'd seen *had* been raised by vehicles. Axel didn't believe it and didn't think the kid did, either, but they had to hope so. And so they walked on, Axel plodding ahead, Cacho trailing awkwardly behind on the staff. . . .

❧

Now they're dying.

All water gone.

Axel's lips are swollen and sore, his tongue feels thick, his throat burns. His scalp is on fire and his vision has a pink tinge. He's queasy even though there's nothing in his stomach to throw up. He recalls having heard another helicopter, the whine of its engine similar to that of the last chopper they'd seen. He has a fuzzy memory of huddling against a low outcrop, glad of the camouflage afforded by their dirty clothes. But he can't say if it happened an hour ago or in the last ten minutes or even if the memory is real.

He hears Cacho cry out and turns to see the kid sprawled facedown. He staggers back to him and rasps, "C'mon, man, *up.*" When he stoops to help him, he loses his balance and falls on his ass.

He sits there a moment, catching his breath. Cacho's face is turned toward him, his eyes shut, his mouth slack, his lips dark and swollen.

"Let's *go,* kid!" he says. "Won't get to a road lazing around like this."

Cacho's eyes open and fix on him blankly. Then they blink a few times, and there's recognition.

"*Heyyyy* . . . Ax," he says, barely audibly. "Go on, man . . . find us . . . taxi."

"Bullshit . . . We're both going." Axel slowly gets on all fours, pauses, then stands up, gets dizzy again, totters sideways, and falls. He's now farther from the kid, whose eyes are again closed. He wants to call to him but hasn't the strength and there's anyway nothing to say. Then everything seems to make a small jump ahead as in a badly spliced film and he senses he has been unconscious for a time. A few seconds? Minutes? He's staring close-up at the hot ground, one cheek pressed to it. He stirs slightly and stops, exhausted.

This is it, buddy boy, he thinks. *Out in the Big Nowhere. Next stop, the Cosmic Nowhere.*

What the hell. At least you're not dying in prison.

Now comes a sound, distant but bearing their way.

The *thwucking* of a helicopter.

He recognizes the high whine of its engine. The same one. Still hunting them. Or maybe only the same kind of chopper.

Don't see us. Don't.

He tries to curl himself into a ball, to embed himself in the ground, to make himself as hard to see as possible. The kid lies as before and seems oblivious to the aircraft.

Pass by, Axel thinks, *pass by. Let me die* here.

The helicopter passes by. It does not sound very high or far off.

Keep going, keep going, keep going. . . .

The chopper keeps going. Its sound diminishing.

Yes!

He releases a long exhalation. His chest hurts.

Dying time. Just lie here and let it come. Won't be so bad, not as worn out as you are. Just let it—

The chopper sound stops fading.

Then again begins to grow.

It's turned back.

Son of *a bitch!*

The aircraft closes fast, growing steadily louder. Then its volume holds and he knows it's circling them.

He sees a flat, hand-sized rock close by and closes his hand around it. *Turn over,* he thinks. *Turn over and point it at them. They can't see what it is from up there. They'll think it's a gun and they'll shoot you dead. Do it.*

He raises his head, moves his feet in search of purchase, tries to roll over, and falls on his face again. He wants to howl his rage at being unable to keep his promise to die free.

The helicopter descends, its engine whine ear-stopping, its downdraft buffeting. He shuts his burning eyes, the raised dust enveloping him as the craft touches down.

Over the engine whine and beating rotors he hears voices shouting in Spanish, the speech too fast and clipped and mingled with the engine whine for him to comprehend.

He cracks open his eyes. Sees figures in dark blue uniforms. Federales?

Crouching over Cacho, picking him up, bearing him away.

He lies ignored. *Leave me,* he thinks, *leave me.*

Then shadows fall over him and hands are at him, turning him onto his back, lifting him by knees and underarms. He squints through the dust as he's borne to the chopper. The lettering on its side reads "Policía de Coahuila."

State cops.

He's carried under the whirling blades and shuts his eyes against the blast of the downdraft. They set him on the chopper floor and someone within drags him further inside. A cop in SWAT gear and dark glasses hunkers just inside the door, an M4 carbine in his hands. Someone puts a wet cloth to Axel's blistered lips and says, "*No mas un poquito! Just a leetle!*" The man squeezes out a bit of moisture that sears Axel's lips but feels wonderful on his tongue, even as he curses his flesh for its limbic desperation to survive. He hears garbled speech shouted against the engine noise. Cacho lies almost within reach, a cop with a medic's red-cross armband crouched beside him, adjusting an intravenous tube from the kid's arm to a solution bag hanging on an overhead hook. He preps a hypodermic syringe and gives Cacho an injection, then turns to Axel and starts rigging a similar IV into him.

Axel wants to yank the needle out of his arm, wants only to die. But he knows they won't let it happen. Both the Mex and the Texas cops want them back alive. The Mexicans will want to put them on display for the news cameras in a grand show of cross-border cooperation and the competence of their police. And Texas wants to remind its convicts that you can't escape the long arm of its law, and if you try it they might have to kill you and wouldn't mind doing it but they'd really rather catch your sorry ass and add to your time and start beating you down some more. That's what's coming—a lot more years in the cage.

The medic says something to him he doesn't catch through the noise of the engine, then holds an index finger in front of his face and moves it slowly from side to side. Axel follows it with his eyes. The man smiles. Then gives him an injection, too, pats him on the shoulder, and moves back to Cacho.

Someone shouts Ready! in Spanish and the chopper engine revs higher and Axel's stomach feels like it's being left behind as the craft rises and leans and accelerates in an ascending climb.

Now a different face looms over him, that of a man crouching. Eyes dark and bright.

"You're pretty goddamn lucky we spotted you," he says in only slightly accented English. "This was our last flyover. If we hadn't seen you this time, the coyotes would have been feeding on you tonight."

If they hadn't seen us this time! If they hadn't . . . he would've died free. He wants to howl his bitterness, but he's beginning to feel dopey and lax. He glances at Cacho, who looks dead.

"He'll be all right," the man says. "Both of you."

"Fug ... fuck you, cob ... *cop.*" The injection is doing its work. It's an effort to form words.

"What?" The man laughs. "Well, fuck you right back, dude. Christ, you got no idea where you are, do you? Who you're talking to?"

"In cob chob ... chopper ... and you're ... fuggen cob."

The man laughs and says something that sounds to Axel like "Pope of Rome."

He's fading out as the man leans closer, his dark face featureless but for a white grin, Axel missing some of what he says, but grasping, "Joaquín Capote, Cacho's brother ... cops with *us ... you fuckers made it!"*

It takes a few seconds more for him to understand, and then he does—and he feels a wild laughter deep in his chest ... feels it bearing him away. . . .

40

Even though Jessie Wolfe has always been confused and ashamed about her father, he has never seemed quite real to her. In grammar school there were early instances of classmates mocking her for her "jailbird" daddy, though all such mockery abruptly ceased after her cousins Eddie Wolfe and Jimmy Quick kicked the asses of the boys she pointed out to them as her main harassers. Her uncle Charlie had often told her about the wonderful times he and Axel had together as kids. Her daddy had made a bad mistake, Charlie told her, and he was sorry for it and was paying for it. She never said anything in response, and whenever he asked if she had any questions about him, she simply shook her head.

The only person she'd ever asked about her father was her 113-year-old great-great-grandaunt Catalina, about whose life she has written a book that she's promised not to publish until after the old woman's death. In the course of their many interview sessions, she once asked Aunt Cat how well she'd known her father. "Well enough to know he was a clever boy with his own secret ways and secret fears," Catalina said—she who was regarded by everyone else in the family as the most

THE WAYS OF WOLFE

secret-ridden of them. "But then, that is true of all the men of this family, whatever their age." She volunteered nothing further, and Jessie asked nothing more.

She's always felt she should hate her mother more than she does her father because he was taken from her by the law but she left of her own free will, just packed up and split for parts unknown and has never to this day been in contact with her.

She's never forgotten when she was ten and went with Charlie to visit her father in prison up in East Texas, but the look of the place scared her so bad she couldn't go in. Charlie wanted her to try again after that but she never would. When she was fourteen she got the only letter from her father she would ever get, and it made her cry. She then lied to Uncle Charlie that she'd burned it, hoping it would hurt her father to hear it, and she said to tell him never to write her again. But she hadn't burned it, and she's read it dozens of times over the years. And she'd only said she didn't want him to write to her to see if he'd do it anyway because he loved her so much he just couldn't help it. Rayo Luna's the only one she ever confided that to, and it was Rayo who made her see she had been putting him to an unfair test and then resenting him for failing it.

When Jimmy Quick came into the Doghouse on the evening of the escape and gave them the news of it, Rayo hustled her out of there and back to the beach house. They had a few beers at the kitchen table and Rayo let her do all the talking, though she had heard it all from her before. They slept together that night as they sometimes did when one or the other was feeling low for some reason, and Rayo held her close and petted her but that was all. They have in fact "fooled around"—as they refer to it—with each other a few times since moving into the beach house. After the first time, Jessie asked with a nervous smile if it meant they were "sapphic." Rayo laughed at her word choice and said no way, because the real thing doesn't care to do it with men and both of them truly preferred to play with cocks. She said not to worry about it, that they fooled around with each other for no reason except they were free enough in their affection to show it any way they pleased, and sometimes it was just fun as hell to be naked together. However, Rayo said, and speaking strictly for herself, she'd never had an inclination to play naked with any other woman. "Me, neither," Jessie said—and they'd laughed like loons.

The next evening came the news that her father was presumed dead. And it was like something in her died on hearing it, though she could not specify what.

PART III

RECKONINGS

41

Axel awakens in a large, four-poster bed, its sheets smooth and fresh-smelling. The room is dimly lighted by a small table lamp next to an overstuffed chair in which a stout Mexican woman dozes, snoring lightly, a shawl over her shoulders. Her dark face is pinched with age, her plaited hair mostly gray. The ceiling is high and wood-beamed. The foot of the bed faces a wall on which is mounted a television with a screen he would guess to be five feet wide and a yard high. On the far wall to his right is a closed set of tall drapes.

His IV has been removed and he's been cleaned up and dressed in short-sleeved pajamas. There's a white terry cloth robe hung on a bedpost. Wherever he is, it's obviously not jail, and he has no doubt that the man who said he's Cacho's brother was telling the truth. But the Coahuila state cops and their helicopter were the real thing, no question about that, either, and while it wouldn't be the first time he's heard of Mexican cops helping out crooks in a big way, he knows they don't do it for small-timers. Whoever Cacho's brother is with, they're big.

He's sore all over. His forearm is bandaged, and his hands, except for the fingers. His face hurts. He lightly touches the thin dressing on his cheek. Every movement of his shoulder pangs it, his neck aches at every turn of his head. But his throat is much better and his lips feel only lightly scabbed. *Not too bad,* he thinks. *All things considered.*

He has a vague recollection of coming partially awake as he was taken off the helicopter by two men bearing the stretcher through an amber haze of rotor-raised dust, another man tending to the IV in his arm. He wanted to look for Cacho but lacked the strength to move his head. He was carried to a black SUV, its windows dark and its backseats folded down to form a floor for the stretcher. When the IV guy saw that his eyes were open he made an adjustment to the drip and it was lights out again. If he has wakened even once between then and now, he has no memory of it.

He hears a rooster crow. Distant wavering bleats of goats. He sits up with a grunt and eases off the bed, works his feet into a ready pair of slippers and goes to the drapes. He pushes one aside to reveal the open shutter doors of a small balcony on an upper floor. It overlooks a large courtyard enclosed by a high stone wall. There are wooden tables and benches under rainbow-striped umbrellas and scraggly mesquite trees. A pair of ravens alight on the rim of a stone birdbath, take a few sips, fly away. Beyond the wall lies a vast, brushy plain extending to a horizon of peppercorn hills, the sun not far above them. Quasi-desert country, rugged but no so starkly as that surrounding the Zanco Unit.

The woman wakes and emits a cry of dismay at the sight of him out of bed. She lumbers from the chair, scolding him for his negligence, and he chuckles as she puts his arm over her shoulders and her arm around his waist as though he might collapse if she did not support him. She guides him to the bed and tries to assist him in getting back into it, chiding him the whole while. She arranges his pillows at his back so he can sit comfortably, then shakes her finger at him in an unmistakable command to stay put and leaves the room. As soon as she's gone, he gets out of bed and puts on the robe and sits in her chair.

Minutes later, Joaquín Capote comes through the door, smiling wide.

"*Buenos días,* Axel! You don't mind if I call you Axel? My brother tells me you speak excellent Spanish, but if it's all right with you I'd rather we converse in English. I don't get much opportunity to practice mine out here."

Axel stands up and they shake hands. Joaquín is taller than both he and Cacho, with thick black hair and a large droopy mustache. He's dressed in jeans, black T-shirt, running shoes. Cacho had said his brother was eighteen years his elder. He looks it.

Axel smiles at the man's good cheer. "English is fine with me, sir. Where are we?"

"In a hell of a lot better place than where I found you. And call me Quino. How you feeling?"

"Little achy is all. What about the kid?"

"Lucky. Ankle's only badly sprained, no fracture or ligament tear. He'll wear one of those removable cast shoes for ten days, be on crutches, then use a cane for another couple of weeks. Otherwise he's pretty much the same as you. A few cuts, bruises, sunburn. Mainly, you guys were dying of thirst and exhausted to the bone. Amazing what a little hydration, some antibiotics and nutrients can do. Except for his ankle, you'll both be fine in a few days. The doc said to take the bandage off your face today, let the air work on it. Use a bandage again tonight when you go to bed, then take it off for good tomorrow. Same for your arm. And let the lip scabs come off naturally, don't pull them off."

Axel goes to the dresser mirror and is surprised by the deep
redness of his face. He carefully removes the bandage. The cheek
cut is discolored but not as swollen as he'd expected. It's been
closed with small adhesive butterfly stitches.

"Won't leave much of a scar," Quino says. "Doc said you
can take the butterflies off in a week or so. Now then, the kid's
waiting on us if you think you can handle some breakfast."

The question of breakfast makes him aware of his hunger,
and he eases out of bed again. "Sounds good, but, ah . . ." He
gestures at his robe.

"No worries. There's clothes your size in the chest of drawers
and the closet, but you don't have to bother to get dressed now.
Everybody's already eaten except for the three of us. But, listen,
before we go, ah . . . I want to express my gratitude. We couldn't
have rigged the thing without your info on the routines, the
guards, all of it."

"To tell the truth, I had no idea Cacho was passing it on
to anybody, and I wouldn't have thought it to be of much use
anyway."

"Well, you would've thought wrong. I mean, the thing didn't
exactly go as planned, but it got you guys out and we got to you
and that's all that counts. That wouldn't have happened except
for you. Another thing . . . the kid says you saved his life. And that
when he went down and couldn't get up you wouldn't leave him.
There's no way I can repay that."

"Repay? Hell, man, he saved *my* ass more than once. Anyway,
I was half-dead myself and couldn't have—"

"Yeah, yeah, I know. He told me everything. You saved
him, he saved you—that's the way things work sometimes, no?
But no more of the fucking self-effacement." He grins. "Pretty
fancy lingo, huh? You're not the only one in this room been

to college, amigo. Look, Axel, I'm just saying thanks, that's all. He's my little brother. Only family I got left. So I want you to know you've got a home here for as long as you want. I mean it. For forever or until death, whichever comes first, as we like to say. Now let's go eat."

42

They pass through a large dining hall—the long tables cleared, the chairs upside down on them, the floor being mopped—then enter a much smaller dining room containing only a single table just off the kitchen doorway. Cacho is already seated there. He, too, is in a terry cloth robe. They laugh at the sight of each other.

"Man, you look like fucking Frankenstein," Cacho says. "Good thing you were ugly to begin with, old-timer, or you'd have something to feel bad about."

"Like you, you mean," Axel says. Cacho's face is dark with sunburn but not as reddened as Axel's, and its many scratches are splotched with iodine. His lips are scabbed, too, his hands also lightly bandaged. His foot is encased in a light blue cast shoe, and a pair of crutches is propped against the wall behind him.

A kitchen girl comes out and asks what they'd like to eat. She's slim and pretty. Axel stares at her and she blushes and looks away.

"Hey, Ax, what'd we say we were gonna have, first thing?" Cacho says.

He returns the kid's grin, remembering their last breakfast at Zanco, and they both say at once, *"Chorizo con huevos!"* and burst into guffaws.

The girl gives them a bemused smile and heads back to the kitchen. Axel watches her go.

"Hate to tell you, but she's unavailable," Quino says. "There are only a dozen women on the place and all of them married to resident workers who are not part of the gang. I've given their husbands my assurance that the women are safe from molestation of any sort. The good news is that the day after tomorrow we're having a party. Have one twice a month. Some very fine-looking young ladies from Monterrey will be on hand from six until midnight. How's *that* sound? Thirty of them, and most not twenty years old. Enough to pair up every guy here and ensure plenty of extras for any guy who wants to enjoy more than one in the course of the evening, and most guys do. You can't have possession of more than one at a time, but you can keep the same girl for the whole visit if you want, just so you get her back to the transport vehicles by midnight. Some of the younger dudes will fuck three of them before the party's over. Me, if I can do two, I'm happy."

⟡

They converse over a breakfast of eggs scrambled with a mixture of ground chorizo sausage, plus refried beans, goat cheese, and flour tortillas, neither Axel nor Cacho deterred from cleaning their plates by the tenderness of their lips, then linger over coffee. Axel learns that the police helicopter and crew that found them had been arranged by Quino's "chiefs," as he refers to them. "They have excellent relations with various law enforcement agencies,"

Quino says, "which of course is configured on a certain quid pro quo."

Axel is curious about those bosses but holds to his ingrained prison rule of not asking questions of someone you don't know well.

"When we spotted you two we thought you were dead," Quino says. "Even after we loaded you in the chopper I wasn't giving better than even odds on either of you making it."

They had refueled at Ciudad Acuña and then flown down-river to a landing site at the outskirts of Nuevo Laredo. They were driven to a private clinic in town where a team of doctors examined them from head to foot. Cacho's distended ankle was X-rayed, found to be only sprained, and put in the cast shoe. They were cleaned up, bandaged, wrapped in robes, and brought here, where they were put in pajamas and tucked into bed.

"Kept you doped to the gills the whole time. I mean, the both of you were *out*," Quino says.

"I still don't know where we are," Axel says.

"Rancho Chivito," Quino says, and tells him it's an isolate goat ranch twenty-five miles west of Nuevo Laredo. It had long ago been a working hacienda, hence the walled compound containing a big two-story main house as well as smaller domiciles and outbuildings. The place produces meat, milk, and cheese for the Nuevo Laredo markets—and is the outland headquarters of Los Malos, a criminal gang of which Quino has been chieftain for the past five years. Before that, his uncle, Alfredo Capote, had been its chief for a dozen years. Because Quino had always been a good student and spoke English, Alfredo had granted his wish to go to college in the U.S.

"UT San Antonio," Quino says. "Economics major, philosophy minor. Some combo, eh? But man, college was a lot of fun. My unofficial major was blondes. That's what you gringos should be smuggling to *us*. Not enough real blondes on this side of the river."

On graduation, Quino came home and became the Malos' head accountant and established a real estate company that has ever since also been the gang's city headquarters. Los Malos had come into being in the 1970s, and in their early years dealt primarily in gambling, prostitution, and extortion, occasionally smuggling wetbacks and sometimes marijuana across the river. However, by the time Quino returned from San Antonio, the drug trade was booming and the cartels had taken possession of the border.

"When the big dicks got in the picture," Quino says, "little guys like us had to choose between getting killed, getting out, or getting in with one of them."

The Malos got in with Los Golfos—the Gulf cartel—whose present territory ranges from the coastal city of Veracruz northward through the state of Tamaulipas to Matamoros, near the mouth of the Rio Grande, and then along the river all the way up to Ciudad Acuña, a 375-mile stretch of border that includes some of the most valuable drug routes into the United States. But rival organizations have long disputed the Golfos' claim on the border upriver of Nuevo Laredo, and the war for control of that stretch of the Rio Grande has steadily grown more intense. The Golfos have held their ground primarily through the might of their enforcers, a paramilitary unit composed mostly of special forces deserters from the Mexican army, most of them trained in the United States.

"Los Zetas," Quino says. "I suppose you've heard of them?"

"Who hasn't?" Axel says. "Inside the walls they've got a rep as one of the baddest-ass bunches in the world."

"They have that rep everywhere, and for very good reason. In any event, a main duty of the Zetas has always been to defend the Golfos' border routes, and all of the Golfo subgangs on the border are under the Zetas' direct command."

"*You* guys work for the Zetas?"

"Not bad bosses, really, as long as you don't fuck up," Quino says. "And very handy ones. Who you think arranged for the police chopper? *We* don't have that kind of pull with the cops. And where you think we got the money for the bribes? To repay it to them, though, we had to get it back, and we did, all but fifty grand of it, which we had to make up out of our own pocket." He looks at Cacho and says, "I don't know if he's worth fifty G's, but what the hell, he's my brother. Started pleading to get in the gang from the time he was fourteen. No way, I told him, not till you finish high school. To his credit, he did. So I let him in."

"Soon as this ankle's okay, I'm back in action," Cacho tells Axel. "Figure to be made a crew chief before long, you watch."

"You're lucky a sprained ankle's the worst you got," Quino says. "I should've let you stew in the joint a little longer to heal your sprained brain. Give you more time to consider the stupidity of getting in such a mess and costing me so much money for no reason except you had to follow your dick over the border after some gringa."

"Oh, man, if you'da *seen* her . . ." Cacho says.

Quino flaps a dismissive hand at him. He tells Axel that Los Malos' principal duty under the Zetas is to guard the Rio Grande smuggling routes between Nuevo Laredo and the upriver town of Piedras Negras—a span of about 110 miles—against incursions by rivals. They have a network of informants in both towns, and there are Malos lookouts patrolling that stretch of Federal Highway 2, the border highway, twenty-four-seven. In both Piedras Negras and Nuevo Laredo, Malos defense crews on rotating shifts are ever-ready to respond to an alert from the lookouts, and there's always a backup defense crew here at the ranch. Whenever the Malos encounter trespassers they deal with them on the spot and confiscate their loads.

"Most of them will fight to the end," Quino says. "They know if they surrender we'll turn them over to the Zetas, who will hang them from some overpass or leave their bodies lined along the roadside, maybe with a dozen knives sticking out of each one, maybe with their dicks cut off, maybe their heads. Sometimes they dump the heads on the front steps of the nearest police station. They know how to make a point, the Zs, and they can be quite theatrical about it."

It was in a riverside fight with a smuggling crew out of Juárez five years ago that his uncle Alfredo was killed, and then Quino took over as chief. At present the gang's membership stands at eighty men. Twenty of them are stationed at the ranch and live in a large dormitory building affording every man a private room; the others all live in either Nuevo Laredo or Piedras Negras, and each of those groups is under the command of a subchief who answers directly to Quino's second-in-command.

"Now you know who you're among," Quino says, "and as I said before, you're welcome here forever. And I mean in the main house, not the dormitory. The quarters you're in right now are yours. You'll have no need of money, but if you ever want a job with a crew, you can have it. We pay pretty good, and you could bank it all for your golden years."

"I think he'll want in," Cacho says. "This dude was a *robber*, bro. Means he liked action. Maybe still does, even if his golden years are just around the corner."

Axel gives him a two-finger "up yours" sign.

"No respect, this kid," Quino says. "Thinks *I'm* old, and I'm only thirty-eight. Got a shitload to learn but thinks he already knows everything."

"I know what the robbers say," Cacho says, giving Axel a look. "The good ones don't get caught."

"Anybody who believes that doesn't know anything about robbery," Axel says. "The truest thing ever said about it is that anytime you go out to pull one, there's fifty things that can go wrong, and if you can think of half of them you're a mastermind."

"I've heard that one," Quino says. "So, assuming you're a mastermind and planned for the twenty-five possibilities you could think of, which of the other twenty-five fucked you up and put you in the joint?"

Axel had not told Cacho any of the particulars of his robbery career, not even about the job that put him in prison. The kid had of course asked about it, and he'd said, "Stuff went wrong. End of story." But he now sees no reason to keep it from them, and so he tells of Duro Cisneros recruiting him and his robbery pal, Billy, for a Dallas rip of three-quarter-million in bonds. He tells how smoothly it all went until they got back to the mall to switch to the other car and rammed into the college kid. Tells of the cop that came along and made the plate of the stolen Ford, of being wounded while losing the cop in the parking lot, of the horde of police that showed up, of sneaking through the parking lot crowd to try to get to their own car. Tells of his leg giving out and how he couldn't get up without help and of his partners leaving him and being chased by the cops and getting away.

"There's no way," Axel says, "to plan for a kid backing out of a parking space at the wrong time."

"Maybe not," Quino says. "But I could argue that the more obvious reason you went to prison is that your partners ran out on you. If they had helped you, you might have gotten away with them."

"Unless stopping to help me would've slowed them down and we all got caught. Must've figured they had no choice."

"But they *did* have a choice. And they chose not to help you. But later on you had a choice, too, no? The prosecutor must've offered you a deal if you named them."

"Yeah."

"And?"

Axel shakes his head.

"And you chose not to. Though they deserted you. Took your share of the money. And one of them a *friend,* you said. The thought must have crossed your mind more than a few times that they might be enjoying themselves somewhere, with your money as well as theirs. I can imagine your bitterness over the years, the size of your enmity."

"'Enmity!'" Cacho says. "You guys!"

"You learn to . . . repress things," Axel says. "Otherwise you can end up bashing your skull against the bars. I knew some who did. Anyway, my bet's they're both dead or in prison."

"Mine as well. But here *you* are, neither dead nor in prison. Perhaps the same is true of one or both of them. Wouldn't you like to know?"

"When the Internet came around, my . . . this good buddy of mine tried to track them down. As time's gone by he's had better and better technical means for searching for Billy's and Cisneros's names in every prison roster in the country, but he still hasn't come up with anything. He was surprised how many William Capps there are in prison. There are even more guys named Cisneros, and I never knew if Duro was his real name or just a nickname or even if either of his names was true. Didn't know either one's date of birth, either, only that Billy was around my age. A few years ago my guy asked me about physical details that might distinguish them from other guys with the same names. Said there are, whatchamacallits . . . databases . . . that include inmates' identifying details like scars, birthmarks, tattoos. Did you know that? Amazing, the stuff that's online."

"It's become a different world the last twenty-four years," Quino says. "You give him what he asked for?"

"Not much to give except Billy had some puncture scars on the back of his shoulder where a guy stomped on him with baseball cleats, and Cisneros, he had a little red mark on his inside wrist. A tat or birthmark, I don't know, looked sorta like a crescent. My guy ran their names again, checking them against those descriptives, and still nothing."

"He got nothing because your partners have undoubtedly been using different names since the day of your capture. In case you should ever rat them. If they've kept to false names, as is likely, you can forget about finding them. Even if they're dead, they could be buried under other names, if their graves are marked at all."

"I know. I told my guy all that, but he still kept at it for about another year before he finally gave up."

"Gave up?" Cacho says. "Shit, man, what about your *money*?"

"I'm not going to spend any portion of the life I've got left trying to get it. You can always make more money, but you can't make more time."

Quino grinned. "Another sage old saw."

"As far as I'm concerned," Axel says, "dead or alive, they're gone for good."

"Just like us," Cacho says.

"Except there's an army of cops hunting for *us* all up and down the border."

Cacho gives him an odd look. Then turns to Quino and says in Spanish, You haven't told him?

"Nobody's looking for you," Quino tells Axel. "Play it smart and they'll never have reason to."

"Not looking for us?" Axel says. "I don't get it."

Cacho leans toward Axel with a wide smile. "They think we're dead, dude. *Everybody* thinks we're dead!"

43

Everybody thinks we're dead.

Back in his room, sitting in front of the open window, he considers how things stand in the light of this information. . . .

❧

Quino had shown them newspapers from Laredo, San Antonio, Austin. Had shown them recorded TV reports, some of them on-the-spot tapings with Zanco Unit in the rainy background. Their most recent prison pictures were in all the papers, were on TV. The getaway Tri-Cross van had been found in the creek and everybody was sure that they had drowned and been carried out to the river. A helicopter then found the stranded owner of the little boat, and the cops thought it possible that they had been the ones to steal it but didn't see how they could have made it alive that far down the river. When they found the boat tangled in riverside brush below the rapids and some thirty miles downstream from where it had been taken, they could only conclude that whoever had stolen it had certainly drowned. Search teams were still combing the banks all the way down to the Amistad

Reservoir, but a state police spokesman said the bodies might never be found, and until such time as they were recovered the state was offering a reward of ten thousand dollars per fugitive.

All the reports, both print and TV, included mention that Axel Prince Wolfe was the son of Harry McElroy Wolfe, the prominent South Texas attorney. Which had come as news to Cacho.

"You said you were an orphan, same as me," he'd said.

Axel had shrugged. "Don't you know better than to believe a convict?"

Quino laughed, and Cacho said, "Jesus Christ, you been keeping secrets even from me. *Lying* to me. You didn't trust me for a minute."

"I do now," Axel said. "Sometimes for even a minute."

Cacho grinned back at him. "It's cool, man. You didn't know me very good yet." He held his fist out and Axel bumped it with his own.

"Will you inform your father you're alive?" Quino asks.

"I don't think it would be a good idea to inform anybody."

"I very much agree."

Quino had then shown them two editions of the *Brownsville Herald* he'd put aside for last. The front page of one edition blared the news of the prison break and manhunt. It carried a two-year-old prison picture of Axel and one of Harry Mack standing on the sidewalk in front of Wolfe Associates. The report included a recap of Axel's conviction for armed robbery and assault, and Harry Mack was quoted as saying he was "deeply distressed" by the escape and hoped that Axel would realize the "irrationality" of it and surrender himself.

A sidebar story emphasized the "local boy" angle, highlighting Axel's once-promising future, his excellent academic record and admirable baseball talent. It contained a yearbook picture of him in his baseball uniform, posing with a bat. It also included the information that he had a daughter, herself a reporter for the *Herald,* but she had refused to be interviewed or to issue a statement. The other Brownsville edition was this morning's and related that although the investigators assumed that the escapees had drowned in either Lonely Woman Creek or the Rio Grande, the search for their bodies would continue. Reporters had again called on Harry Mack, who said the family was grieved by the news and he asked the media to respect their privacy.

Scanning the Brownsville papers, Cacho had said, "Damn, man, you're a real hoot! Some shrink could have a pretty good time poking around in your brain trying to figure why a smart college kid would become an armed robber."

"Ask your brother with the degree in economics but who's working as a border guard for the Zetas," Axel said.

"More whistle in the work," Quino said.

⁘

Everybody thinks we're dead.

He had not until now attempted to summarize how things stand beyond the fact that he's free—and now even freer than he'd thought, since the bastards are no longer looking for him.

He's not badly hurt. He has a comfortable place to stay for as long as he wants. A job if he wants it. One that pays well and keeps the adrenaline flowing.

That's how things stand.

And everybody thinks he's dead.

Everybody. The cops. Charlie. Harry Mack.

Jessie. His daughter thinks he's dead.

Was she grieved by the news too?

He had not yet given thought to how he would go about trying to see her, to talk to her if possible. But now there are new factors to consider. Even though everybody thinks he's dead, there's a reward on him, and to the vast majority of border residents ten thousand dollars is a fortune. His picture has appeared everywhere. *Everybody* knows what he looks like. Countless total strangers can recognize him on sight. Any of them could spot him and call the cops before he even knew he'd been made.

And if he was identified and yet somehow avoided capture, the first thing the cops would think was that somebody in the family was harboring him. They'd go banging on the doors of every Wolfe residence and business, search every foot of them, barge into everybody's life. They'd for damn sure go snooping in Wolfe Landing and maybe inadvertently stumble onto shade trade evidence of some kind. Which could be big trouble for Charlie.

He cannot risk making trouble for Charlie.

A disguise might work, but you never know. A stranger in a small town can draw close scrutiny, too, just for being a stranger, and he still might get found out someway or other. And there's the question of how Jessie might react if he shows himself to her and tries to talk to her. What if she freaks and calls the cops? Or the other one does? Rayo Luna? Only one road in and out of that beach where they're living. They might see him coming toward the house and call the cops without even knowing it was him. Either way, he'd be cut off from all escape routes.

So . . . better not to go there just now. And that's okay. He's waited for so many years, he can wait a little longer. The thing to do is let the hoopla die down. Let the escape fade into old news. Let his face get forgotten in the public mind. It will anyway give him more time to figure the best way to see her and not just go at it catch-as-catch-can. And before he does go there, he should let

Charlie know. Give him a chance to wipe down the Landing in case anything goes wrong and the cops came poking around. And if there's anybody who'd be glad to know he's alive, it's Charlie.

That's how things stand, too.

⌑

He takes a short nap, then a walk in the courtyard, wearing a cap against the brute sun. He strides briskly along the perimeter walkway, working up a sweat. Back in his room he takes a shower, careful not to soak the cheek and arm bandages but lingering under the cascade of cool water for the wonderful sensation of it, then puts on fresh clothes and joins Quino and Cacho for lunch. He tells them of his workout walk and Quino says, "I told you you're not hurt that bad. In no time you're gonna be agile, mobile, and hostile, like the Zetas were taught at Fort Benning."

"Hell of a thing to be jealous of an old guy because he can walk without crutches," Cacho says.

⌑

Later in the day Quino presents Axel with a cell phone and acquaints him with its operations. He gives him Cacho's number and Axel calls him. The kid laughs at his excitement about the little phone's capacities. "Welcome to the twenty-first century, amigo," he says.

44

They take supper that night in the main dining room and in the company of the resident Malos, a raucous affair, as Axel will find it to be every night. Few of the men know English, and most of the Spanish in the room is of rustic dialect and erratic grammar. He sits at a table with Quino and Cacho and three others, the eldest of them Quino's *segundo,* his second-in-command, a one-eared man named Sino. The other two men are Sino's personal operatives, Vaquero and Alto, neither one much older than Cacho. They both speak English well and much better than Sino. The three of them live in Nuevo Laredo and spend most of their time there and in Piedras Negras, but they pay frequent visits to the ranch to confer with Quino and they often attend the semimonthly parties.

All the Malos have been told that Axel provided the information essential to Cacho's escape and that he saved the kid's life in the course of the getaway. He has thereby proven himself and is accepted as one of them without question. When Sino hears his precise diction and faultless grammar, he says, Fucking guy sounds like a professor. And so is he nicknamed by the Malos—El Maestro.

He'd been unsure if beer would still afford him pleasure after such long absence from his life, but his first sip from a cold bottle of Negra Modelo is so gratifying that he chugalugs half the bottle, then burps, eyes watering, and says, *"Jeeesus!"* The table grins in appreciation of his pleasure. Supper is a savory repast of roast kid and rice topped with grilled tomatoes and peppers.

The conversation throughout the meal is animated and largely concerned with women. Everyone is in high anticipation of the party the day after tomorrow and the girls it will bring, and Axel is an object of awe and much joking about not having had a woman in twenty-four years. Cacho says his own deprivation of nine months has been unbearable and he can't conceive how Axel has been able to stand it all that time. Quino says he's known guys who were in prison for so long that when they got out they couldn't enjoy a woman except in the ass, and some couldn't even work up a good boner anymore except with their own hand. Axel says he still prefers pussy and has never buggered a guy in his life. The assertion is met with skeptical hoots and grinning insinuations that maybe *he* was always the one to get buggered. Vaquero quips that even if the Maestro never put it to a guy, he bets his hands have calluses like cowhide from all the years of jacking off. Axel picks up a fork and fakes stabs at his palm, feigning frustration at his inability to puncture it, raising another chorus of laughter.

Near the end of the meal, it comes as a shock when he overhears Joaquín asking Sino if it was really necessary to kill one of the bribed guards. He tried to make fools of us, Sino says. Alto and Vaquero nod in affirmation. Redhead prick had it coming, Chief, Vaquero says. Thought he could fuck us out of the money. *Mason,* Axel thinks. *Dumb bastard took a hell of a beating*

*for the money and got killed trying to keep it. The Zanco word on him
was right. Bad gambler.*

After supper they all repair to the lounge at the other end
of the house, where there is a room-length bar, tables along the
other walls, a jukebox, a bandstand, and a dance floor that gets
much use on the two nights a month the girls from Monterrey
come to visit. An adjacent room contains three pool tables.

The evening is full of good cheer and drinking, Axel taking
care to sip his beer and pace himself so that he won't get drunk
but simply achieve a mellow buzz. The general congeniality is
only briefly interrupted by a fight between a man who begins
talking about the terrible things he's going to do to the Nuevo
Laredo son of a whore who stole his woman last month and
a man who calls him a fool because nobody can steal another
guy's woman unless she wants to be stolen. The antagonists are
quickly separated, both of them bloody-nosed, and five minutes
later each has an arm around the other's shoulders and they
are in loud agreement about the universal perfidy of women.
Let a woman know you love her, they agree, and it's like giving her a license to lie. She'll know she can get away with just
about anything. There ensues a general discussion on the eternal
question of what women want. There is much postulation and
bafflement and disagreement.

On the other hand, what men want is easily answered.
They want to be respected by other men—to be feared is even
better—and to have sex with pretty women, a desire that persists to the end of a man's life. They all know it's a lie that old
men lose interest in sex. They all know it because they have
been told so by old men. The main reason they don't have sex
anymore, the old men have said, isn't a loss of interest but that

their sexual interest remains in young and pretty women, but young and pretty women, by and large, do not want to have sex with old men, and so the only sex available to old men is, very by and large, with their wives, who are, extremely by and large, old women, and not even an old man wants to have sex with an old woman.

45

He rises early the next day, already feeling stronger, his aches much abated. He removes the cheek bandage and the one on his forearm. The arm wound is scabbing nicely and he's pleased to see that his palms are so much better they don't really require another gauze wrap. He takes a walk around the compound and admires the tidiness of it. Then spies a circular watchtower atop the roof of the main house—it had not been discernible from the courtyard below his room—and for a moment is suffused with a sense of being back in prison. The guard holds a rifle in the crook of his arm, but his face is indistinct in the shaded booth and under his hat brim, and Axel cannot tell if the man is looking at him. Then the guard raises a hand in greeting and Axel returns the gesture.

⚬∞⚬

During breakfast with Quino and Cacho, he remarks that the kid's bruises are fading even faster than his.

"Always been a fast healer," Cacho says.

"Always been young is what you always been," Quino says. "There's no curative more effective than youth."

"Means your bruises oughta start fading in about a year," the kid says to Axel.

Their plates are cleared away and they are finishing the last of their coffee when Quino tells Axel that he and Cacho are going to do some target shooting tomorrow. "If your hands feel up to it," he says, "you're welcome to join us. Kid says his hands don't hurt too much to shoot, and since it's been a while since you handled a gun, I thought you might want to check yourself out."

"Hands are fine," Axel says. "I'd like to go along."

⸎

He spends most of that day with the rancho's tech expert, who tutors him in the operations of a personal computer. Through reading, he had kept abreast of computer innovations during his years inside, but it is revelatory to actually use one and discover for himself the seemingly limitless scope of digital processes and possibilities, the ease and speed with which information can be accessed, messages sent and received, all of it.

When he gets back to his room he finds that a small refrigerator has been installed next to the television. It is filled with beer, cold cuts, sundry snacks. There is a large bowl of fresh fruit atop the dresser.

⸎

After another loud supper in the big dining room, they again go to the lounge to drink and bullshit, play cards, shoot pool. At the bar Axel and Quino converse about their college studies, Axel recalling that they mainly bored him, Quino reflecting on them mostly with affection, especially his philosophy classes. "The most fun I had in class," Quino says, "was giving an oral report about Death, capital D, as the only true god because she's the only one who every hour of ever day gives us copious, visible, irrefutable proof of her omnipotence. She gives it mostly by way of her most powerful emissaries—disease, famine, natural catastrophe, and especially by way of the human race itself. *We* are her most industrious archangels, and we do her work everywhere and in so many ways. The class didn't know what to think. Some thought I was crazy, some wanted to beat the shit out of me, some thought I was a hell of a lot more fun than reading Bertrand Russell."

"*She?*" says Axel.

"Of course, she. And an unsurpassable knockout. Why do you think so many men hurry to her, *run* to her with open arms?"

46

After breakfast the next morning they go shooting. They usually shoot at a makeshift range a hundred yards or so outside the compound, Quino says, but he recently bought a brand-new Dodge Ram 1500 pickup truck and feels like putting it to the test, so they'll go out on the plain to shoot.

The Ram truck is a huge quad-cab model and Axel gets in the backseat. Quino cranks up and revs the big Hemi engine, its roar monstrous. As they approach the front gate, a guard with a carbine slung on his shoulder opens it and raises a hand as they pass by. Quino then stomps on the gas and the Ram accelerates like it's been let off a chain.

In less than a minute they're moving at a hundred miles an hour, the brush flashing by to either side in a gray-brown blur, a great tan billow of dust rising behind them. It's a graded dirt road of mostly straightaways and long wide curves, though some of the curves are tight enough that the truck skids off them and onto the rougher ground and rocks so wildly that Axel is sure they will overturn and be battered to pulp as they go rolling and bashing over the ground like some great wild beast shot down in full stride. Feeling a kind of freedom he cannot name, he lets out a shrill cry of maniacal glee.

"*Grítalo, Maestro!*" Quino yells. "*Howl it, Wolfe man!*"

They're on a straightaway and the speedometer reads 105 when Quino eases off the gas and says, That rock stand up ahead will do.

They've brought a trash bag full of empty beer cans, and Axel and Quino set several dozen of them along the top of a waist-high outcrop while Cacho hobbles on his cane around to the back of the truck and retrieves a large gym bag. Quino unzips it and takes out a Beretta M9 pistol and shoves it into his waistband. He passes another one to Cacho and then hands one to Axel, saying, "The preferred sidearm of your country's military forces."

"You get them direct from American suppliers?"

"No. A Mexico City outfit. Los Jaguaros. Very hush-hush bunch, and they charge top dollar but are always very dependable."

Axel hides his smile at the thought of what a small world it truly is.

Quino gives him a full magazine and Axel snaps it into the gun butt and chambers a round. It's the first firearm he's held since the day of the bonds robbery, and nothing else since the escape, not even the wild drive out here, has made him feel as liberated as he does at this moment. From a distance of ten yards, he shoots a can off the outcrop and exults at the feel of the recoil against his sore palm.

"Get a load of this guy!" Quino says. "First time in twenty years and he's a goddamn deadeye. No flies on him."

And a one-hand shooter! Cacho says. Goddamn *cowboy*!

"Like swimming," Axel says, backing up another five yards. "Riding a bike." He shoots another can off the rock. "You don't forget."

They back up another five yards and each of them uses up two magazine loads with the Berettas. Axel declares it a very nice pistol. Quino takes it from him and hands him a Glock 17, which Axel recognizes as the make of gun with which Cacho shot the CO at the creek. He shoots up two magazines with it and says he likes it more than the Beretta because of its lighter weight and smaller grip. The brothers agree. "Which reminds me," Quino says. He goes to the truck and comes back with a Colt .45 1911A and hands it to Axel. "The kid tells me these old bastards are your favorite. Still true after the Glock?"

Axel smiles at his own daffy notion that the gun feels like he's gripping the hand of an old friend. He draws the slide back enough to see there's a bullet in the chamber. Though the .45 holds fewer than half the number of rounds that either the Beretta or the Glock do, it's heavier than either of them. He turns toward the remaining cans on the outcrop, raises the cocked pistol, and fires eight times in quick succession, smacking away a can with each shot, emptying the magazine, the slide locking open after expelling the last shell.

"Wooo!" Quino says. "With *any* gun he shoots like Pancho Villa."

"It's still the one, gents," Axel says, wagging the .45.

"No way," Cacho says. "Thing weighs a ton and only holds seven shots. Eight if you carry one in the chamber. I'll take the seventeen in the Glock."

"There's some who *need* seventeen," Axel says.

He extracts the empty magazine, lets the slide snap closed, and extends the pistol butt-first to Quino, who waves it off, saying, "It's yours, hombre. There's a damn good shoulder holster for it in the truck."

Quino next withdraws an M4 carbine from the bag. It is a smaller, lighter version of the M16 rifle, a type Axel often fired at the Republic Arms, and he is impressed by the M4's lightness and easy maneuverability. "It's a better weapon than the M16 for close fighting," Quino says. "Every Malo at the ranch has one, every man on a crew." The selective-fire switch permits a choice between shooting one round with each trigger pull or a three-round burst with each pull. The bursts are more fun, and Axel makes quick work of shooting up three magazines in acquainting himself with the weapon. Quino offers to show him how to fieldstrip it for cleaning, but the carbine is so similar to the M16 that Axel quickly breaks it down, and then as swiftly reassembles it. Quino grins and shrugs and says, "It's yours, too. Keep it close."

On the roaring drive back to the compound they hit 110 miles per hour on a straightaway, all three howling like wolves.

⌘

At lunch, Quino tells them he's received a report that a gang working for the Sinaloa cartel is planning to smuggle a load of cocaine across the Rio sometime soon in the Malos' sector. "Supposed to happen not too far from here, right in the heart of our territory," Quino says. "The brass balls on those fuckers! Nothing definite yet on exactly where they'll do it, but the word is it'll likely go down within a week. If the spot's within fast enough reach of the ranch, I'll be taking a team to deal with them myself. If you're feeling up to it, Maestro, you'd be welcome to come along, see how we earn our keep."

That's why the target practice, Axel thinks. The man wouldn't ask him to go out with a team without first finding out if he can shoot. He was wasting no time putting him to the test. "I'm up to it," he says.

"It'll get dicey, I can promise you that," Quino says.

"All the better. Count me in."

"Me, too," Cacho says. "I can give cover fire from—"

"You don't go anywhere until you can walk from point A to point B without assistance," Quino says. "End of discussion."

47

As always on the evenings when the girls come to the ranch, the Malos have supper early, then get spruced up. The girls will already have eaten, too. As the men see it, the visit will be brief enough without wasting time over a dining table. The music is provided by Los Jóvenes, a band as adept with a slow-dance number as with a rousing conjunto to set the dancers whirling. They are highly popular with the resident Malos and have played at each of their last six parties, coming all the way from Monclova, more than a hundred miles away.

All day Axel had been increasingly nervous about the party, wondering if maybe he'd become one of those guys Quino had mentioned at supper the first night. What if after all those years of using his own hand and growing accustomed to its manipulations that was the only way he could get off anymore? Maybe the only way he could even get it up. He was afraid he might embarrass himself terribly. He'd finally chided himself for being a damn fool who was simply nervous because it'd been so long, that's all, and he'd been holding tight to that thought since.

The girls arrive at the circular driveway of the main house in a caravan of five chauffeured Chevrolet Suburbans. The lead vehicle stops where Quino is standing a few feet from the head of the line of men, who greet the girls with cheers. Axel had come out to the driveway at twenty minutes to six, thinking it early enough to be close to the head of the line, but many of the men were already waiting and he is somewhere near the middle, and despite all his self-assurances of there being nothing to worry about, he is keenly nervous again.

Quino has told him that some of the girls will be making their first visit, but most will have been here before, and some of the men have favorites among them. But there is a rule that no one can stake a personal claim on any girl and no girl can deny herself to any man, and as always Quino will be selecting girls from the vehicles at random and allocating them to the men in the order that they have lined up. In the years that he has been chief, there have been very few fights over a party girl, and in every case but one he punished the men involved by banning them from the next party. The exceptional case was an instance in which one of the antagonists killed the other with a knife before the fight could be stopped. Quino punished that man with a bullet in the head.

He opens the back door of the first Suburban and assists a girl in getting out, then takes her over to the first man in line, who leads her off to his room in the dormitory. All of the girls are pretty mestizas, caramel-skinned and black-haired. Most of the men will take their girls straight to their room and then later to the lounge for drinking and dancing and maybe to select another girl for another round of sex. Only a few couples will go to the lounge before heading to the dorm.

When Axel reaches the front of the line, Quino is whispering into the ear of the next girl. Her hair touches her shoulders. Her minidress reveals trim legs and the tops of her breasts. He steers her to Axel and turns her over to him and gives him a wink. She smiles and seems to take no notice of his wounded cheek and sore lips. He takes her hand and asks her her name as they go into the house. Celinda, she says.

He had intended to have a drink with her first, then a slow dance or two, but he now decides that such delay would only make him even more anxious and so chooses to go directly to his quarters. As they pass through the large main room and various hallways, she looks all around trying to see everything at once. This is not the way to the dormitory, she says. No, he says, I don't live there. Ah, she says. He lets go of her hand and tries to dry his sweaty palm by pretending to brush off the front of his jacket.

Then they're in the dimly lit room and staring at the bed, whose covers he'd turned down before going out to the driveway. She says that Quino told her he has been in prison for many years until very recently and she does not want him to worry, everything will be fine.

She puts a hand to his face and gently kisses the butterfly stitches on his cheek and then his sore lips and presses her belly to him and her perfume is dizzying and his heart begins to race and everything seems to be moving too fast and he feels himself responding weakly and his fear of failure is like a fist in his gut and she steps back and removes the little dress with a fluid overhead action and drops it on a chair and slips off a pair of tiny panties and goes to the bed and slithers onto the sheets and beckons him with both hands as he undresses and he's dismayed by the obviousness of his mere semi-readiness and he gets into the bed and she takes him in her arms and kisses him and insinuates her tongue in his mouth and he desires her madly but is still not ready and if he could only use his hand he knows he could set himself right but

he's afraid of what she would think and then her hand is on him
and her fingers are moving artfully and as he responds to the talent
of her touch she neatly maneuvers herself under him and guides
him into her and enfolds him with her legs and works her hips
and then they're rocking and rocking and everything is exactly
as it should be and then he suddenly feels as if he's falling and a
tremulous moment later collapses on her in gasping exhilaration.

And then he's laughing and laughing and she's laughing with
him and kissing the tears on his face.

⟡

More than two hours later, after dancing naked to a CD of Sinatra
songs and making love again, this time taking it slow, after drinking a few beers from the fridge and conversing about the kinds
of music they like and the many DVD movies she recommends,
they finally get out of bed and get dressed.

But at the door he embraces her from behind and presses
himself to her and she feels his revived readiness yet once more
and says, *"Dios mío,"* and again takes off the dress. This time they
go about it even more languidly, Axel in no hurry at all, wanting
to prolong the union as long as possible, and they do. Then he
gets another two beers and they drink them sitting up in bed,
their backs against the headboard, idly stroking each other and
talking of this and that. When she asks if he thinks he might have
had enough now, he gets out of bed and affects a slouching limp
as he crosses the room to where his clothes lie scattered, and she
cackles with delight.

In the lounge, where most of the Malos and their girls have
already gathered, he touches his bottle of Bohemia to hers and
toasts her in a whisper as the finest lover in the world. She thanks
him very kindly and toasts him as the world's second-finest lover,

and they both laugh. When it's time for the girls to go, he walks her out to the row of Suburbans, where the drivers hold open the doors. He would like to kiss her good night but is mindful of the silliness of that impulse and so puts the tip of his finger to her nose and thanks her for a good time. She grins and pretends to snap at the finger and says she had a good time too. Then she's in the vehicle and the driver shuts the door and goes around and gets behind the wheel and the little caravan departs. Axel and the few other men who came out to see the girls off, including Quino and Cacho, watch the vehicles until they pass through the front gate and their taillights turn to the north and vanish.

The moon has not yet risen, and the sky is a brilliant crush of stars. *You've never really seen the stars,* Axel reflects, *until you've seen them from far out at sea or deep in the desert.*

As they go back into the house, Cacho places a hand on Axel's shoulder and says, Well, old man, how was it? As good as your hand?

I don't know about that, but it was definitely better than a stick in the eye, he says.

Which gets a big laugh from the brothers.

48

Barely an hour later he's awakened by Quino, who's shouting at him from the bedroom door to grab his gear and get out to the driveway, *fast.*

In minutes Axel is dressed and out the door, the M4 in his hand, three thirty-round carbine magazines in the ammo belt at his waist, his shoulder holster holding the .45 under one arm and a double-magazine pouch under the other, his phone in his jacket pocket.

Quino's Ram pickup truck and a black SUV—a Jeep Grand Cherokee—are idling in the driveway. He glimpses Vaquero at the wheel of the Cherokee, Alto in the shotgun seat, two other men in the back. "*Move* it!" Quino yells at him from the truck. Axel scrambles into the backseat and the truck roars away, its sudden acceleration slamming the back door shut. In the front passenger seat, Sino is speaking into a satellite phone. With the Cherokee following, they speed through the already opened front gate and turn onto a narrow trail bearing to the northwest.

Axel braces himself against the front seats as the truck gains speed, rocking over the rough road. The Cherokee's headlights are hazy orange in the trailing dust. He leans forward and sees a half-folded topography map on Sino's lap in the glow of a dashboard lamp. Yes, I've got it, Sino says, pressing the phone hard to his intact ear against the rumble of the truck. He draws a small circle on the map with a ballpoint pen, then states its coordinates and asks for a verification, listens for a moment. How fast are they going? he asks. Axel follows his glance at the speedometer—the Ram is doing 80, the truck swaying and jouncing, leaving the ground at every roll in the road.

I estimate forty minutes, Sino says into the phone. Let me know immediately if *anything* changes. He sets the phone on the console and says to Quino that the call of a few minutes ago was correct, the transfer will be at Dos Burros. They're in two vehicles, he says, one security, one the payload. Our contact's tailing them in a Volkswagen bug. He started out of Piedras Negras in the traffic ahead of them so they've got no reason to be suspicious that he stayed behind them after they passed. They're sticking to the speed limit and he's holding a long way back but keeping them in sight. He'll let us know if they speed up. If they don't, we'll get to Dos Burros twenty minutes to a half hour ahead of them. Plenty of time to get set. The tail will let me know when they make their turnoff onto the trail to the clearing, then he'll head back.

Quino nods and says, Very good.

Where and what's Dos Burros? Axel asks.

Sino tells him it's a riverside clearing about eighty yards off the border highway and well concealed by an extended stretch of high, dense brush. It's a fairly narrow and shallow crossing with solid footing to permit the load to be hand-carried across. It was a popular crossing point for wetbacks before the Golfos took it over for drug shipments.

Quino slows down, makes a turn onto the northbound trail, and then they're doing 80 again, then 85.

❦

Crouched in the thick scrub growth on the river side of the two-lane border highway, Axel awaits the coming smugglers, M4 in hand. Mosquitoes whine at his ears. Quino's pickup and the Cherokee are hidden in a clump of mesquites on the other side of the road, which is twenty yards behind him. Even if he stood up to look back he wouldn't be able to see the highway for the foliage. This is an isolate stretch, sparingly traveled at night, and the few vehicles that whoosh by seem in a great hurry to be away from here.

By the frail light of a low crescent moon and through gaps in the foliage, he can vaguely discern where a rude trail bends into the narrow entry to the clearing. The smugglers will be coming on this trail after exiting the highway at a gap in the brush a couple of miles westward. Quino and the others are hidden in the scrub along the west edge of the clearing, set to ambush them. Axel's assignment is to ensure that nobody escapes by retreating through the clearing entrance. Positioned as he and the other Malos are, all their lines of fire will be eastward to some degree, reducing the possibility of shooting each other.

A breeze kicks up and rustles the riverside reeds and he catches the ripe, mucky smell of the Rio. Another vehicle whisks by behind him. Minutes pass. Then he hears an engine, guttural and revving low, approaching from his left along the trail. He thumbs the M4's selector lever from "safe" to "burst."

Headlights appear out of the darkness, moving slowly. As the bulky vehicle passes abreast of him, not ten yards distant, he sees it is a pickup truck about the same size as Quino's, several men standing in its bed. The security unit. The brake lights flare and the truck stops at the clearing's entrance, and the men, five of them, debark from the bed. The truck's headlights brighten and dim into the forward darkness three fast times, and a moment later there is a single spark of white light through the obscurant brush and from somewhere beyond the truck. The buyers, responding from the other side of the river. The men on the ground advance into the clearing and out of Axel's sight as the truck's brake lights flare one-two-three times, and seconds later he hears the rumble of another vehicle coming up the trail and then sees another set of headlights. Another pickup, this one carrying the payload. Two men in the bed. It stops a short distance from the first truck, engine throatily idling, and then the first truck proceeds into the clearing.

Long seconds pass. Over the sound of the idling engine of the payload truck he hears a loud but unintelligible voice. Someone calling across the river? Another minute passes and then a man appears in the headlight beams of the payload truck and beckons it into the clearing. The truck advances and slowly turns into the entry and the man hops onto the rear bumper and then this truck, too, vanishes into the clearing. Axel eases forward, closer to the trail, finds a spot with a better view of the entry and with more room to move to his left or right.

It happens fast. A pair of M4 three-round bursts shatter the silence—and then the night erupts into a raging fusion of gunfire, curses, screams. The thick brush between Axel and the clearing permits him only a few glimpses of muzzle flashes. He hears the rising roar of an engine and in the next second the payload truck comes barreling out of the clearing in reverse, a lone man in the bed, leaning over the cab and shooting back into the clearing with a handgun.

Axel fires a burst at him, the carbine muzzle flaring whitely, and the man lunges sideways and tumbles from the truck as it crosses the trail and plows rearward into the heavy brush to Axel's right. Axel shoots at the driver's obscure form through the window and he slumps out of view and the truck keeps moving in reverse, slowly rocking and lumbering through the heavy scrub for another few yards before it jams in a denser thicket, its wheels spinning in mud. Axel moves over a few feet for a better angle at the front of the vehicle and shoots two bursts through its grille, and the truck sputters and quits. The rear right-side door swings open and someone drops to the ground in a crouch and fires three rapid-fire pistol shots before Axel triggers a burst at him and the man flings back in a supine sprawl. Keeping the carbine pointed at him, Axel is astonished to hear him wheezing. Then realizes all other gunfire has ceased, all screaming. Now the man is gasping, speaking softly to who knows whom. Praying? Axel starts to walk up to him, then halts. *He tried to kill me,* he thinks. Then shoots him with another burst, the man flinching, and the gasping ceases. He then goes up to the truck window and peers in and sees the driver's crumpled, soundless form.

Quino comes out of the clearing, his M4 trained on the man Axel shot out of the truck bed. He prods the man with his foot, steps back, and shoots a burst into him, then comes over to where Axel is standing beside the disabled payload truck and the dead smuggler on the ground. He looks into the cab and says, Excellent work, Maestro, he says. *Three* of them.

Two, Axel says. You just did the third one.

Him? He was good as dead, I only hurried him along. He's your kill.

The Malos come out of the clearing, jabbering and laughing, describing to each other how well the ambush worked, how fast the buyers across the river hauled ass when the shooting started. Too damn bad. Woulda been nice to kill them, too, get the money. Their only casualty is Alto. A bullet through the outer part of a calf. In and out without touching bone. Won't sideline him long.

Quino sends Vaquero and another man to retrieve their vehicles from the other side of the highway, then checks out the load in the shot-up truck. It consists of four duffle bags full of tightly wrapped two-kilo plastic packs of what is supposed to be cocaine. Quino removes one of the packs and has Axel hold it directly in front of a headlight. With a pocketknife he makes a small cut in an upper corner of the pack, extracts a little of its content on the blade, presses a finger to one nostril, and snorts the powder with the other. He wipes at his nose and sniffs as if testing the air. Then says, Excellent! The Zetas will be pleased.

Their vehicles come around and the men make fast work of transferring the heavy duffles to the Cherokee. Quino appoints Axel to drive the Ram and gets in the backseat and they drive off on the little trail, headed for the gap in the brush and then onto the highway, then the back-road ride for home.

⌀

The Ram's great power is palpable in the steering wheel under Axel's hands, in the accelerator under his foot. He had thought to remind Quino that he hadn't driven in more than twenty years and maybe wasn't the wisest choice of driver for a speeding night drive through the desert. Then thought, *What the hell, Quino knows that.* And he anyway *has* been wanting to drive. *And a chance to drive something with as much muscle as* this? *Bring it on.*

He's holding their speed at a hair above 70 when Quino says, *Move* this thing, Maestro! I'm hungry for a steak and want to get to it!

He presses the accelerator and the truck surges up to 80, 85. They're flying through the night, the headlights swaying over the low-rolling road, the truck seeming to dance its way over it in skips and hops, wagging its ass, the Cherokee lost in its dust behind them.

"*Wooo!*" Axel yells.

Sino laughs and withdraws a small bottle of tequila from his jacket, takes a drink from it, and passes it to Quino, who takes a swallow and returns the bottle. Sino starts to hand it to Axel, then draws it back and says, No, it is against the law to drink and drive. Axel snatches the bottle from him—the truck veering off the road for a moment, jarring hard—and Sino says, For the love of God, man, don't kill us! They all laugh and Axel takes a sip, starts to give the bottle back to Sino, then jerks it away and takes another drink before giving it up. He's never cared much for tequila, but at the moment it tastes glorious.

49

Not until they're back home and have eaten steaks and had a few cold beers and relived the fight yet again and have all sworn they're going to sleep until mid-afternoon and he returns to his room and strips to take a shower does he see the bloody patch on the left side of his shirt and then the two holes, one where the bullet entered and one where it exited. Then he finds the small clotting gash on his left-side ribs where the bullet brushed him. And only now feels its mild burn.

He stays under the shower a long while. After drying off, he disinfects the rib wound and affixes a small bandage over it, then removes one of the butterfly stitches to examine the cheek cut, decides that it has sufficiently healed, and removes the rest of its stitches as well. He puts on pajamas, gets a bottle of beer from the little fridge, and starts toward the chair in front of the window. Then stops and looks at the still-tousled bed. He goes to it and picks up a pillow and holds it to his face. It contains the scent of her. Of her skin, her hair. The wonderful perfume smells of a woman, so long denied to him.

He settles into the balcony chair and stares out at the vast and ghostly moonlit country and sips the cold beer. It seems inconceivable that a week ago he was in prison, and that within the last ten hours he's had sex with a woman for the first time in twenty-four years—had it *thrice,* with a lovely young woman—and for the first time in his life killed a man. Two men. *Three,* by Quino's estimation. Any of whom, given the chance, would have killed *him,* and one of whom had come within inches of doing it. All he's ever wanted was a life of . . . *sensation.* That's as well as he can define it. He is not unmindful of the actual smallness of such a life, of its paltry essence. But the truth's the truth. It's all the life he's ever wanted . . . and here it is. *This* is it. And he can have it for the rest of the ride. How did Quino put it? Forever or until death, whichever comes first.

What more could he ask?

Except to see Jessie.

Yes, well. That particular objective, he reminds himself, is currently on hold. He wonders if his worry of maybe being recognized and rousing the cops, making trouble for Charlie, maybe for others in the family, is overblown. The beach house is way back in the dunes. If all he wanted to do was *look* at her, he could go there at night, leave the car on the beach, sneak up to the house, peek in a window, have his gander, and get gone. She wouldn't be any the wiser. He smiles at the thought that it could also be a good way to get his ass shot off for a burglar or Peeping Tom. Not so much by Jessie—though Charlie had told him he taught her how to shoot when she was fifteen and that she'd gotten quite good at it—as by that Jaguaro cousin, Rayo, whose style for damn sure would be to shoot first and ask later, if she asked at all. Still, if he could settle for just a *look* at Jessie andforget trying to talk to her, it might just work.

He goes to bed as the sky shows the thin light of false dawn.

⌒◇⌒

The following afternoon he accepts Quino's invitation to go with him and Sino in the Cherokee to turn over the confiscated cocaine to the Zetas. Midway between the ranch and Nuevo Laredo, they turn off into a winding trail that takes them to an isolated spot in the wooded hills. A large green SUV with black glass, a GMC Yukon, is already there and waiting. Five men step out of it, two of them holding small submachine guns pointed at the Cherokee. Axel recognizes them as Uzis. Quino halts the Cherokee and gets out and raises a hand in greeting, calling, Hector, how's it going? One of them smiles and flicks a hand at the guys with the Uzis and they lower the muzzles. The man wears a T-shirt that says in English, "It's Only Funny Until Somebody Gets Hurt—Then It's Hilarious." He comes over to Quino and they embrace. Quino says something that Axel doesn't catch but that makes both men laugh, then opens a back door to expose the duffle bags. Hector smiles and asks if he's sampled it and Quino says that of course he has, and it's top-grade. Hector pats him on the shoulder and signals his other two men, and they get busy transferring the duffles to the Yukon.

Hector's gaze suddenly fixes on Axel, and he says, Who's the gringo? The guy who helped my little brother escape from prison, Quino says. I told you about him. Glowering at Axel, Hector walks up to within a few feet of him, saying, You sure he's not some gringo cop *spy*? He draws a snub-nosed revolver from behind his back and points it squarely at Axel's face. Axel raises his hands at his sides, saying, Hey, man, easy. Hector's eyes blaze. I think he's a fucking spy! he says, and cocks the hammer. Axel believes he's going to be shot and he's about to try to slap the gun aside when Hector lowers it and laughs. Oh, man, he says, the *look* on your face! The other Zetas laugh too. Hector claps him on the shoulder and says, You're okay, pal. You didn't piss or shit your pants. He whirls a hand at his men and they all get in the Yukon and a moment later are gone. Quino tells Axel that the accusation of spying is a game Hector loves to play with new men. It's why he keeps that little revolver, Quino says, so he can cock the hammer for effect. Not a lot of people are aware of it, but some of the Zetas have a pretty good sense of humor.

"Oh yeah, no question," Axel says.

50

The next day, another sizzler, the bodies at Dos Burros are discovered when an enlarging flock of vultures circling low over the river prompts a pair of passing state policemen to pull over and make their way through the brush to determine the attraction. That evening the Malos at the lounge bar watch the TV footage and whoop at the sight of the draped corpses—eleven of them, according to the report—and the two shot-to-hell vehicles. The report is followed by an editorial lamentation about the continuing violence of the drug wars, with much finger-pointing at the United States and its insatiable appetite for drugs and much reiteration of the need for the Americans to legalize them and thereby deflate their value and financially cripple the cartels.

Quino and Axel, buzzed on beer, hoot at the editorial. Except maybe for weed, Quino says, you gringos will never legalize drugs. Too many of your politicians are being bribed to *keep* them illegal, which of course keeps their prices high. And the politicians need only to hold to a moral stand. They have only to say that their love for America's children, their desire to do the right thing for American families, will not permit them to support legalization of such an evil product that has done so much great harm to so many families. It's win–win for the fuckers. With one hand they pound the table in high-minded dedication to the war against drugs, and with the other they receive money under that table to keep that war going. The truth is, you can't afford to legalize drugs. Hell, man, what would happen to the DEA and all of its employees? To the thousands of police departments whose budgets depend on federal money to fight drug trafficking? To all the private prisons making all that money for keeping all those poor bastards locked up for possession, for dealing?

What would happen to all the school drug counselors? Axel says, signaling the bartender for another round.

Exactly! Quino says, thumping the heel of his fist on the bar. The simple truth, my gringo friend, is that the illegal drug trade has become an essential component of your economy. Every American who tokes up or shoots up or snorts up is doing his patriotic part to sustain your country's financial well-being and preserve its employment rolls.

Hear, hear, Axel says, raising his bottle to Quino.

The TV is now reporting yet another discovery of bodies, this one near Monterrey, the screen displaying a quartet of charred corpses that were dumped in a city park.

Now, things like *that* don't really help to promote international notions of smiling Mexican benevolence, Axel says.

"Oh, I don't know. It's really a matter of perspective," Quino says in English. He points at the burned bodies on the screen. "From a certain point of view, that sort of thing can be seen as an act of high altruism. It's like the difference between giving a man a fish and teaching him to fish. I mean, if you build a man a fire, you warm him for a night, but if you set a man on fire you warm him for the rest of his life."

51

Two weeks pass and there is another party. Cacho has been freed of the cast shoe and now has no need even of a cane and is eager to dance again. At the greeting line for the girls from Monterrey, Quino pairs Axel with a pretty and very amiable girl named Azuela. Axel has sex with her in his room before taking her to the lounge, where he looks around for Celinda but doesn't see her. He isn't surprised, because surely any man paired with her would want to have her for the full length of her visit. But neither is he disappointed. Which he is pleased to discover. He then dances with a girl named Rosa Blanca, takes her to his room, and again has a grand time.

As he would have with two different girls at the next party as well.

⟨⟩

Now they are into September. Quino has a photographer take Axel's picture in front of a portrait screen backdrop. "For your passport and license," he says.

Five days later he hands Axel a Mexican passport with his
picture and physical description and bearing the name "Alejandro
Xavier Capote Lobos." Plus both a Laredo and a Nuevo Laredo
driver's license with the same photo and ID.

"Social Security card's gonna take a while longer," Quino
says.

⟨∞⟩

He takes target practice almost every day at the little range outside
the compound, as often as not accompanied by Quino and Cacho.
Several times a week, with one or the other Capote brother, Axel
goes for a long drive out on the open plain, each time in a different vehicle so he can get acquainted with all of them.

One day they take him to Nuevo Laredo for his first visit.
They dine in an excellent seafood restaurant, Axel relishing his
first oysters since preprison days, amazed at their freshness. Flown
in every morning from Corpus Christi, Quino tells him. They
stroll through the streets and ogle the girls, take a walk along the
river. At a sporting goods store Axel and Cacho buy running
shoes, and the next day begin a daily routine of jogs around the
ranch compound, ignoring the gibes of other Malos, who call
them lunatics and mad dogs.

⟨∞⟩

A week later, at breakfast, Quino says to Axel, "By the way, it
might interest you to know that Duro Cisneros may still be alive."

Axel sets his fork down and clears his throat. "What makes
you think so?"

"You said he had a red mark on his inside wrist like a crescent
moon. I asked around and found out that such a tattoo had been
the sign of a robbery gang along the Lower Rio Grande many

years ago. La Luna Roja. So I asked the Zetas to put the word out that anyone who knows anybody who was a Luna Roja or who has such a tattoo was to inform me of it. Because it was a small gang and has been out of existence for nearly thirty years, it's no surprise that only three men were located. All three were taken to Nuevo Laredo, and when I went there yesterday to meet with Sino I also went to talk to them. You said Cisneros was probably between thirty-five and forty when you knew him, which would now put him in his late fifties, mid-sixties. One of the three guys was eighty-five years old and looked it. He was able to provide a birth certificate, and I cut him loose. The other two were in their sixties, but one of them could prove he'd been in the army during the time you were with Cisneros, and the other swore he couldn't speak English, and you said Cisneros spoke it well. We gave that one a little test that proved he really doesn't know the language. However, in the course of our Q&A, that man, whose name is Azcal, told me there was guy in the gang named Jesús Gallo whose nickname was Duro. Hardly an uncommon name, of course, but, according to Azcal, Duro Gallo could speak English very well. Azcal and Gallo were the same age and both from Monclova, and after the gang broke up they sometimes ran into each other back home. The last time Azcal saw him was about twenty-five years ago. Gallo told him that he and a partner had been doing well pulling robberies in New Mexico and Texas. He said he could use a third man, but Azcal had quit the life. He didn't hear anything about Gallo again until eight years ago, when he heard that he had been working as a money courier for the Juárez cartel and tried to steal a transfer somehow or other. To make a lasting example of him, they crippled him severely. The way Azcal heard it, they placed him in a Monclova apartment and the people paid to care for him were under orders to put him on display on the balcony for an hour every morning and again in the late afternoon. As far as Azcal knew, Gallo might still be there, though of course he might long since have died or been taken somewhere else. So I had it checked out. He's still there. Apartment number eleven-F."

"You put a lot of effort into this," Axel says.

"I'm still thanking you for my brother, but I don't want to discuss it. The only question is, do we go see this guy?"

They hold each other's eyes a moment.

"Let's do it," Axel says.

52

They leave at sunrise, Quino at the wheel, Axel beside him, Cacho and a man named Rico in the back. It's a two-and-a-half-hour drive and they don't talk much on the way.

For much of the previous night, Axel had deliberated on the state of things. After many prison years of aching for revenge against Duro and Billy, he had come to believe he had at last made peace with that desire. Had at last decided that their desertion of him no longer mattered, he no longer cared, it was in the past, and the past could never be changed and so it was best forgotten. Now comes the possibility Duro is alive and in Monclova. If that's true, it raises the additional possibility that he might know if Billy Capp is alive as well—and if so, where. Such possibilities have sundered the peace he'd made with himself and exposed it for the lie it was. Because he *does* care and the past *does* matter and can never be left behind, never be forgotten.

That is the state of things.

They get there at mid-morning of what is already another searing day. The four of them enter the apartment house lobby and Quino gives the doorman a pair of hundred-dollar bills and directs the man's attention to Rico, who opens his jacket just enough to permit him a glimpse of a holstered pistol fitted with a suppressor and then seats himself in a chair next to the doorman's desk. Quino tells the doorman to phone the people in number eleven-F in three minutes and tell them a package from Ciudad Juárez is being delivered to their door. Then they take the elevator to the eleventh floor.

They've been informed that Gallo's resident attendants are a middle-aged married couple, and at the door to the apartment they hear the sounds of television voices within. Quino gives the door two solid raps and says, Delivery! The man opens up and Quino puts the muzzle of the silencer in his face and backs him into the living room. Axel and Cacho come in behind them, pistols in hand, also with silencers, and Axel closes the door. The woman stares at them wide-eyed from a sofa facing the TV, and Quino puts a finger to his lips. No one else is in the room. Along the far wall are two doors, both closed, and Cacho holds his Glock pointed in their direction. There's a faint stink in the air. The telenovela cuts to a commercial and the sound volume automatically rises. Quino gives the man a quick pat-down with one hand and motions for him to sit on the sofa, then gestures for the woman to stand, frisks her too, and has her sit again.

He leans down to the man's ear and says, Point to where Gallo is.

The man points to the nearest of the two doors.

Quino signals Cacho to cover the couple, and he and Axel go to the bedroom door. They stand to one side of it, pistols ready. Quino slowly works the doorknob, then pushes the door open and crouches into it in a sidewise move, pistol raised and ready.

Who's there? a husky voice asks.

Mother of God, Quino murmurs. He stands up and they go in and close the door.

Gallo is in a wheelchair in a corner, skeletal but for a small potbelly, his gray hair thin and scraggly, his gray face noseless and turned toward them. Gallo's eyes are closed, the lids strangely sunken, and then Axel understands that there aren't any eyes under them. They've been removed. As have both legs at the knee, and one arm at the elbow. And the digits of his remaining hand except for the thumb and forefinger. Colostomy bags are attached to both sides of the chair. The room reeks.

Gallo's sudden laugh is a half-screech, the man's open mouth revealing a total absence of teeth. Getting a first look, eh? he says. I can always tell . . . and there's two of you.

At first sight, Axel hadn't thought this creature could be the man he'd known as Duro, but it's his voice. Raspier than before, but his voice. It's him. He lowers his pistol and goes over to Gallo and says in English, "Are you Duro Cisneros?"

Gallo lifts his face to him, the nasal bores large and black and rimmed with mucus. "You speak English . . . like a gringo," he says in English. "Who are *you*?"

"Axel Smith. I was a partner with Duro Cisneros on a robbery back in 1984. In Dallas. Me and Billy Jones."

The man's head tilts sideways as if he's pondering, searching his memory. Then his toothless mouth opens in what may be an attempt at a smile. "*Yes!* . . . Smith and Jones! Dallas! . . . You're . . . the college guy!" There is a breathless aspect to his speech.

Axel trades a glance with Quino. "That's right," he says to Gallo, "the college guy. And you said you were Duro Cisneros."

"I have been many people. . . . The college guy! Yes . . . We hit a jewelry store . . . but not for jewels."

"It was bonds."

"Oh, man, yeah . . . *Long* time ago! A good take but went to hell . . . in a fucking parking lot. . . . And *you,* you went down and . . . oh shit . . . we had to leave you, get out fast. . . . And they got you. Was on the TV, the papers. . . . They lock you up long?"

"Yes."

"Ah, yes, I see, yes. . . . Now you are *here* to . . . *settle* things, no?" Duro emits another screechy laugh and gestures at himself with his two-fingered hand. "Well, my friend . . . there is not much left of me for you to punish . . . not much to cut off, even a dick. . . . But what the hell, you can still *kill* me, eh? It's like they left . . . the best part for you. The best . . . satisfaction." Gallo leans forward as if preparing to depart the chair, his breath coming faster. "So take your . . . vengeance, college guy. . . . *Do* it."

"Tell me about Billy," Axel says. "What happened to him? You know if he's alive?"

Duro leans back in the chair and expels a hard breath. "*That* cocksucker," he hisses.

"What about him? When was the last time you saw him?"

The laugh again. "The *last* time? Oh . . . five or six hours after . . . the last time I saw *you.*"

"What happened?"

"Ah. You want to know . . . what happened. . . . I will tell you if . . . you make a promise to me."

"What?"

"Kill me after. . . . Immediately. Kill me."

"All right."

"*Yes?* . . . You *promise* this to me?"

"Yes. Now tell me."

In his laborious, gasping manner, Duro tells him that he and Billy fled the parking lot in the Mustang with the cops on their ass. There was shooting and he was hit in the back of the shoulder. They lost the cops but the wound hurt like hell and he couldn't drive much farther and they anyway had to get rid of the Mustang. They ditched it a couple of blocks from a little plaza where Billy stole a car and they headed for San Antonio. Duro had a friend there who could get him a doctor and put them up for a while. They kept expecting to see flashing lights behind them any minute, maybe even a roadblock up ahead, but no, nothing. Couldn't believe their luck. They pulled in at a rest stop and parked way the hell at the end of the lot where Billy could check the wound without attracting attention. The bleeding wasn't very bad but the bullet had hit bone and it hurt like a sonofabitch. Duro bit into a rolled handkerchief to keep from screaming and nearly passed out from the pain as Billy used his T-shirt to bandage the shoulder, but it was a good wrap and they drove on. They were almost to San Antonio when Billy said they should make sure Duro's friend was at home and let him know they're coming so he'd stay there till they arrived. They pulled in at a rest stop just a few miles north of the San Antonio loop road and Billy put a jacket over Duro's shoulders to hide the wound and gave him coins for the call and he went in to use a pay phone.

"*That's* how stupid I was . . . how stupid the pain had made me," Duro says. "I go inside to make the call and . . . leave him in the car."

"And he took off," Axel says.

"Of course! I come out, he's gone. . . . I walked around the parking lot again and again . . . looking for the car. Gone. . . . Bonds in the briefcase, briefcase under the seat. Fucker got it all. . . . Felt like the biggest asshole in the world. How *stupid* the pain had made me! . . . But if I had insisted . . . he go in with me when I called . . . he could have shot me there in the car. Got rid of

my body somehow, someplace. . . . He was going to win either
way. . . . All I could do was call my friend again . . . tell him to
come for me."

"You ever hear from Billy again? Hear anything *about* him?"

"Nothing. For a long time I asked . . . about him here and
there. . . . I asked other robbers, described him. . . . Nothing. Not
a whisper. . . . Have no idea what happened to that . . . queer son
of a bitch. I should have known better . . . than to trust a faggot."

"What're you talking about? He was no *faggot*."

"Fuck he wasn't."

"Bullshit, I knew the guy."

"Yeah? Well, let me . . . tell you something *I* know. . . . Two
nights before the Dallas thing, him and me . . . we got pretty
drunk at an eastside cantina . . . start talking about women. . . . First
time we got laid, first blow job . . . all that, right? . . . I tell him
the best kiss I ever got was from Mariana Rivera. . . . I was fourteen. First French kiss. . . . And *he* says best kiss he ever got . . . was
from *Rocky*. . . . Had his head on the table, eyes closed . . . talking
all slurry like in his sleep. Said he *loved* Rocky. . . . Well, I never
heard of no girl named Rocky, but hey, there's all kinds of odd
names . . . so I figured that was his girl. . . . But then he mumbles
something about 'not enough money for him, or . . . *get* enough
money for him,' some shit like that. . . . 'Him.' Said it clear enough,
'him.' . . . Then it was like he suddenly realized what he's saying . . . and he sat up and shut his mouth. Didn't mention any
of it again. . . . Me neither . . . I mean, what the hell, a man can't
help what . . . stiffens his dick. . . . All that really mattered was the
job in two days and . . . him doing his part. But . . . don't tell *me*
he wasn't queer. . . . In love with a guy named Rocky . . . best kiss
of his life. . . . *Shit!*"

But Axel's not listening to him now.

Rocky, he thinks. *Of course.*

"Let's go," he says to Quino, and starts for the door.

Your *promise!* Duro cries.

Axel turns and looks at the maimed and sightless remnant of Duro Cisneros. The sorry bastard got no more than he deserved. But still, enough is enough. He shoots him in the heart—the suppressed gunshot sounding like a light door slam—and Duro rebounds off the chair and pitches free of it.

∞

They're back on the road and heading for home, Quino at the wheel again.

Feels pretty good, eh? he says to Axel in the shotgun seat. Worked out for both of you. He's for sure a hell of a lot better off, and you squared it for keeps. Too bad he couldn't give you anything on the Billy guy.

Wish I'd seen him, Cacho says. Pretty bad off, huh?

Almost nothing left of him but a voice, a few stumps, and bags of piss and shit, Quino says.

Jesus, Rico says. Sounds like a hospital garbage disposal.

∞

The ranch is in sight when Axel says, "I need to borrow a vehicle. I have to go to Matamoros."

"Matamoros?" Quino says. "When?"

"Today. This afternoon. There's something I need to see about. Won't take long, but hard to say just how long. Might be back before dawn, might take a couple of days."

"What's going on, man? The garbage disposal say something I missed?"

"Tell you about it when I get back."

"If it's gonna be dicey, we'll go along for backup."

"Don't need backup, I need a vehicle."

"At least let *me* go with you," Cacho says.

"Thanks, kid, but no."

"You're sure?" Quino says.

"Absolutely," Axel says. "Got it covered."

53

In the early afternoon he departs the ranch in a dark green Dakota pickup with custom lighting—roof lights, front bumper lights, a tailgate light bar. The vehicle has valid plates and registration, but the owner of record is a fabrication. In the extended cab behind the front seats is a plastic cooler with bottled water and ginger ale on ice, plus some sandwiches. He wears a black T-shirt, dark jeans, black running shoes. He carries his passport on Quino's advice to take it with him whenever he leaves the ranch. Because it's the rainiest time of year in the delta, there's a lightweight rain jacket back there, too, also black, with a roll of duct tape in one zippered pocket and a half-dozen flex cuffs in the other. Just in case. He is again armed with the silencer-fitted .45, is again carrying two extra magazines in the holster pouches. He cranks up the AC, then flips through the CDs in the console, finds a collection of Willie Nelson, slides it into the player, and starts tapping the wheel in time to "Nothing I Can Do About It Now." At the border highway he turns right and heads downriver and stays just under the speed limit. The idea is to get to Matamoros right around sundown.

It's on account of I got no money, I know that's why.

He'd never have enough money to satisfy her daddy, Billy had said on the night of the graduation dance. Never enough for *him.*

Well, he damn sure had some money after he split from Duro. Three quarters of a mil. At the time of the bond robbery it had been three years since the graduation dance. Raquel would still have been in college. In Austin. Would he have gone to her? And if he had, would she still have felt the same way about him? And if she did, would the money have been enough to sway daddy to let her marry him? And if it was, would they have settled somewhere near her parents, maybe even *with* her parents? And if they did, was Billy Capp still alive and still there? And if they lived somewhere else, was Billy still alive and still *there*? Lots of *ifs.* Lots of questions.

But the only ones that really matter are whether he's alive and, if so, where? The first thing to find out is whether he's at the Calderas house, and the best way to do that is go there and see.

Be a damn shame if he's dead. You can't get even with a dead man.

But if he is there . . . imagine his look when you put the pistol in his face.

⁕

He'd been to Raquel's family home only once. Near the end of their senior year and a week before the graduation dance at which she turned down Billy's proposal, she had hosted a pre-commencement party and invited all her friends. She'd asked Billy to be her date and he had accompanied Axel and his date, a girl named Violeta whom Raquel had introduced to him as her best friend and doubles partner on the school tennis team. The estate was fifteen miles east of Matamoros, out in *"el campo,"* as the countryside was called by locals. The property encompassed eight hundred acres and its south boundary abutted the border highway.

They turned off onto a junction road that went snaking for almost a mile through stands of hardwoods and palms and wild scrub before coming to a gated entrance at a white stone wall a dozen feet high that completely encompassed the forty-acre residential grounds of the estate. The top of the wall was lined with large glass shards cemented into the masonry. The spiked, iron-barred gate stood open to the coming guests, and a brick guard hut was unoccupied. The guard hut, Raquel would inform them, dated to the estate's original owner, an old-time cotton merchant, but her father posted an attendant there only at night.

She had said she would be happy to show them around the estate if they arrived ahead of the other guests, so they'd made it a point to get there early, passing through the open gate and following a winding, smoothly paved lane for almost a mile through heavy stands of trees before arriving at the house, a large two-story structure with a wide verandah. She greeted them at the front steps and introduced them to her parents—her mother a lovely woman of charm and poise, her black-bearded father tall and imposing in a white linen suit, his manner courteous, his dark eyes intense as a hawk's.

After giving them a tour of the house she drove them around the grounds in her open Jeep, showing them the stables and corrals and horse pastures, the magnificent horses of various breeds, the scattering of oak-shaded gazebos and fountains and lily ponds, the swimming hole at the east end of the estate. Coyotes and wildcats still roamed the property outside the walls, she told them, and she had often seen deer carcasses when she'd gone hiking out there with her father. The nights abounded with owls calling to each other through the shadows of the trees. She was just a child when her father had acquired the place, and he'd bought guard dogs to patrol the walled grounds at night, but after several weeks of their crazed barkings at every animal sound or feral scent, and realizing there was little actual danger of robbers intruding onto the grounds, he'd sold them in order to grant everyone a decent night's sleep.

The residential grounds' main lane ended at the rear wall, where deliveries were brought by way of a side trail to the only other entry to the residential area, a barred gate like the front one except that its spikes were longer. This gate was chained and padlocked every night and in no need of an attendant. Axel had noted the side trail she spoke of. It branched off the estate road about halfway to the front gate, well before the gate came into view.

When they returned to the house, other guests had arrived and were being entertained by Señor and Señora Calderas. The house was lavishly appointed and the evening was loud with laughter and music and dancing. Axel had very much enjoyed his date with Violeta, who during a slow dance whispered to him, "Look how our friends are entranced by each other," and directed his gaze to Billy and Raquel as they swayed close by. And then he'd noticed Señor Calderas off to the side and watching them too, his hawk eyes narrowed.

54

His timing is excellent, and he passes through Matamoros as the orange sun is setting behind him. But dead ahead, miles out over the Gulf, storm clouds are building. By the time he turns off the highway and onto the Calderas estate road, night has risen and the eastern sky is entirely black. Though there's little likelihood a front gate guard might glimpse his headlights through all the foliage flanking the road, he cuts them off and uses only the bumper lights. And sees that the road is now flanked by small amber ground-lights along both shoulders, clearly marking the lay of its passage and making a lack of headlights or even bumper lights no problem at all. He proceeds slowly in order not to miss the entry to the side trail. The foliage is denser than it was those many years ago, but the road is in good shape and has probably been repaved more than once. He has considered that the layout of the estate may have changed a great deal over the years and the side trail may no longer exist.

But then there it is.

⚮

He arrives at the rear gate, ready with a story, should there be a guard there, about having taken a wrong turn and gotten lost, needing directions to get back to the highway. He would then force him to open up and kill him if he didn't. But there's nobody posted at the chained gate. He's hoping to engage with no one but Billy, but if others step in he's ready to deal with them however necessary.

He wheels the truck around so it's facing back down the trail, cuts off the bumper lights and the engine, and sits there a minute, letting his night vision adjust to the encompassing darkness. Then he gets out and puts on the rain jacket and his cap. Flickers of lighting show in the distance, followed seconds later by barely audible thunder. The wind has picked up, stirring the trees, bringing the ozone odor of the storm. He scales the fence and with great care eases over the spikes, then descends its other side and stands motionless, listening, looking all about. Then withdraws the .45 and starts walking up the main lane, heading for the house.

∝∞↶

The lower floor lights are on. Some front windows show light, too. Most do not. There are no vehicles in sight, but he recalls a garage at the end of a long driveway on the far side of the house. A short distance past the garage had been a row of small cabins where the resident employees lived—about a dozen of them at the time Axel was here, though now there might be more or fewer. He advances through the trees to the near side of the house, then moves around to the back of it and again halts, peering all about, listening hard, hearing nothing but the wind and the trees.

A narrow gallery runs the length of the rear of the house. He mounts its steps and goes to the rear door, prepared to jimmy

the latch with his Buck knife, but is not surprised to find it un-
latched. People who live within the protection of twelve-foot
walls with iron-spiked gates have little cause to lock their doors.
He eases inside and silently closes the door. He's in a small sitting room, lit only by a weak glow from the dining room ahead.
The dining room is lighted by a lamp atop a sideboard. Here
had refreshments been offered buffet style at that long-ago party.
He's startled by the sound of muted laughter off to his right.
The direction of the kitchen, as he recalls. He guesses the cook
and her helpers at their ease. He's prepared to use the tape and
cuffs on them, on anybody he runs into other than Billy. But
where's the family? He goes into the main living room. The
furniture is different from before, but the huge wall mirror is
the same one, as is the black fighting bull's head mounted over
the fireplace. He goes up a staircase to the second floor and
pauses at the weakly illumined top landing. The only sound is
of windblown trees brushing against the house. It appears that
only the kitchen help is at home.

Now comes the first loud crack of thunder.

There are two doors to his left, but neither shows light at
its bottom. To his right, toward the fore of the house, is a single
door, a bright strip of light at its foot. He goes to it, hears no
sound within, opens it quickly, and enters the room in a crouch,
the .45 straight out in front of him. There's no one there.

It's a large room. Venetian blinds closed on the windows.
Tall bookshelves with more gimcrackery and magazines on them
than books. A rowing machine in a corner. On a spacious, littered
desk is a closed laptop. Set into the wall to the right of the desk
is a small fireplace whose mantel holds a trio of similar metallic
objects and a few framed photographs. Almost the entire wall behind the desk is covered with framed pictures. He closes the door

and goes to the mantel and sees that the three metallic objects are bronze cremation urns with etched plate inscriptions. One reads, "Mercedes Rivera de Calderas, 1928–1993," another "Ricardo Elias Calderas, 1925–1997," and the third, "Elena Mercedes Mc-Capp Calderas, 1987–1991."

Axel's pulse jumps. . . . *McCapp* Calderas.

And there, next to the urns, stands a picture of young Billy and Raquel at a church altar. The first time ever he's seen Billy in a suit. Raquel beautiful in a dress of white lace. The whole story's right there. He *did* come back, *did* go to her, she *did* still love him, then he went to the father and said look what I can offer and dumped the bonds in his lap. All I want is your daughter and a job. And the father had opened his arms and said welcome to the family, my son. He changed his name to McCapp and married Raquel and they had a daughter, Elena. And she died. So too had Raquel's parents. And unless they bequeathed the place to Raquel, it's Billy's.

All this time Charlie was hunting him, he was just across the river.

He regards another mantel photo, this one of Raquel in a hospital bed, smiling and holding a swaddled newborn. The handwritten inscription says "Elena, 2/4/87." The dead child. Next to that photo are two others of Raquel in different hospital beds and in both pictures holding an infant, one inscription reading "María Susana, 5/18/88," and the other "Anita Flor, 8/10/90."

Three daughters.

The thunder is coming faster, growing louder.

He goes behind the desk to look at the images on the wall. There are portraits and studio shots and candid photos of the surviving girls. There are childhood snapshots of them—helping their mother build a sand castle on the beach, assisting her in setting a picnic table, clutching to Billy and the teddy bears he's won for them at a carnival shooting gallery with the rifle he's yet holding. There are pictures of them as skinny pubescents attempting vixenish poses in their bathing suits, and in goggles and snorkels and standing in seawater to their waists. Pictures of them on saddle horses, in soccer uniforms.

Here's a captioned newspaper picture of María Susana Mc-Capp Calderas at age twelve receiving a plaque for winning a citywide spelling bee, and here one of her at sixteen, on a tennis court and being presented with a singles trophy. There are newspaper photos of Anita Flor McCapp Calderas as well. At age nine as she waves at the street-side crowd from a parade float belonging to "Frontera-Mexica Investments" during a Charro Days festival. At thirteen and grinning at her first-prize medal at a science fair for her three-dimensional model of something to do with genetics. Here the girls are in prom dresses, here in high school graduation gowns and being hugged by Billy and Raquel and everybody beaming.

In the very center of the wall is a photograph of Billy sitting before a birthday cake blazing with candles, his teenage daughters hugging him, all three of them laughing, the picture inscribed, "Happy 40th, Daddy!" There are pictures of Billy and Raquel in their youth, in middle age, on horseback, on a day sailer, toasting each other in a kitchen, dancing at a party. A gun range snapshot of Billy standing at Raquel's back and helping her aim a Browning pistol. There are several shots of Billy together with his father-in-law, Ricardo Calderas—both of them grinning wide in dirty ranch clothes, smiling on a golf course, looking serious in suits as they confer at a dockside restaurant table, posing with shovels at a groundbreaking and next to a sign proclaiming, "A Frontera-Mexica Development." In another picture they are sitting at a café table in the company of a wizened and dapper Mexican whom Axel recognizes as Manuel Sosa-Magón, a Matamoros gangster he had once seen at the Doghouse Cantina in conference with Henry James Wolfe, the photo lending support to the old rumors of Señor Calderas's illicit sidelines. Indeed, he might very well have appreciated the assistance of a son-in-law with Billy's outlook and experience. Not to mention his 750-thousand-dollar contribution to the Calderas holdings.

He returns his attention to the pictures of Billy with his daughters. The girls would now be how old? Twenty and eighteen, thereabouts. Only a few years younger than Jessica Juliet. In college, most likely.

Three daughters. Their first one dead. At four years old.

The edges of the venetian blinds flare with lightning and the windows shudder in the following thunder.

He'd never had any money till he stole the whole bundle from the Dallas rip, and look what he's done with it. Made a family whose love for each other is all over this wall. More than you could do. Let it go. What would be the point now? Really? He didn't estrange you from Jessie. He didn't run Ruby off. So what do you want from him if not his blood? Your cut? If he doesn't hand it over except at gunpoint and then you don't kill him, he could be of a mind to retake it—he's got his pride too. You want that, wake up every morning wondering if today's the day he finds you? And if you kill him to make sure he doesn't hunt you, you'll be partly killing those girls. And Rocky. His daughters, man, his wife. What's killing him going to satisfy?

Let it go.

As he starts back to the door, there's the sound of a vehicle pulling up in front of the house. He goes to the corner window and fingers the blinds aside just enough to see a dark SUV in the verandah's light near the front steps. The first fat raindrops are ticking against the window. The vehicle's front and back doors open and three women hasten out of the vehicle, their laughter audible. Two of them dash up the verandah stairs and out of Axel's sight, but the other one abruptly turns and goes back to the vehicle, calling, "Wait!" She opens a rear door, laughing and saying something to the driver. *"Mommmm,"* one of the women yells from the porch, "come *onnnn!"*

Raquel and the girls. Must be Billy driving. Raquel retrieves a large handbag from the front seat, and now the rain comes harder, clattering on the windowpanes. She holds the bag over her head for cover and scoots to the verandah, the girls shrieking with laughter and warnings not to get hit by lightning. Then she's out of view too. The SUV passes directly below Axel and turns down the driveway to the garage.

With the women downstairs, he can't chance trying to get out the same way he came in. But he recalls drainpipes at the corners of the house. He slips the .45 into the holster and opens the window—the sudden influx of wind batting the venetian blinds crazily and slinging rain into the room and scattering papers—then sticks his head out and his cap sails off and he sees a drainpipe not two feet away. He reaches out and tests its stability with his hand and thinks it will hold. He straddles the sill, leans over, and clutches the pipe with both hands, the rain pasting his hair to his crown, then rolls to his right and falls free of the window.

The downward swing and tug of his weight on the wet pipe nearly breaks his hold on it and he feels it pull partly loose of its moorings, but it holds. He starts shinning down, hand under hand, each hold tenuous, his feet pressed to the sides of the pipe. He's six feet from the ground when the pipe lurches outward and he loses his grip and falls, striking heels-first and then smacking onto his back in the mud, hearing the breath heave out of him.

For a moment he's unable to breathe and the rain is running into his nose and he remembers the sensation of nearly drowning in the rapids. Then his lungs inflate and he rolls over and gets up just as a jag of lightning finds the metal rod affixed to the rim of the verandah roof and ignites a great crackling blast of white sparks that draws Axel's gaping stare and makes the verandah lights flicker.

And then he's running down the dark lane and back to the rear gate.

55

Billy Capp is heading for the side door of the house—flinging aside an umbrella blown inside out the second he stepped out of the garage, his fine suit soaked before he's gone ten paces, his head hunched against the wind and rain—when the bolt hits the lightning rod. He flinches and looks up to see the spray of sparks and the drainpipe angling awkwardly from the corner of the house and shaking in the wind. Directly below it a man is getting to his feet and gawking upward, his face starkly illuminated by the verandah lights.

And even at this distance, even after all this time, he recognizes him. Even if he hadn't seen the recent prison pictures of him in the papers and on television, he would have recognized him. He grabs under his coat for the .45, but, without having looked in his direction, Axel Wolfe is already sprinting out of sight into the rainy gloom.

Billy runs after him, pistol in hand, squinting against the wind-slung rain, now unable to see more than a few feet ahead but feeling he has an advantage in that Axel didn't see him. He runs and runs down the lane—sporadically pausing for a moment to listen for him, try to figure which way he's gone—and then it strikes him that he has to be heading for the back gate and will climb out the same way he climbed in, then hop in a waiting vehicle and be gone before he can even catch sight of him. He whirls around and runs all the way back to the garage, heaving for breath, and gets in the SUV, a 4Runner. He guns it in reverse down the driveway and onto the lane, turns on the lights and windshield wipers, and heads for the front gate, calling the guard on his cell, telling him to open the gate *right now*.

⌒∞⌒

Anita Flor sees the 4Runner speed rearward past a window and says, "What in the *world*? Where's *Daddy* going?"

⌒∞⌒

He supposes Axel was climbing up the pipe when it gave way. Wanted to avoid having to deal with anybody he might run into on the lower floor. *Who the fuck knows and what difference does it make? Goddamnit,* he *knew* he'd be coming. He'd read about his capture, about his trial and conviction for some robbery they *didn't* do, and he'd known that if Axel didn't die in prison he would one day be released and find out where he was and come for him. And then all these years later came the news of his escape, and the first thing he thought was, *He's coming.* He drowned, they'd said, him and the other convict. But they didn't find either body, did they? Since last month he's been on guard, always alert, going armed all the time, even on the estate, putting up a good front for Rocky and the girls but feeling as jumpy as he had for weeks after the Dallas thing. He'd been sure Axel would rat them for cutting out on him, leaving him for dead, which is the only way he woulda seen it. But it was leave him or go down with him.

Axel for damn sure woulda done the same thing in their shoes. He'd never worried about Duro looking for him. The guy didn't know anything about him except he'd been a pal of Axel's. Never a word about Duro in the news. Had thought maybe the cops nailed him at the rest stop. Hadn't had any choice about the rest stop, either. All bloody like Duro was, if they'd been pulled over for any reason—roadblock, faulty taillight, whatever—they'da been had.

God damn *it,* Billy thinks, *if all he wanted was his cut, all right, no problem, he had it coming, I'd give it to him quick. But if the cut was what he wanted, all he had to do is get the word to me, let me know, even be hardnose about it if it made him feel better . . .* my cut or else.

"Oh hell, Ax, no need for 'or else,' here's your money."

Could've been that easy. But no.

Because the money's not what he wants.

What he wants is to kill me.

Came for me in my home*! My* family *right here!*

He curses the poor visibility and the narrow winding lane that forces him to hold down his speed, though he nevertheless goes too fast and slews off the pavement twice, once almost miring but for the four-wheel drive, the second time scraping the right side of the 4Runner against a tree. The gate attendant is standing by the open gate when Billy's headlights swing around the curving lane and fix on him. The man hops into the guard shack just before Billy tears by.

He cuts off his lights, the flanking ground-lights sufficiently outlining the road. His intention is to get to the trailhead before Axel does, then pull over, jump out, and start shooting as soon as Axel comes wheeling off the trail. Just shoot and shoot till the magazine's empty and he's crashed into the trees, then slap in another mag and shoot it all up too, just to make sure. Then call his service people to come and take away the wreckage and the body and dispose of them utterly. End of problem.

Too late. As he comes out of a curve, he sees Axel's headlight beams swing out of the side trail and onto the road up ahead, sees the bulky silhouette of his vehicle against them, and then his brake lights flash and he goes into a curve and out of sight.

Billy passes through the curve and spies him again and slows down. No way Axel can spot him this far back in the dark and the rain and running without lights. He anyhow doesn't have any reason to think anybody's chasing him, just wants to get the hell out of here. He notes the horizontal row of small red lights along the rear of Axel's vehicle. Tailgate strip lights. A pickup. Those lights'll make it easy as pie to keep a fix on him, even in rainy traffic.

Axel's brake lights brighten before each curve and again when he reaches the main highway, where he turns west. Billy halts at the junction and sees a lone set of headlights coming fast from the east. He waits until the car goes by and then pulls out behind it, using it as a visual buffer against Axel, and turns on his lights. Traffic is sparse. When they come to a long curve farther down the highway, he can see past the car ahead and spies Axel's strip lights. He's holding to the speed limit. *Because he thinks he's all clear now. Probably already planning his next try at him.*

Only there ain't gonna be no next try, old buddy. Not gonna happen.

He moves his hand to the comforting feel of the .45 beside him on the seat. *Play the thing by ear. If he stops at a traffic light and there's no one around, just pull up alongside and toot the horn and when he looks over . . . boom! If he turns in somewhere—gas station, plaza, bar parking lot—ease in there too and when he gets out stop next to him and give the little toot and . . . boom! Do it however it presents itself, but get his attention first. So he can see who it's coming from.*

56

Nobody saw him, Axel's sure of it. No one made an outcry. No vehicle came after him on the estate road.

It's over, and he's glad of it. Glad he didn't encounter anybody in the house. So very glad he didn't have to frighten Billy's girls, his wife.

It is truly *over*. He bears him no malice anymore. No . . . enmity. He thinks of Quino and smiles.

❧

The ferocity of local thunderstorms is often short-lived, and when he reaches the eastern outskirts of Matamoros the thunder and lightning have dwindled to a few last muted rumbles and glimmers, though the wind yet sporadically gusts and the rain is still steadily falling.

He hasn't been able to get Billy's dead daughter out of his mind. He has two others, yes, and the pictures on the wall tell of his love for them and theirs for him. But thoughts of the dead one bring up an old question . . . what if something were to happen to Jessica Juliet? Something can happen to anybody anytime. If she got

killed in a car crash tomorrow, what could he tell himself except he'd
been a goddamned fool to wait for a better time to try to see her.

*The river's right there. And the Gulf just a little ways back. That's
where she lives. She's not thirty miles from you right this second. At this
hour she's probably home. With this rain, be easy to slip up to the house
unseen, unheard, sneak a look at her somehow, slip away again. One
look, that's all, and you'll have it the rest of your life. This could be your
best chance ever. And if she's not there, she's not there, and what the hell,
you tried, and you can still try again another time. Nothing to lose.*

He turns north into the heavy traffic on Avenida Cinco de
Mayo and it takes him to the river and he crosses the Veterans
Bridge into Brownsville—the first time he's been back in his
hometown since Charlie's high school graduation day.

～∞～

What the hell's this? Billy wonders when Axel makes the turn onto
Cinco de Mayo. Then follows him at a distance and over the bridge,
staying several cars behind him. Then they're on the interstate for
a mile or two before Axel exits onto the Boca Chica road. Billy
stays more than a quarter-mile behind him, thinking he might be
going to Port Isabel or Padre Island. But Axel passes the junction to
those places just before an old Volkswagen microbus turns off of it,
and Billy slows to let it meld in ahead of him. The road now leads
nowhere but the beach. It's the only way there, the only way back.

*Why would he be going to Boca Chica? No matter. Press on and
see how it plays. Might never get a better chance at him.*

The microbus's interior lights are on and he sees four people
in it, kids, one couple in the front seat, another in the back. All of
them gesticulating, seeming to be talking at once. Going to the
beach on a rainy night. Have a few beers, share a joint, get it on.

He envies them their youth.

57

Where the highway terminates at the beach—most of which is part of a state park—it faces the Gulf. Between the dunes and the highest reach of the tide, the sand is firm enough to drive on. Roughly four miles to the left—northward—the beach ends at a jetty at the entrance to the Brownsville Ship Channel, with Padre Island and its rows of condominium towers on the channel's other side. About three miles south of the highway's connection with the beach is the mouth of the Rio Grande, with Mexico just across the way.

Axel turns right. The wind has reduced to a fitful breeze, the rain slackened to a drizzle. He proceeds slowly, his mirrors showing only the vague glow of the Padre Island condos. He lowers his window a little to admit the mild spray of rain and the sound of breakers swashing onto the beach. He's almost to the river and no longer on state park property when a small yellow glow slightly upriver comes into view. He knows it to be from Harry Morgan Wolfe's house way back in the dunes. Somebody's at home. Jessie or Rayo or maybe both of them. His pulse picks up.

He hasn't been to the house since he was fifteen years old and Harry Morgan hosted a barbecue for the family. It's a single-story, mounted on pilings a dozen feet high and three feet thick, deep-rooted and cemented into the riparian ground, with a narrow covered gallery along the sides and rear of the house and a spacious covered porch. It was built by Harry Morgan's grandfather, Morgan James Wolfe, in the 1920s, and has withstood every hurricane since. Its twenty-acre ground has been known to the family as "Playa Blanca" since the time of its acquisition, shortly after the founding of Wolfe Landing, and its southern and western boundaries abut the Rio Grande. All the locals know who the place belongs to and none would dare to trespass on it. For those who don't know, there is a sign affixed to one of the shoulder-high iron posts on either side of the property's trail entrance, a pair of padlocked barrier chains hung between them, one at chest level, the other thigh-high. The sign advises, "Private Land. Trespassers May Incur Regret."

The sign comes into the side glow of his headlights and he parks the truck just past it, then gets out and goes to the barrier. The narrow trail beyond the chains is just wide enough for a large vehicle. It is composed of a dense layer of hard-packed clay and was ingeniously constructed by Morgan Wolfe and some engineer friends way back when. The chains came much later and are impossible to sever with anything less serious than an acetylene torch. Both of the padlocks are equipped with a digital sensor that triggers an alarm in the house should anyone tamper with them.

The rows of dunes to both sides of the trail are high and softly yielding and the only vehicle that might negotiate them without bogging down is the sort of blatantly loud dune buggy that anyone at the house could hear coming long before it got there. The only way a trespasser might make it to the house undetected is on foot, and over the decades there have been a few such incursions, all but one by nosy beachgoers in bright daylight who were gently rebuked and sent back the way they came.

The exception was a pair of late-night robbers whom Harry Morgan had heard as they came up the gallery stairway. He unlocked the front door and positioned himself in the dark living room with a twelve-gauge pump and waited until they stepped inside before blasting them both dead and then notifying the police. He refused to grant the newspaper an interview but was pleased that it put the story on the front page. It was a sign of wider reach and stronger import than even the one at the trailhead promised.

Axel ducks between the chains and starts up the trail, advancing slowly and carefully, ready to spring aside and hunker behind a dune should somebody come driving toward him.

58

Billy sees Axel's lights turn south at the beach entrance and vanish behind the dunes. The microbus goes out of sight in the other direction. He cuts off his own lights before turning onto the beach and following Axel toward the river. But for the shrinking taillights of the microbus in his mirror, there's no sign of other beach traffic. When Axel's brake lights brighten and halt, Billy stops too. He judges the truck to be forty yards ahead. He's certain Axel can't see him back here in the blackness. Then the truck's lights go off and Billy can no longer see him either.

What's he doing? Waiting for somebody?

Can't just sit here.

Billy backs up in a semicircle and behind the cover of a dune, the 4Runner facing the sea. He waits a moment, then turns on his lights and wheels back onto the beach and heads toward the river. He could be anybody . . . a guy and his girl looking for a more private fuck spot. He lowers his right window.

You got the advantage on him with your lights, he thinks. *You'll be able to see him in the cab as you move in, but he can't see you. Pull up next to him, toot the horn, and ask real loud if there's a public toilet around. Soon as he starts talking, turn on the interior light and give him one good second to see you before you raise the .45 so he can see it . . . then* boom!

When he draws close enough for his lights to illuminate the cab, he doesn't see anyone in it. He stops alongside the truck, holding the .45 pointed out the window. He scans in front of the truck and spies a yellow gleam deep in the far-off dunes. House lights? In the red cast of his taillights he sees the sign on the chain post. He backs up to put his headlights on it, sees the chains and the trail it's blocking.

Goes to the house, he thinks. *That's where he's gone.*

He backs the SUV into a space between dunes and cuts off the lights and motor, grabs an extra magazine from the console, and gets out into the soft rain. *No telling who else might be there, but so what? Move fast enough and you might catch him before he even gets to them. Best if he could see you before you do him, but fuck it, put him down first chance you get and split quick.*

The .45 in hand, he hustles up the trail at a jog.

59

The trail ends where the dunes curve back around and to the river. Morgan Wolfe had not wanted anyone to be able to drive right up to the house and therefore built it a couple of dune rows farther in from the end of the trail. The only way to get to the house from here is over those dunes, on foot. Some years ago the dunes had become too laborious for Aunt Christy, Harry's wife, and rather than extend the trail to the house, Harry had bought a residence in town.

Parked at the trail's end are a truck and an SUV. *The girls' vehicles? They both at home? They alone? With boyfriends?* He clambers up a dune, the wet sand sticking to his hands, getting in his shoes. From its crest and beyond another row of dunes, he sees the house directly ahead, one of its front windows bright with light. The open area under the house is dark but for the vaguely lighted stairway off to his right.

She's here. He knows she is, he can feel it.

Cat-foot it up the stairs, start checking windows, and you'll see her. Really see her. And that'll be that.

He slogs down the dune and starts up the next one.

⠶

Somebody's *here,* Billy thinks, breathing hard when he comes trotting in sight of the two vehicles. He sticks the gun in his pants and scrabbles up the dune on all fours and sees the lit window of the piling house. And in the cast of its light sees the dark form of someone moving in a crouch over the top of the next dune. *Him.*

He pulls the .45, but Axel vanishes down the other side of the dune before he can take aim.

Shit.

Can wait right here till he comes back. Or by the vehicles. Pop him soon as he shows up.

And if he doesn't come back till tomorrow sometime? Gonna stay awake out here till then? And what if he's not alone when he comes back? These are somebody's *vehicles. Can't be too many of them, though, and you can maybe do them all if you go up and take them by surprise. But if they catch you down here in the daylight . . .*

He sticks the gun back in his pants and half-walks, half-slides down the dune and starts up the next one.

⠶

Axel arrives at the bottom of the dune, then sprints through the rain mist and into the deep shadow under the house, then makes his way to the stairs. They're illuminated by an outer light just above a door at the landing at the top of the steps. He slowly ascends to the landing and pauses there, under the roof's wide eave. There are two windows on this side of the house, a dark one to the right of the landing, near the rear corner of the house, and one midway ahead along the gallery, open to the breeze and showing bright light. He hears music.

He starts toward the window ahead and then flinches at the
soft *thunk* of his foot glancing against an overturned plastic bucket
in a shadow by the door. He holds stone-still. Seconds pass. The
music persists. He hears muted voices. A low, brief laugh.

He moves up to the window and carefully leans and peers in
with one eye. A kitchen. Nobody in it. Dishes in a sudsy sink. The
music clearer here. He recognizes it. A Cuban song. "Siboney."
There's a drone of voices in another room and then laughter.
Women's laughter. Probably just her and Rayo here.

Then one of them is approaching the kitchen as she asks
the other if she wants another beer. Axel draws aside from the
window because whoever's coming will be facing it directly and
might see him and if it's not her, what then? The other voice
says no thanks, and the voice in the kitchen says she's going to
take a bath. Axel ventures another one-eyed peek and glimpses a
woman with short black hair and wearing a thin green robe just
before she rounds the kitchen door and goes out of view. Rayo
Luna. Then the window near the rear corner comes alight and
the sash is raised. The bathroom.

⟨�֍⟩

From the top of the dune Billy sees Axel hurrying under the
house and loses sight of him. He stares hard and barely discerns
the poorly lighted stairway at the north side of the house. Then
catches the shadowy movement of Axel's dark figure just before
it goes up the stairs and out of view. He scrambles down the
dune and scurries under the house, halts, and listens hard. Then
wends his way around the pilings and to the stairway. Gripping the .45 in both hands, he steps out from under the house,
aiming upward and ready to shoot, but the stairway is bare. He
starts up the steps.

⎧∞⎫

Axel advances along the gallery to the front corner of the house, takes a peek, then goes around it and onto the porch. The door is flanked by large windows on both sides, the near one dimly lit, the farther one very bright and casting a rectangle of light on the porch floor. He eases up to the near one. It's draped with a gauzy material through which the room within is a smeary vision of colors and shapes. He sees an indistinct form standing by the far wall and softly singing along with the Spanish song.

It's her, he knows it is. He moves over to the other window and takes a look around the frame.

And sees her. At a CD player on a table by a bookcase. She's in a white robe, her red-blonde hair in a ponytail. More beautiful than in any picture he has ever seen of her.

The song ends. She removes the disc and replaces it in its case. She moves to the center of the room and he sidles over a little further into the light of the window, the better to watch her as she gathers magazines off the sofa and arranges them in a neat stack on the coffee table, pausing at times to scrutinize a cover.

⎧∞⎫

At the top of the stairs, Billy stops and listens hard. Faint music. He regards the closed door, the two windows on this side, both of them showing light. *He's in there. But there's still the question of who else and how many.*

He starts toward the forward window to have a look, lightly kicks the bucket by the door, and freezes. The only sound is the continuing music. He moves up to the window and looks into a deserted kitchen. Hears somebody singing along with the song. A woman. *No one to worry about.*

As he quickly moves up the gallery, the music stops. He pauses at the front corner and carefully peeks around it and sees Axel at the far window, no weapon in hand, staring at something inside, looking a little drunk.

Got you, he thinks.

He steps around the corner, thinking, *Don't hit the heart with the first one,* and says, "Hey, Axel!"

Axel makes a flinching half-turn, stepping back into the full light of the window, seeing a dark figure pointing a gun at him, feeling his own holstered gun a distant world away. Jessie hears it distinctly—"Hey, Axel!"—and whips around to the window to see him standing there, her impulse to shriek stifled by his name, by her immediate and astonished recognition of him . . . the TV and newspaper pictures . . . the photos on Uncle Charlie's walls . . . and the word is out of her mouth before she can think to say it. *"Daddy!"*

As he starts to turn to her, Billy's .45 blasts with a yellow flare and the slug smacks him in the chest and knocks him flat.

Jessie screams.

Axel can't breathe. Can't raise his head.

Billy Capp walks up and stands over him in the light of the window, wanting Axel to see him clearly. He smiles down at him. "Come to kill *me,* huh?" He points the pistol at his face.

A gunshot disintegrates Billy's forehead in an outward spray of bloody bone and brain, and he's dead even as he pitches past Axel and falls.

Rayo Luna stands at the corner of the gallery, naked and dripping wet, a large revolver in her hands. She'd been in the tub and heard the *thunk* of the bucket and lunged out of the bath and to the towel closet and grabbed up the .44 Magnum she kept there. Then came out the back door and to the stairway side of the house and saw a man sneaking up to the front corner and going around it. She was racing down the gallery when she heard the shot and Jessie's scream.

Jessie comes out, her face anguished, and looks down at her father. His eyes are open and moving over her, wide with desperation. He wants to tell her everything that he has wanted to tell her for so many years, but cannot now muster the breath. He can only behold her a moment more. Then die.

60

It isn't easy for Rayo—now wearing jeans and a T-shirt—to convince Jessie they have no other choice, that it's the only way. There's no place in the entire delta they can bury them where the first tropical storm or hurricane won't bring them up again. Body pops up, gets DNA-tested, its dental work X-rayed, and chances are good it'll get made. Cops of every sort would come poking around and asking questions of everybody in the family and maybe raising some serious problems. "They can't be found," Rayo tells her, "not ever, neither of them. Not a scrap."

Jessie can't stop crying, intermittently shaking her head as if she's trying to rid it of something, until Rayo finally grabs her and shakes her. "*That's enough,* for Christ's sake! *Enough!* I know it's hard, but goddamnit, you've been through worse than this! We have to do this, and do it now! You gonna help me or pussy out?"

Jessie helps, though she still weeps softly as they go about the preparations, cleaning out the men's pockets of keys, IDs, money, putting it all except the keys and the money in a plastic bag, together with their pistols. They strip the bodies, wrap them in blankets and tie them in place at the feet and above the head with cloth strips, then push the bodies off the porch. They slosh the blood off the porch planks with pans of water, then go down and begin the arduous task of lugging each body in turn over the dunes and to the vehicles. It takes both of them to transport each body, with panting pauses in the process. They open the back of Jessie's Durango SUV and push aside the jumble of gym bags and golf club bags and cardboard boxes full of old newspapers, then lay the bodies inside and cover them over with the clutter.

They make one more trip to the house to collect the bag with the men's guns and personal items, plus the long pole they use for knocking wasp nests off the underside of the house. They then go on foot to the trailhead and find the men's vehicles and drive them back to the trail end. Tomorrow Rayo will speak to Jesús McGee at Riverside Motors at the Landing and—no questions asked—he'll arrange to get the vehicles to the garage, attach new VINs, work up new registrations, and sell them off.

With Rayo at the wheel of the Durango, they head for the beach entrance and turn onto the Boca Chica road. It's a bit tense when they stop at the Border Patrol checkpoint on the return side of the road, but they're well acquainted with all the guys of the local unit and the only reason they're ever stopped is so the duty officers can flirt with them for a minute before waving them through.

⌦✖⌫

A little before eleven o'clock, they roll into the Landing, the rain now no more than a mist. All business places are closed at this hour except the Doghouse Cantina. They turn onto Gator Lane and follow it past the place, the light over its front door still on, its parking lot holding but a half-dozen vehicles, then turn onto the narrow lane that leads into the deepest thickets and tree stands in the Landing. They proceed slowly through the greater darkness along the misty, winding track. They see a small light deep in the trees—the light over the doorway of Charlie Fortune's piling house, the most isolate residence in the Landing. But they know he'll be at the Doghouse until he closes it at midnight. His house is as far as Jessie has ever come this way before.

⁓⊗⁓

Now they're there. At a reed-cleared portion of bank on the Resaca Mala. Rayo leaves the headlights on and shining out over the dark water and against the cattail reeds on the opposite bank. Jessie had long before heard of how Doghouse kitchen scraps are disposed of here, but had never cared to witness the spectacle, and not until Rayo informed her earlier this evening did she learn of the other sort of disposals that sometimes occur here. Rayo herself had learned of it shortly after moving here from Mexico City and going to work in the shade trade.

They work quickly in the illumination of the interior lights and the reflected glow of the headlights. The surrounding shadows are long and deep and loud with the ringing of frogs, the heavy air rife with the smells of decayed vegetation. Rayo gets the bag with the men's guns and other belongings, cuts slits in it with a pocketknife, then slings it far out into the water and it vanishes in a splash. They drag out one of the blanket-wrapped bodies and lug it over the edge of the bank, turn it facedown, and then retrieve the other one.

Rayo says she can handle the rest of it by herself and suggests that Jessie go off a ways and wait. But Jessie says, "No. I can do it. It isn't him anymore, like you said. I *know* it isn't."

"Okay, get the pole."

While Jessie does that, Rayo cuts away the ties holding the blankets around the bodies and then loosens the blankets so that they simply drape them. Jessie returns with the pole, and Rayo sets one end of it against one of the corpses and they both take hold of the other end. "Push!" Rayo says, and they shove forward in concert and launch the body off the bank with enough force to send it bobbing out into the water. They then do the same with the other. As the bodies drift toward the opposite bank, the loosened blankets slip off them and sink and Jessie can't restrain a small cry. Rayo turns her away, but she wrests free and says, "I can *do* it!" And remains in place, watching.

There's a sudden agitation of reeds on the opposite bank, and then the alligators come crashing out of the shadows. They tear into the corpses in a wild froth, rending flesh, crunching bone, the men's blood mingling in dark billows, their sundered remains mixing in the bellies of the beasts. Jessie covers her mouth with both hands, but she's unable to look away from the carnage. Rayo hugs her close.

It does not take very long, but Jessie refuses to leave until there's nothing left to see. After a time, the last of the gators vanishes into the reeds and shadows of the other bank, and the water slowly gentles, and then again becomes placid.

"It's done, Jess," Rayo says. "Come on."

They get in the Durango and head for home.

It's a silent drive until they're almost to the beach and Jessie says, "I never went to see him. I never wrote to him. So I don't understand . . . why did he come?"

"I don't know, sweetie," Rayo says. "I guess he just couldn't help it. That's the way with some men. Some people."

❦

They will make a pact not to confide to anyone else what they have done, and the rest of the family, like everyone else, will continue to believe that Axel Prince Wolfe was drowned in the Rio Grande rapids while attempting to evade capture after escaping from confinement.

61

Raquel and the girls will wait for three fretful days before they report Billy missing. He has never gone away for more than a day without telling her in advance, *never*, and has never been gone more than a day without calling her. The police will issue a bulletin and promise to keep an eye out, but after another week, and knowing the utter incompetence of the local cops, Raquel will hire private detectives in Matamoros to try to find him, and then engage the services of even more expensive investigators from Monterrey. Both companies will exploit her hope with false reports of possible leads, billing her steadily, until the daughters lose all patience with them and fire both firms and threaten legal action if they submit even one more invoice. Neither the girls nor their mother ever knew the particulars of Señor Calderas's or Billy Capp's private enterprises, but none of them are fools and they have always suspected that many of the men's dealings were of an illegal nature involving dangerous people. Still, they keep hoping for word from him or about him, but when he has been unheard from for six months, the daughters accept that he is dead and put on mourning dress. So, too, their mother, although for the rest of her life—another four years, before she succumbs to breast cancer—she will harbor a secret hope and wake every morning with the thought, *This is the day he will return.*

⌀∞⌀

After two weeks without word from or about him, Quino's only certainty regarding Axel is that he was not captured by police. Had he been, it would have made the news. Cacho bets that he has returned to his family. Quino accepts the bet and sends his best men to Brownsville. Days later they report that Axel Prince Wolfe is not living with any of his family, nor has anyone claimed to have seen him in either Matamoros or Brownsville. Quino and Cacho agree that he is either dead or, for whatever reason, has gone somewhere else and deliberately chosen not to come back.

Why did he go, you think? Cacho says at the breakfast table.

Quino shrugs. Something personal, I would suppose.

Wish he had let us in on it.

So do I. But as you know, he was one for keeping secrets.

Cacho nods. Yeah. Had some funny ways. Ran in the family, he told me.